"I can't imagine why Carrie's husband is here."

"Really?" Glenn's speculative gaze made Beth Ann turn away.

She shook her head and then guilt pulsated in her stomach. She didn't want to lie to her dearest friend. "He might have mentioned something about Bernie inheriting a software company...."

Glenn was silent for so long that Beth Ann looked up. Eventually he asked, "Does he want Bernie?"

Beth Ann shrugged. "Do you think he knows the truth?"

"I don't think so, but you should probably tell him anyway."

"Are you nuts?" Beth Ann whirled around, then burst into tears, the thought sending terrible waves of dread through her. What if Christian did want Bernie? With his money, his clout, he'd cream her in court.

Glenn enveloped her in a warm hug. "I know you don't want to hear this, but you need to tell him. Now—while you've got nothing to lose."

"I have everything to lose. I could lose Bernie."

Dear Reader,

In our ever-changing world, the definition of *family* shifts, as well. Families expand and contract as people come into our lives or sadly, leave. But every person in the family, whether present or not, contributes to the wisdom, love and laughter shared by all.

In this story, the family is held together by the grit and love of Bethany Ann Bellamy. Caught between the energy of a youngster at the beginning of life and the needs of an elder nearing the end, Beth Ann doesn't have the time to nurture her own life, her own dreams. Then she meets Christian Elliott, a man of great wealth and power but little understanding of what is truly important.

Please join Beth Ann and Christian as they journey together to discover that what is most real is often least appreciated.

I love to hear from my readers, so feel free to write me at P.O. Box 2883, Los Banos, CA 93635-2883 or visit me at www.superauthors.com.

Sincerely,

Susan Floyd

MR. ELLIOTT
FINDS A FAMILY
Susan Floyd

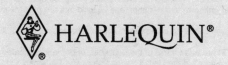

HARLEQUIN®

TORONTO • NEW YORK • LONDON
AMSTERDAM • PARIS • SYDNEY • HAMBURG
STOCKHOLM • ATHENS • TOKYO • MILAN • MADRID
PRAGUE • WARSAW • BUDAPEST • AUCKLAND

ISBN 0-373-70919-6

MR. ELLIOTT FINDS A FAMILY

Copyright © 2000 by Susan Kimoto.

Visit us at www.eHarlequin.com

Printed in U.S.A.

For my dear friend, Annie, who's found a family all her own.

A special thank-you to Lynne Collins, Darylee Ishimatsu,
Trix Peck, Brenda Latham, Suzanne Davis, Apryl Smith,
Leslie Grigsby and Melinda Wooten, who have all
generously shared their journey through
motherhood and their children for observation.

To Mom, Mother Bate and Grandmother Lucille—
we are forever in your debt.

To my own Fluff, a special pink elephant named Eledent.

PROLOGUE

RAAAH! Raaah, raaah! *Raaaahhh!*

Bethany Ann Bellamy woke to the wail. She rolled over and groaned, steeling herself against the sound, vowing she wasn't going to be the one to get up.

Not this time.

Just ten days old, Bernadette was Carrie's responsibility. Beth Ann shut her eyes tightly in a vain attempt to ignore the plaintive cry of the small infant. An ache throbbed behind her left temple. She had been painting nonstop for the past month, her career as a watercolor artist just beginning to flower. With a small show in Sunnyvale opening in a matter of weeks, she didn't have time—

Raaah! Raaah, raaah! Raaaahhh!

Beth Ann pulled the pillow around her ears. Couldn't Carrie hear that?

Raaah! Raaah, raaah! Raaaahhh!

The unhappiness in the cry propelled Beth Ann out of bed. If she didn't get Bernie, Iris surely would. At eighty-seven, Iris needed every moment of rest she could get. Having Carrie, pregnant and cranky, around the past months had taken its toll on all of them. Pushing her feet into worn slippers and pulling on a faded green chenille robe, Beth Ann stumbled out into the hall, her eyes bleary with sleep deprivation, her subconscious still wrestling with a problematic sap green splatter in the center of a near perfect watercolor wash. She heard a creak in Iris's bedroom.

"I've got her, Grans," Beth Ann whispered as she shuffled past.

Raaah!

Poor Bernie. It wasn't her fault. Beth Ann padded quietly to the small room where Bernie and Carrie slept. At the sound of the door squeaking open, Bernie stared up at her, distress in her large eyes. Then her tiny mouth opened.

Raaah! Raaah, raaah! Raaaahhh!

Beth Ann scooped up the infant, gently cradling her head, pressing her close to her chest. Bernie instinctively sought to connect with a nipple.

"Shh. Bernie-Bern-Bern," Beth Ann crooned as she rocked her, supporting her head, pushing her higher up on her shoulder. "You're okay, sweetie. Shhhh, shhh. Bernie's okay."

Raaah, raaah, raaaahh, raaaahh.

"Let's go find your mommy. Where's your mommy?"

Raaah, hiccup, raaah?

"I know, sweetie. You're so hungry."

Still rocking Bernie, Beth Ann swiftly negotiated the narrow halls and sharp angles of the sixty-year-old, one-story bungalow that she and Carrie had grown up in. In the large kitchen, she took out a bottle of prepared formula from the fridge, shook it vigorously and popped it in the microwave, her hand automatically pressing buttons. As they waited, Beth Ann tickled Bernie's rounded cheek. Twenty-eight seconds later—*ding!*

"Where's your mommy, sweetheart?" Beth Ann whispered as Bernie fought against the rubber nipple, her tiny head turning away in her frustration to find suction.

Raaah, raah. Gulp. Success.

Bernie sucked greedily and stared intently at Beth Ann, her infant, frog-like eyes, protruding and blurry. Beth Ann kissed her small pink forehead, still peeling, and ran a gentle finger across the fine dark fuzz that couldn't conceal the pulsing soft spot.

Then Beth Ann saw Carrie's carefully formed round letters on a thick, manila legal-sized envelope lying conspicuously on the kitchen table.

I'm going crazy! I've got to get out of here.

I'm going back to Christian. Bernie will be fine with you.

I owe you one.

Caroline

Careful not to jostle Bernie, Beth Ann sat on a kitchen chair stunned.

No. She hadn't. Even with postpartum depression, Carrie wouldn't— Carrie couldn't—

With one hand, Beth Ann opened the envelope and stared in disbelief at the quarter-inch stack of crisp, new hundred dollar bills. *Back to Christian.* Bernie suckled away, none the wiser, her seven pounds heavy against Beth Ann's arm.

Yes, she had.

Her half sister had abandoned her baby.

CHAPTER ONE

Two years later

IN HER TWO-PIECE, yellow ducky pj's, Bernie scuttled past Beth Ann with a toddler's gleeful scream. The plastic no-slip on her feet slapped against the hardwood floor as she sought her ultimate destination—the out-of-doors, where the fog, thick with late spring chill, socked in the tiny one-story Victorian bungalow so badly Beth Ann couldn't see the large gnarly oak tree twenty yards from the back door. Smothering the California Central Valley in a silent blanket of thick wet mist, the low ground Tule fog was almost comforting, protecting their home in blessed anonymity—anonymity that would be gone in one short hour, when Christian Elliott was supposed to arrive.

''Bernie.'' Beth Ann tried to make her voice sound stern, but Bernie's infectious laughter caused her lips to twitch, as the toddler, on her tiptoes, successfully turned the knob on the back door only to be stopped by the locked screen. Beth Ann thought she could actually see the heat of the house along with the precious pennies needed to provide it being sucked out by the fog. However, in a scant two weeks, when the temperatures soared into the nine-

ties, they'd be wishing for the chill the fog brought
in.

Since Carrie's death eighteen months ago, Beth
Ann had talked with Carrie's husband twice. Once
at the funeral and once last week. She had only met
him a single time before Carrie's death, the day after
she had flown down to San Diego nearly nine years
ago with two purposes in mind—to meet the man
Carrie had eloped with and to discuss their grandmother's long-term care.

Surrounded by paperwork, barking terse orders
into the phone, as his large hand swiftly signed documents, Christian Elliott gave her a rather obscure
gray stare and a quick, surprised nod from his executive teak desk, before answering yet another
phone line. Dressed in her comfy jeans and a San
Jose Sharks T-shirt, Beth Ann felt like the dowdy
country cousin in his opulent penthouse office, especially in relation to Carrie—called Caroline by
everyone in her new life—who was carefully coiffed
from her professional makeup to the precision cut
of her raven dark hair. Her coordinated linen pant-
suit merely acted as an elegant backdrop to her
breathtaking, almost untouchable, beauty.

Rather than giving her new brother-in-law a
hearty welcome to the family as she intended, Beth
Ann was rendered speechless as she gawked at the
spectacular floor-to-ceiling panoramic view of the
San Diego harbor.

At lunch, Carrie seemed anxious for Beth Ann to
be on her way, declaring halfway through Beth
Ann's pastrami sandwich at the corner deli that she
absolutely could not miss her tennis lesson with
Pierre. She promised they would get together later.

After three days of touring San Diego by herself, Beth Ann took the hint and left.

At Carrie's funeral, even though Christian had arranged for her, Grans and Bernie, who was just six months old at the time, a suite at his family's five-star hotel as well as unlimited limousine service, he did not recognize Beth Ann until she introduced herself. Even then, with over five hundred mourners at the funeral patting him on the arm, it was easy for her and her small family to fade into the background. They didn't blame him for his inattention. After all he had just lost his wife. She'd felt a tug of pity for the man, his too handsome face somber. He had everything the world could offer, but even that couldn't shield him from the most tragic of losses.

Bernie squealed again, her intentions obvious, momentarily distracting Beth Ann from the oppressive thoughts of Christian's terse phone call, where he more or less commanded her to be home because he would be in the area briefly on his way to Napa for an important business engagement. He needed to talk to her. Thank goodness, he didn't plan on staying long. Bernie, her face pressed against the screen door, oblivious to the damp chill, contented herself with several loud flat-palmed pounds on the screen, laughing as her hand bounced back at her.

"Go garden," Bernie declared with extraordinary enunciation and another big pat and squeal.

Beth Ann grimaced as a small rip in the side of the screen got larger. She quickly got up and closed the door, steering Bernie back into the kitchen.

"We can't even see the garden. Maybe when the

sun says hello, we'll go. Besides it's time for you to visit Mrs. Potty.''

''No!'' Bernie protested automatically and then looked to Beth Ann as if her reaction would tell Bernie whether or not she, in her nearly two-year-old mind, really objected.

''Bernie.''

''*No!*'' Bernie reinforced her position with a shout. ''No want potty! No like Mrs. Potty.''

''You love Mrs. Potty,'' Beth Ann reminded her gently. ''Mrs. Potty is your friend. Remember every day you need to give Mrs. Potty your poop and pee.''

The phone rang.

With no warning and a playful growl, Beth Ann picked up the two-year-old, smothering Bernie's fat cheeks and squirming neck rolls with kisses. Bernie screamed, giggled, but didn't renew her objection as Beth Ann pulled down her pajama bottoms, stripped off the still clean diaper and plopped her on the potty before answering the phone on its fourth ring with a breathless, ''Hello?''

Bernie made a move to get up, but Beth Ann gave her the evil eye and Bernie settled back down.

''Bethy.'' A familiar, deep voice chuckled.

''Read me that,'' Bernie commanded loudly, pointing like a queen to her pile of books next to the potty.

''Why don't you read the book?'' Beth Ann suggested. ''You sit on the potty and read to Fluff while I talk to Pop-pop.'' Beth Ann pushed Bernie's favorite stuffed bear and a book into her outstretched arms.

''Fuffy!''

"Glenn." Beth Ann breathed a sigh of relief as Bernie babbled behind her, instructing the ragged brown bear to listen carefully. "Am I glad to hear from you. You were supposed to be here by now."

"Is he there yet?"

Beth Ann looked out the window, searching for an unfamiliar car, but the fog obliterated any view she could have of the driveway. "No. Not yet. Where are you?"

"Stuck on 101 by Morgan Hill. A big rig spilled something and they're taking their sweet time cleaning it up."

"Morgan Hill?" She tried not to sound disappointed. "It'll take you at least an hour to get here."

"At least," Glenn agreed. "You going to be okay?"

"I suppose. I just have nothing to say to him." Beth Ann tried to make her voice neutral, but noticed that her hands shook as she cleared away the breakfast dishes. She wiped a hot dishcloth over Bernie's high chair and sighed as she stepped on a soggy Oatie-O. And then another. Cereal everywhere. It was a wonder Bernie got any sustenance at all. Beth Ann used her thumbnail to scrape a mashed oat round off the well-worn hardwood floor. "I'm just nuts. I can't wait until he says his piece and then moves on. What could he want anyway? He didn't even ask about Bernie. I don't want to see him—"

"He's your sister's husband."

"Was," Beth Ann corrected, blinking back her tears. "And we know what kind of husband he was."

"Actually, we don't," Glenn said reasonably.

"We know only what Carrie wanted us to know. You have no idea whatsoever what kind of husband or what kind of man he is."

"I'm not listening." Beth Ann began to hum loudly.

"So are you about eleven now?" Glenn asked with exasperation. "Carrie wasn't perfect."

"But she shouldn't be dead," blurted out of her mouth before she could stop it.

She had waited a long time for Carrie to come back and get Bernie. After two weeks, she had called and was told by the maid that Carrie hadn't yet returned home but was expected back in six weeks. Just six weeks, Beth Ann had told herself. During that turbulent time of adjustment, Beth Ann tried the best she could to meet her art obligations so her first show would open on time, strapping Bernie to her chest as she painted. To Bernie's credit, she slept most of the time, seemingly comforted by the close proximity to Beth Ann. By the end of the six weeks, even though Beth Ann had not carried Bernie in her womb, she carried her in her heart. So much so, that Beth Ann secretly hoped Carrie would never return. Then, more weeks slipped by and they received the phone call from the Elliott's family attorney.

There was a long silence. Glenn cleared his throat, his voice subdued. "Yes. You're right. She shouldn't be dead."

"I know we weren't close anymore, but I miss her—"

"I done," Bernie announced, threw Fluff and the book onto the floor and stood up.

"Wait," Beth Ann said more sharply than she

intended, putting a restraining hand on Bernie's shoulder and peering into the potty-chair bowl. "Just a minute, Glenn. Bernie, you're done when there's poop or pee in the potty."

"I done," Bernie repeated, her voice a hairs-breadth trigger from a tantrum.

"When there's poop in the potty," Beth Ann said firmly.

"No poop," Bernie insisted in a plaintive whine.

"I think you do. You always have poop after breakfast. Can you make a poop for Mommy?" she cajoled, willing Bernie's bowels to move in the potty rather than the diaper.

"Poop, poop, poop, poop, poop," Bernie chanted.

Beth Ann could hear Glenn hold back a laugh. The sound of a bedroom door creaking made Beth Ann turn quickly. The bright ruffle of a pink petti-coat caught the corner of her eye as it whizzed past the open entryway to the kitchen and down the hall. The front door opened and then banged shut.

"Oh, jeez! Grans! Stop!" Beth Ann called fu-tilely and then spoke hurriedly to Glenn, "Iris just took off. Be careful when you get on this side of Pacheco Pass. We're socked in."

"I'll be there as soon as I can," Glenn assured her, his voice patient. "Everything's going to be fine."

Beth Ann wished she could believe him. She poked her head out the front door and craned her neck to see if she could spot Iris but the only thing she saw was opaque fog. For a woman a year from ninety, Iris could travel alarmingly fast, even in a pink petticoat with ruffles. It was no small conso-lation that their bungalow was surrounded on three sides by vast parcels of farmland belonging to the family dairy behind her. There were a thousand places for Iris to hide. The fog only created more of a problem.

"Come on, Bernie. Let's go get Nana," she said hurriedly. She peeked into the potty, relieved to find a small tinkle if no poop. "Good girl, Bernie. You tinkled in the potty."

Beth Ann grabbed a wipe and attended to Bernie, refastening the disposable diaper around the toddler's chubby legs, pulling up her pj's, stuffing her arms into her winter coat with practiced speed. Setting the toddler on a hip, Beth Ann raced out of the house desperate to find some sign of Iris. She could be lost for hours in this fog, wearing only a petticoat. It was insane. Not insane, Beth Ann corrected herself, feeling a muscle strain in her right shoulder from Bernie's weight. Touched.

Beth Ann took a deep breath willing herself not to panic. Iris had good days and bad days. On good days, she was an older version of the same woman who had single-handedly raised two unruly, prepubescent girls during a time when her peers were enjoying their retirement. On Iris's bad days, Beth Ann could only mourn the woman Iris had been, a small part of Beth Ann dying with every subsequent episode Iris experienced. At those times, Beth Ann was partly grateful Carrie wasn't present to see Iris's decline and partly resentful that she now bore the burden alone. She bore many of Carrie's burdens, the least of which wriggled impatiently on her hip.

After having surveyed the boundaries of the acre parcel, looking up in all the fruit trees, checking the storage sheds—all of Iris's favorite hiding places—

Beth Ann realized with a sinking heart that Iris must have left the property to hit the high road. The isolated country road was a long one, nearly three miles, but at the end was a major east-west freeway that connected Highway 5 with 99. With a rapid walk, she hauled Bernie to the street at a half trot, hoping to get a glimpse of the direction Iris would take. With a leaping heart, Beth Ann thought she saw a flash of pink, but wondered if it were simply the play of light off the fog.

Trying not to become disoriented, Beth Ann gingerly made her way in the direction of the truck and breathed a sigh of relief when it came into focus. With practiced hands, she stuffed Bernie into the car seat, digging the car keys out of her jeans pocket and willing her heart to stop beating so fast so her throat could open up. Beth Ann held her breath as she turned on the low beams and carefully backed out onto the road. She couldn't see more than ten feet in front or behind her and the last thing she wanted to do was unwittingly knock Iris over. It was ludicrous to drive in this stuff. But it was even more ludicrous to try to chase Iris down on foot.

She cranked the steering wheel left and had no visibility as she shifted from reverse to drive. She slowly, slowly pulled onto the road, driving as far right as she could, creeping at five miles an hour, praying Iris would come into sight. The muted screech of tires and a blunted scream sent shivers down Beth Ann's back and she resisted the urge to accelerate, her heart pounding in her ears and dread shooting up her neck. She didn't want to become a victim or, worse, add to any injuries.

Bernie sat unusually silent as if she knew something was wrong, terribly, terribly wrong.

"Nana?" she whispered.

"We're going to get Nana," Beth Ann said reassuringly, hoping it wasn't nearly as bad as it sounded.

"Nana, okay?"

"I hope so."

"Nana, careful?"

"Maybe not so careful this time."

"Careful, careful," Bernie told her, her large blue eyes solemn.

"I know, Bernie-Bern-Bern, careful, careful."

It seemed to take forever to get to the accident, the headlight beams of a car were angled awkwardly off the side of the road. Miraculously, Iris was still standing when they arrived at the scene, the right side of a chrome bumper just inches from her bony legs. Beth Ann pulled over, unhooked Bernie, her back and shoulders feeling the strain of Bernie's weight. She shifted the toddler onto her hip, snagged an old zip-front housecoat that she'd learned to keep in the truck for just these episodes and hurried to Iris.

"I wet myself," Iris said, looking down at her soaked bunny slippers.

Beth Ann nodded sympathetically. "If I were almost hit by a car, I'd wet myself, too. Here, sweetie, put this on. It's freezing out here."

"I want to wear my pearls."

"You can wear your pearls when we get home. But put this on now," Beth Ann repeated, deliberately keeping her voice low and soothing.

"Nana, put on," Bernie echoed insistently, as

Beth Ann pulled the housecoat over the frail woman with one hand and then shifted Bernie further up her hip. Thank goodness, Iris was being cooperative today. She obediently put one arm in the blue sleeve and then the other, then looked down to find the zipper. With shocked horror, suddenly aware of her state of undress, she pulled the zipper all the way up to her chin. Her thin, pale cheeks flushed with embarrassment.

"Beth Ann, what am I doing out here?" she asked, anxiety crowding her voice. She looked around, searching for something familiar in the landscape but the fog obliterated any view at all.

"Going for a walk, I imagine," Beth Ann said equably, her heart rate finally slowing. At this point, she couldn't even look at the driver who had reversed and straightened the car, a Jaguar no less, and had gotten out. Now that the crisis was over, Beth Ann felt absolutely drained, not inclined to explain anything to anyone, her mind only focused on holding down the fort until Glenn got there.

"Is she okay?" the tall stranger called, the deep timbre unfamiliar, the annoyed tinge in his voice belying how shaken he was.

Beth Ann nodded with a casual wave and a quick glance over her shoulder, and said with a dismissive nod, forcing her voice to be cheerful, "She's fine, thanks. Sorry about that."

"She shouldn't be wandering about by herself."

Beth Ann could hear his condemnation mixed with agitation but said nothing as she led Iris to the passenger side of the truck.

He continued walking closer, his voice now with a sharp edge of authority to it. Beth Ann took a deep breath, bracing herself for the onslaught of words. "I could've killed her. Are you sure she's all right? Maybe you should get her checked out by a doctor."

Beth Ann sighed and nodded, impatient to have him on his way. Then she opened the passenger side of the truck and helped Iris clamber in. When she had safely belted the older woman in, closed and locked the truck door, Beth Ann called as brightly as she could, "She's fine. Not a scratch on her. I'll get her home, clean her up and she'll be as good as new."

"Bethany Ann Bellamy?"

Her head snapped up in surprise at the formal use of her name, her eyes narrowing with dread as he came closer out of the fog. She was startled by his bearing and presence. She shouldn't have been. Carrie always favored the austere type.

"Yes?" Beth Ann deliberately made her voice clipped, masking her recognition.

"Do you know me?" he asked.

With long easy strides, the man walked toward her, looking her over from head to toe. She returned his assessment with cool detachment. He was dressed impeccably. Buff-colored casual linen slacks, well-fit to his long legs, a button-down light green cotton shirt and fine brown leather jacket accentuated his lean, powerful frame. She looked down at his feet, not surprised by the expensive shoes. They matched the look of the vintage Jaguar. She could smell a rich, spicy cologne and swallowed hard as she met his compelling gray eyes, eyes the color of fog and just as chilly. She glanced at his left hand. He still wore his wedding band.

The best defense was a good offense.

"No," she lied, badly at that, her voice trembling. "I have no idea who you are."

Christian immediately stopped in his tracks when the woman glanced at him nervously, tightened her hold on the child and then looked furtively at the truck, ready to disappear into the fog. He studied the angles of her pixie face, her narrow chin, the damp brown, almost red, curls made unruly by the wet of the fog, searching for a resemblance to Caroline.

He found none.

While Caroline had been tall, nearly five-ten, with model-like proportions, the top of this woman's curls would probably just brush the bottom of his chin. Maybe, if he stared at her hard enough, he could see some likeness around the nose and forehead. Her eyes were unfathomably dark, so dark that he couldn't tell where her pupils ended and her irises began. So unlike Caroline's sky-blue eyes. Maybe they shared the same nose. But, then again, maybe that was just the fog, his nerves or wishful thinking.

"Who are you?" Beth Ann repeated, her tone tough and uncompromising, even a shade rude for a woman so petite.

Christian cleared his throat. "Christian. Christian Elliott. Caroline's husband."

Beth Ann stared at Carrie's husband, scanning his face. Her pulse thudded at the base of her throat. Even though she'd had a week to prepare for this meeting, she felt as if she were being choked and the shock made the back of her eyes water. For the briefest of seconds, she believed if she looked around this tall, remote man, she would see Carrie hiding in the car, laughing and saying her death was all just a big joke and Beth Ann shouldn't take her so seriously and these past two years had only been a terrible dream. Her heart thumped against her chest in anticipation, as she shifted around, trying to peer through the fog at his car. But the Jag was empty.

She glanced up at the man, her bottom teeth plucking at her top lip, biting down hard to keep the tears back.

"You're early," she said, wincing at the roughness of her tone. Beth Ann put Bernie down, keeping a firm grip on a wiggling wrist as the toddler immediately tried to break free. Then Bernie looked up, way up, into the face of the handsome stranger and with a fit of shyness, turned away to clasp her arms tightly, very tightly, around Beth Ann's knee almost buckling her leg as she buried her face in Beth Ann's thigh. Beth Ann straightened herself and loosened Bernie's squeeze as she smoothed back the little girl's brown curls.

Christian stared at both of them, then surprisingly retreated two steps to put a more comfortable distance between them. He stared hard at Bernie, who ventured a peek and then dug her chubby cheeks deeper between Beth Ann's legs.

"I didn't know how long it would take to get here," he said by way of explanation, then added, awkwardly, "Your directions were good. But the fog and all."

Beth Ann blinked.

"Oh," she said abruptly. "Well, come on. I have coffee ready." She picked up Bernie again, who remained uncharacteristically silent, as if she sensed Beth Ann's rising panic. Beth Ann turned to get into the truck.

A firm voice added behind her, "Carrie's husband is always welcome at our house."

Iris, the real Iris, had returned, her gray head poking out of the truck window, the confusion gone from her face, the authority back in her voice. She gave Beth Ann a matriarchal look of reproach. Beth Ann breathed a sigh of relief with Iris's return to reality. Perhaps it wasn't going to be that bad a visit.

"Yes," she agreed quietly, finally remembering her manners as she shifted Bernie higher up her hip and opened the driver's side door. She glanced at him, noting how out of place he looked standing in the middle of the road, the fog just beginning to clear around him. He belonged behind a teak desk in a penthouse office in San Diego, not on a dirt road in Mercy Springs with newly plowed fields surrounding him. "Carrie's husband is always welcome at our home. Follow me. It's just down the road."

With Bernie strapped into her car seat, Beth Ann noticed her hand shook so badly she could barely put the key into the ignition. She felt a reassuring pat on her shoulder.

"All is well," Iris said, her voice soothing and clear. "This is just what is supposed to be happening."

Beth Ann gave her a watery glance and a half smile, wondering how many times Iris had said that to her, until it had almost become Beth Ann's personal mantra. All is well. All is well. Beth Ann took a deep breath and tried to remember what peace felt like. All was well. But it wasn't well. If it were, Bernie's adoption would be signed and sealed and Christian Elliott wouldn't be sitting twenty feet behind them in a car that cost twice her annual salary.

"He can't have Bernie," Beth Ann said tightly, as she started the engine.

"He doesn't want Bernie. He wants Carrie," Iris responded, her voice clear and unperturbed. And then she said, the focus in her eyes drifting away again, "I want to wear my diamond tiara today. I want you to put my hair up."

Beth Ann glanced in the rearview mirror as she guided the truck onto the road. Christian Elliott was looking down, his thumb and forefingers pressed between the bridge of his nose and his eyes. Then he looked up and blinked rapidly before following her.

When Beth Ann turned into the driveway, Christian pulled in neatly beside her. Unhooking Bernie from the car seat first, she took the toddler and scrambled to get Iris who had opened the truck door. By the time she got around to the other side, another surprise. Christian, with a small formal bow, cordially offered his arm to assist Iris down, his large hand wrapped securely around Iris's frail one, giving her complete support, catering to her as if she were a queen disembarking from a horse-drawn carriage rather than a faded pickup truck. He murmured something in her ear that made her laugh, her embarrassment miraculously forgotten.

They all trooped silently into the house, then across the living room and through a swinging door that led into the kitchen. Beth Ann immediately put Bernie down and said to Christian, taking advantage of another adult, "Do you mind watching her for a minute, while I go help Iris?" It was easier to watch Bernie when she was confined to a limited space.

Christian shook his dark head, his gray eyes unreadable. "Not at all."

Bernie was furiously digging in a pile of toys. "Stay with this nice man, Bernie," Beth Ann instructed the back of the toddler's head. "Fluff is under the chair. Remember, where you threw him? Why don't you read a book to him?"

She looked up and politely addressed Christian as she opened the creaky baby gate that blocked the kitchen's open entry to the hall, using her head to indicate the room directly across that hall. "We'll be right there, never out of hearing. Call if you need anything. I'll be back in a minute." She carefully secured the gate behind her and followed Iris into the bedroom.

Christian shoved his hands in his pockets and rocked back on his heels, looking around and seeing much wear on the old bungalow, more evident by the clutter that had the stamp of decades of habitation on it. A far cry from Bella Grande, his family's estate, which he had left just the day before. Even when he was young, the only decoration in the mansion besides the art on the walls was the great vase of flowers his mother arranged every morning in the cathedral entryway.

No clutter anywhere. Not even snapshots of the family unless one counted the looming oil portraits of his grandfather and father, so creepy that Christian had avoided walking down those particular halls until he'd learned not to look at them. He shook his head. Why was it that his mother had never allowed the natural paper trail of life in the house? The memorabilia young children might collect, like the first edition *Superman* comic book that had cost him three weeks of kitchen duty in military school. Christian's throat closed at the arbitrary memory, indignation rising like bile. It should have been safe next to his father's evening paper. She never discarded his father's paper.

Now as he looked around the dilapidated kitchen covered with happy scrawls, predrawings if one could call them that, on the refrigerator, bundles of herbs dangling upside down over the kitchen sink, an edge of bitterness caught in the back of his throat. The warm aura of the disarray was powerful. He clearly remembered Caroline telling his mother, right after she met him that she had no living family, then backtracking hastily when her sister had showed up at his office unannounced.

The timing of Beth Ann's unexpected visit those many years ago couldn't have been worse. He'd been in the middle of closing a two hundred and fifty million dollar acquisition that wasn't being acquired as neatly as he had expected, his staff of lawyers and accountants scrambling to tie up the loose ends of a poorly constructed contractual agreement, which he was loathe to blame on his longtime school friend and executive vice president, Maximilian Riley. When the deal had been finalized a day later, he specifically asked Caroline about taking Beth Ann to see the sights, because he remembered her mentioning that she would be in town until the end of the week, but Caroline had coolly replied that he was mistaken, her half sister, emphasis on the half, was only in town for the day.

Now, Christian Elliott studied an old photograph propped up on a shelf that held an assortment of well-used cookbooks stuffed full of pieces of aged paper and felt a small ember of anger in the pit of his stomach add to the bitterness in his throat. He focused on the photograph, squelching, as he'd been taught so effectively, the residual resentment toward his mother and his wife, willing himself to see Caroline in the past. He barely recognized her, her long dark hair in crooked braids, her dress too small, her bony wrists sticking out from the cuffs, her front teeth much too big for her mouth. Caroline must have undergone intensive orthodontia.

In this picture, Beth Ann was substantially taller, her clothes too loose, her arm draped protectively around Caroline's thin shoulders, her curls bushy with frizz. Caroline hadn't grown up under even modest circumstances, he noted dryly, wondering how Caroline had managed to transform herself, allowing others to believe she had come from an affluent family, carrying with her the taste and confidence of the very rich. Yet another lie. Christian nodded, the bitter taste still in his mouth. Apparently, his money had supplied her with all the props she'd needed to carry off that confidence.

"Go 'way!" A loud voice startled Christian out of the past. He looked down at the little girl, no taller than the top of his kneecap, who stood poised in the middle of the room, her finger in her mouth, staring up at him with great dislike. She glanced around and when she saw that Beth Ann was not in the kitchen anymore, shrieked, *"No!"* and ran to the baby gate. *"Mommy!"*

"It's okay, sweetie," Beth Ann crooned from across the hall. "Mommy's helping Nana. I'll be right back."

"Noooooo! Want come." The wail was mournful, heartbreaking. Bernie started to climb the baby gate, which moaned and creaked under her weight. Chris-

tian moved to pull her off the old gate, convinced it would collapse with Bernie on it.

"Stay right there," Beth Ann told her sharply, then said, "Why don't you ask, uh, Uncle Christian to read you and Fluff a book."

Christian smiled uneasily. He had never been around very many children, especially of this stature. What could Fluff be? He looked around the room and deduced the well-used bear—though more matte than fluff—forlornly stuck on its side under a weathered kitchen chair must be Fluff. With a quick swipe Christian retrieved the bear and said in the most reassuring voice he could muster, "That's okay, uh, Bernadette. Your mom'll be back soon. She's just helping your grandmother. I'll read you and, er, Fluff a book. Which book would you like me to read?"

He held Fluff out as a peace offering.

Bernie wasn't impressed and clung to the gate, mutiny in her eyes. She ignored Fluff and resumed her climb.

"No," Christian said in a firm gentle voice that came out of nowhere. He tried to be reasonable. "Your mom is busy now. Let me read you a book."

Bernie turned a suspicious blue eyeball toward him. A two-second pause had Christian thinking he'd successfully negotiated a signature worthy agreement, until Bernie's face screwed up, her button nose almost disappearing as her plump cheeks turned redder and redder with her indignation. Her cherry lips opened and the loudest screech that Christian had ever heard in his life came out of her tiny lungs. *"Go away! No want book! Want—Arrgghh!"*

As Christian shook his head to clear his ears, Bernie stopped scaling the baby gate and plopped on the floor, the stress of not getting what she wanted far too great for her two-year-old tolerance. *"Arrgghh!"*

"Bernie! Stop that!" Beth Ann barked from across the hall. The sound of her mother's voice was enough to bring Bernie out of her tantrum and she looked at him with a resentful gaze. Then her bottom lip quivered and her baby blues pooled with tears the size of Arizona raindrops in the summer.

"I'm right here," Beth Ann called, her voice so soothing Christian felt his own tension slip away from his spine. "I'll be right with you, Bernie-Bern-Bern. Nana's almost done."

"Mommmmy!" The wail was heartbreaking, full of genuine emotion and distress. The tears spilled over and Bernie peered at Christian. At that moment she looked so much like Caroline that Christian's heart stopped. He bent down, staring intently into her eyes, then picked her up to hold her at arm's length so he could study her features more closely. Bernie was so startled by his movements she stared back at him, almost in awe. It took only a second for her to decide she was having none of this either. She started to thrash, madder now she was off the ground. He studied her face, the resemblance now gone, and wondered if he'd only imagined it.

"Thank you," Beth Ann said quickly coming back, hopping over the baby gate, holding her arms out, almost snatching Bernie from him. "I'll take her now."

"Mommy!" Bernie uttered with relief and gave

Christian a baleful glance as she clung to Beth Ann's neck.

Christian was shaken. Why would he see Caroline in this child? Why?

CHAPTER TWO

BETH ANN CLASPED the small body next to hers, trying to calm the beating of her own heart. She knew the panic was caused by the image of Christian holding the squalling Bernie. In two months, Bernie's adoption would be final, but he didn't know that and he wasn't going to know that. She willed her heart to stop pounding. She was getting upset about nothing. There was nothing in his behavior that indicated he even knew Bernie was Caroline's. Beth Ann hugged Bernie tighter until the toddler protested with a wiggle and another indignant yelp. Beth Ann relaxed her hold and then said in an overly bright tone, "Can I get you anything to drink? Coffee? Tea?"

Christian continued to stare at Bernie. And then he shook his head, "No, no thank you." After a pause, he asked, "How's, uh, Iris?"

"Grans is fine. I've given her a sedative, which puts her right to sleep. She's had a busy day. Been up since four." Beth Ann glanced at the clock, surprised it was only nine. "This is about the time she takes a nap."

"Iris is your, er?"

"Have a seat," she offered while Bernie clung to her neck. Beth Ann winced and shifted Bernie's grip to her shirt. With one hand, she poured herself a cup of coffee, carrying it well away from Bernie.

She watched as Christian looked around and then sat, but only after meticulously picking an Oatie-O off the seat.

Beth Ann smiled nervously, putting her hand out to take the piece of cereal from him, and apologized. "Sorry. Professional hazard. They're probably stuck to the bottom of your shoe as well."

To his credit, he didn't look, but merely grazed the hollow of her palm with his fingertips as he deposited the Oatie-O in her hand, which she tossed away before settling herself across the kitchen table from him. She pushed the coffee out of Bernie's reach, then leaned over to grab Fluff and put him in her daughter's hands.

"You sure I can't get you any?"

Christian shook his head.

Self-consciously, she scooped four heaping teaspoons of sugar into her mug along with a generous splash of milk, left over from Bernie's cereal. She caught him staring and grimaced. "I use it for the drug it is. I like the smell but hate the taste." After a minute, she added, "Iris is Carrie's grandmother."

His elegantly arched eyebrow raised. "Caroline's grandmother? Not yours?"

Beth Ann shook her head and looked outside with a small laugh. Iris was Carrie's grandmother, Bernie was Carrie's daughter and here she was sitting in her kitchen talking to Carrie's husband, suddenly feeling responsible for all three of them.

"No, not mine," she said softly. "We were half sisters. We had the same mother, different fathers. Iris is Carrie's father's mother." Smiling, she asked,

"So, what can we do for you?" Beth Ann tried to make her voice neutral, but it came out more chirpy than she intended. "It must be important if you couldn't talk about it over the phone." She tightened her hold on Bernie.

"Do you know what DirectTech is?" he finally asked, his tone slightly patronizing.

"It's a software company," Beth Ann replied. Her head was beginning to pound. She took a sip of coffee, and Bernie wriggled to get down. Beth Ann let her slip to the floor, where she immediately clambered to get up again.

"A software company we acquired eight years ago—"

"We?"

"My family's business."

Beth Ann looked at him warily and asked, "What exactly is your family's business?"

"We acquire things."

"Venture capitalists?"

He shrugged. "If you want to call it that. We invest in companies—or buy them—build them up, then sell them when the timing's right."

"Do you keep anything?"

"Some things. We have a couple of resort hotels that we've held for two generations."

"Oh." Beth Ann glanced down, suddenly noticing how grubby and rough her hands looked. Just yesterday she had tried a new painting technique she'd read about in *Watercolor* magazine and hadn't been able to get the stains out from under her fingernails. She pushed her hands under the table and surveyed the kitchen, noticing its shabby appearance, and was thankful she had taken yesterday afternoon to clean the house from top to bottom. At least Bernie's fingerprints weren't prominently displayed on the door of the faded avocado-green refrigerator. She then looked up at Christian completely at a loss for something else to say.

The silence stretched between them. Christian stared at the two people across the table from him. Beth Ann stirred her coffee, tasted it and added another two scoops of sugar. She gave him a half smile before her gaze danced away. She kissed the top of Bernie's unruly curls and then took another sip. He felt slightly uncomfortable, as if he were the cause of her silence. What was he supposed to do but tell her the truth? Why suddenly, sitting in this kitchen, did he feel a deep sense of embarrassment about what his family owned? His eyes followed her gaze, as she now stared at an old china cabinet stuffed full of paper, cards and envelopes. Lots and lots of mail. Much of it unopened, he realized.

He cleared his throat. "I was asking whether or not you were familiar with DirectTech."

"Oh, yes." She turned attentively toward him.

"It's worth quite a bit these days."

"And tomorrow it could be worth nothing," Beth Ann replied.

Christian smiled and said politely, "That's possible, but not likely. We don't generally acquire duds."

"So what does this have to do with me?"

He paused, wondering if she ever read her mail. He glanced back over to the cabinet. Apparently not. Then he said, "I'd like that coffee now."

Beth Ann put Bernie down and headed to the coffeepot. Bernie followed, frowning at him as she went. He gave her a tentative smile. She scowled.

Beth Ann handed him a mug of coffee and then pushed the sugar in his direction. She gestured to the old refrigerator. "There's milk in the fridge."

Christian nodded his thanks and said, "I take it black."

"After you drink that, you might want to reconsider," she advised and sat down. She looked impatiently at the clock.

"Expecting someone?" he inquired.

"What?" Beth Ann asked, her cheeks flushing.

"You keep looking at the clock."

Beth Ann turned away guiltily. She was wishing with all the power in her that Glenn would sprout wings and appear on her doorstep. Then she shook herself. Why couldn't she face Carrie's husband by herself? Why did she need reinforcements? He seemed to be a perfectly reasonable man. She should just let him say his piece. After all, he had to be in Napa for an important meeting. She perked up at the idea. Wouldn't Glenn be impressed if she handled this on her own?

"I do have a friend coming," Beth Ann admitted cautiously. "But you were telling me about DirectTech."

"It's hers."

The words were spoken so softly Beth Ann didn't think she heard him correctly. Beth Ann noticed him staring intently at Bernie who scowled back at him. As Bernie tried to climb onto her lap, her sharp elbows dug into Beth Ann's thigh. "Ow. Uh, excuse me?" Beth Ann asked as she helped Bernie up.

"It's hers." He jerked his head toward Bernie.

"Bern's?" She sucked in a deep breath. "What do you mean DirectTech is Bernie's? You must mean you've brought Bernie the software. Well, thank you very much." She flashed what she hoped was a friendly smile. "We certainly appreciate it and we'll save it for when she's keyboard literate."

"Not the software," he said, his voice abrupt. He took a sip of coffee and grimaced. "The company. It's hers."

"No."

"Well, yes. Don't you read your mail?"

"Yes, I read my mail."

"Didn't you get something from my attorney for Bernadette?"

Beth Ann searched her memory, and then remembered the fat envelope. "Bernie got something from *a* lawyer," Beth Ann corrected him, her face growing hot from his scrutiny. "But I thought it was a hoax. Bernie's much too young to receive mail. I tossed it." She was lying. It was actually in a safe pile along with Bernie's legal papers. She'd planned to have the lawyer handling Bernie's adoption look over the document the next time she saw her.

"Do you always toss documents worth several million dollars?"

"Routinely," Beth Ann said blithely, wondering if there was a way to buy more time. She didn't need his involvement right now. She changed the subject and asked, "So why are you here? I'm sure it isn't just to remind me to read my mail."

"Call it idle curiosity," he replied, his voice almost amused.

"About?"

"About Caroline's other life."

Other life. Beth Ann swallowed hard and cursed Carrie for putting her in such a position. Bernie had inherited a fortune. She glanced out the window surprised to see the old oak tree. The fog must have lifted.

When was it, exactly, that her life had become so complicated?

In college, free and single, working on her Masters of Fine Arts, all she'd had to worry about was the soft blur of colors and trying to control, cajole really, the wet medium to fit the impressions in her head. Too much wet and mold grew on the paper. Too little, not enough blur. She spent hours, chasing the elusive values of light that plagued her even in her sleep, especially as she tried to infuse some spark of life into a painting already long dead, flat and mottled from her vain attempts at repair. There was a time, just before a depressed and pregnant Carrie arrived, when Beth Ann had had the promise of a lucrative career in art.

But not today.

The offers had waned because first she couldn't deliver her paintings on time and later because there was nothing new even to deliver. Between Bernie and Iris, she just couldn't maintain the momentum she needed to paint, to finish what she had already started.

Beth Ann had gone from painting six hours a day to six hours a week to six hours a month. And then she'd stopped painting altogether when Bernie came down with the croup and was in the hospital for five days. Beth Ann had frantically tried to call Carrie, but she was nowhere to be found. The hospital bills wiped out both her and Iris's savings and

Beth Ann had been forced to take out a mortgage on Iris's long-paid-for house to pay the balance of the bill and to get herself and Bernie insurance. At least, Iris had Medicare. Between Iris's social security and university pension, the residuals still dribbling in from Beth Ann's sporadic sales and the drawing and painting classes she taught for the city's parks and recreation program, they were doing okay. Not great, but okay. Okay enough that Beth Ann could stay home most of the time.

Bernie wriggled impatiently on her lap. Beth Ann stared at the man sitting across from her and took another sip of coffee. Finally, she said, "What do you mean by Carrie's other life?"

When Bernie squirmed more and slid to the ground, Beth Ann used the opportunity to put some distance between herself and the piercing gray stare. She went to the ancient dryer tucked in the corner of the kitchen and rifled through the clean laundry, looking for clothes for Bernie. Half a kitchen away, she could now safely ask, "Why do you want to know about Carrie's other life? Don't you think that it's a little late now?"

The second question slipped out before she could stop it.

She was surprised at how bitter she sounded and she suppressed a feeling of guilt, ashamed she'd allowed her anger to show. She pulled out a small T-shirt and frowned at the hole under the sleeve and the brown splotch she couldn't get out. She looked for something newer and matching and swallowed hard when she realized she had neither. Bernie's clothes were mostly hand-me-downs supplied by Elena Marquez, the dairy farmer's wife. With a quiet sigh, she quickly assembled a small outfit for Bernie, a faded green monster-truck T-shirt and a pair of loose blue toddler sweats, pants that Bernie could easily pull on and off. She returned to the kitchen table, avoiding the gaze of the almost oppressively silent man sitting there. She focused her attention on the little girl, well aware that his silver eyes were fixed on Bernie's faded blue striped socks and palm-size tennis shoes.

"Nana?" Bernie asked as Beth Ann stripped off the toddler's pajamas, tugging the top over her head. She pulled on Bernie's little T-shirt, glancing up and flushing when she met Christian's pale eyes, withdrawn and shuttered close. She felt a chill run down her spine. How could Carrie have ever married a man whose humorless expression bored into a person, as if he was dissecting every part of her?

"Nana's napping now," Beth Ann replied making her voice as even as she could. "Give me your arms." Bernie's arms came up immediately.

She finally addressed Christian. "I'm sorry. I shouldn't have said that."

"She looks like a boy," Christian said suddenly.

Beth Ann's back stiffened.

"Dressed like that, I mean," he added.

"My friend has three boys and the clothes were perfectly good," Beth Ann replied, not able to control the defensiveness in her voice.

Christian stayed quiet, but his eyes followed her every move.

Beth Ann caught Bernie between her legs. "Give me a foot," she instructed and Bernie put her foot into the pant leg. "Other foot."

"*I* pull up!" Bernie insisted.

"Yes, you pull up your pants, just like you do after you go poop," Beth Ann agreed and watched Bernie's chubby hands fight for coordination as she grasped the elastic and tugged with such toddler might that the waist ended up at her armpits. Beth Ann fixed them, pulling out Bernie's self-inflicted wedgie, paying more attention to the smaller details of Bernie's attire than she normally would. With a small pat on Bernie's behind, Beth Ann opened up the baby gate and sent her off to get her hairbrush.

Christian forced himself to relax, mentally surveying the layout of the small bungalow. The house went back a lot further than he thought, the hall cutting the house in half lengthwise. Bernie's room was near the back—he could hear the direction of her footsteps. The grandmother was directly across the hall from the kitchen. So by elimination, that made Beth Ann's room the one up front across from the living room. Which had been Caroline's room?

After he and Caroline had gotten married, he'd wanted to find a place of their own, but Caroline had quickly fallen in love with Bella Grande along with the well-trained staff. Declaring he was absolutely crazy to want to live anywhere else, she'd halfheartedly toured the homes he'd arranged for her to see, then convinced him that his parents' estate was the best place for them to settle. Perhaps an early sign that their marriage was disintegrating.

Now, he caught a small glimpse of the reason behind Caroline's driving need to reside at Bella Grande. She denied her ordinary beginnings and used him to reinvent herself to the point of obliterating her family, her sister, her grandmother. First it was the mansion, then it was the cruises. When two-week holidays had turned into three-month or five-month journeys, he'd known Caroline had stumbled upon a life-style.

When she'd return home, she'd always declare she wasn't going to travel again, that she was sick of the crowd, of the food. But after about three weeks, he saw the brochures, found the tickets on her dresser, felt her restlessness. He'd responded by working harder, ridding himself of the fanciful notions of children gleefully screaming on the vast lawns of his parents' estate, adjusting to the fact that when Caroline was in town, her cruising friends would slobber over him because of his family's name.

It had been almost a relief when Caroline would call to say she was extending the cruise of the hour for another few weeks. In the seven years they were married, Caroline had traveled for probably five of them, if all the months were strung together. It had happened so subtly that even if Christian had wanted to, there was no way to protest. When he finally did, she'd spoken so bitterly he'd had to force himself to walk away.

Their arguments weren't about money.

He had enough money for God knew how many trips. Even with all her excesses, Caroline had never made a dent in his personal fortune, much less the vaster family one. No, she'd sharply pointed to several of his flaws—his failure to engage in verbal combat, his grueling, self-imposed work schedule, his lack of affection, his inability to fill the bottomless pool of adoration Christian perceived she needed in order to maintain her self-esteem.

His jaw tightened and he pushed away the

thoughts that caused his stomach to churn. He didn't want these feelings. He hadn't wanted to come here. But Mrs. Murphy, his battle-ax of a personal assistant, more surrogate mother than secretary, had insisted. Told him to get the signatures once and for all so he could put Caroline to rest. Meanwhile, she would change the locks on the entire building and shut down his private elevator to ensure that he would continue to travel north to Napa Valley to take his physician's prescribed three-month vacation—far, far away from work.

Mrs. Murphy knew leaving the office wasn't easy for him. She knew how much he resisted the endless days filled with nothing but the guilt that haunted him. For too long, work had been his one constant, the only element that could seal up the cracks left by Caroline's death. Even though they hadn't passionately loved each other at the end, Caroline had been his wife and her death had affected him much more than he would have ever anticipated.

Many times he wanted to believe that she was just away on an extended cruise. But the image of Caroline's body, crushed in her beautiful, brassy-red convertible was permanently etched in his mind. He carried it with him every day, saw it during his sleepless nights. Thank God Mrs. Murphy had stepped in during the crisis and had steered the financial conglomerate through competitive waters. Max—who was paid more and was supposedly his right-hand man—had been practically useless during the turbulent days that followed Caroline's death.

Weary, ready to be on the road, away from this small bungalow, away from the woman who looked at him so suspiciously, Christian forced himself to focus on his main objective. Once he had her signature, he would deal with the feelings, the long days ahead of him.

He repeated, "DirectTech, the company, is Bernadette's and we need you to sign some paperwork. I've got copies in the car."

Beth Ann sat at the table, her face averted as she began to tame Bernie's wild curls with firm strokes. He watched her spritz Bernie's hair with some sweet smelling detangler and then pull half of it into a pigtail. Eventually, she looked up and asked cautiously, "Why is it hers?"

"DirectTech was Caroline's. She willed it to Bernadette. You wouldn't know why, would you?" When he received no other answer than a brief shake of Beth Ann's head, Christian continued, "My parents gave the company to her as a wedding present. They thought it would be nice if she had an income of her own." He pointed at the toddler whose head bobbed as her mother fastened the other pigtail securely. "She's going to be guaranteed an income for life."

"And?" Beth Ann's eyes were wary.

"And you were named as the trustee." He gave her a hard stare, that she deflected by looking away. She was very good at not making eye contact.

"Oh, that's easy. I won't sign," Beth Ann said, her voice almost relieved, as she stood. "If that's all you need to know, I guess you can leave now." She started to walk to the front door. Christian stayed solidly seated, ignoring her obvious signal that he should make his exit. She couldn't physically oust him, could she?

"I'd like to have another cup of coffee," he said politely, draining what was left, and holding out his mug. It was awful, but it would keep him here until he had what he wanted.

Beth Ann's face turned red and she said tightly, "I'd rather you left. I have a friend coming soon."

"Poop!" Bernie said urgently, tugging at the seat of her sweats, frozen where she stood.

"Poop? You're kidding!" Beth Ann yelped with wide eyes and scuttled the toddler across the kitchen floor. "Let's go, Bernie-Bern-Bern. Let's go give the poop to Mrs. Potty."

Christian got up and poured some more coffee. Beth Ann looked up and frowned silently as she watched his actions, her hands pulling Bernie's sweats down around her knees and releasing the tape on her diaper. He met her brown gaze directly and she glanced away.

"Potty training stops for nothing," she commented abstractly.

He couldn't help but be mildly interested in what they were doing, the communion between mother and daughter clearly apparent as she helped Bernie onto the low potty.

Then they all waited.

The combination of Beth Ann's wry smile and her nurturing care of the toddler stirred feelings he'd buried away in a very deep part of his soul. This small part of him secretly wished he and Caroline had shared such moments. Maybe then they wouldn't have drifted so far apart. As an envious outsider, he watched Beth Ann gently rub Bernie's back. If he squinted hard enough he could imagine the woman was Caroline not her sister. In his fantasy, he wouldn't be a stranger in such a loving household, but an integral part of it.

The image placed before him—Beth Ann talking reassuringly to Bernie, her little face scrunched as she bore down—was an intimate snapshot reserved for family. Only family cared enough to celebrate the triumphs of proper waste disposal. He'd never seen his mother look at him so lovingly and although he couldn't remember the event, he had no doubt she wasn't even remotely involved with his toilet training. He wondered if she had even changed a diaper.

"I pooped!" Bernie announced loudly, as she stood and looked into Mrs. Potty, while Beth Ann cleaned her off with a wet wipe.

Beth Ann nodded with a beaming smile that took his breath away. It was the smile of an angel, sending deep dimples into her cheeks, crinkles around her eyes. Even the light dusting of freckles across her nose glowed. Christian couldn't help but be jealous of the attention and admiration that Bernie was getting. He wondered why Beth Ann's smile seemed to have the effect of a low-grade volt of electricity, stimulating some distant physical impulses that he'd assumed had died long before Caroline.

"Yes, you certainly did," her voice deepened with affection. "You pooped in Mrs. Potty and now what do we have to do?"

Bernie looked at her, her face pensive with concentration.

"Remember," Beth Ann said, her voice prompting. "We wash our hands. Wash our hands, wash our hands, wash our hands."

"Wash our hands, wash our hands," Bernie sang.

She scrambled to the kitchen sink, up onto a chair and pushed her hands under the faucet. *"Soap!"* she commanded.

"Soap, just a little." Beth Ann handed her a half-used bar of hotel soap. "Scrub, scrub, scrub."

"Scub, scub, scub."

After Bernie finished rinsing, the window was cracked slightly to ventilate the room, and the evidence of her latest achievement was properly flushed away. Then Bernie ventured to him, staring up at him with great blue eyes, the exact same color as Caroline's, fringed with the darkest, longest eyelashes he had ever seen. She placed a chubby, still damp hand on his thigh, leaned forward and informed him, "I pooped in Mrs. Potty."

Christian had never been so touched in all his years. He could see her earnestness and smell the strong soap that mingled with her baby scent. Her plump cheeks just invited a touch or a pinch. What did one say to capture the significance of the occasion?

"Sweetie," Beth Ann interrupted, steering Bernie away from him. "I think he knows."

Christian wasn't sure he liked Beth Ann's not-so-subtle attempts to keep distance between himself and the toddler.

"But poop!" Bernie was obviously proud of her accomplishment. She then tilted her head and batted her eyelashes at Beth Ann. "Garden? Sun says hello."

Beth Ann looked out the window. "You're right. The sun does say hello. Okay. Where's your jacket? Go get your jacket and we'll go out in the garden." Christian thought she looked relieved, using the excuse to take Bernie to the garden as a way to avoid their inevitable conversation. Bernie went to find her coat, her feet pounding on the hardwood.

"Beth Ann!" came the plaintive wail from across the hall.

Christian watched as Beth Ann stood still, her face torn as she was pulled in two directions. If he noticed her glow before, now he saw the haggard dark circles under her eyes, the fine lines that would deepen with age, the tightness around her mouth. Why did he suddenly want to kiss that mouth, soften the edges—

Bernie came back, dragging her coat across the floor, a chubby fist clutched around a sleeve.

"Let's go check on Nana," Beth Ann said, grasping Bernie's wrist.

Bernie fell to the floor, coat and all, legs splayed in a skater's death spiral. Christian blinked and watched her face shrivel up again. He braced himself for the inevitable onslaught.

"*No!* Garrr-dennn!"

"We need to check on Nana," Beth Ann insisted as she tried to untangle Bernie from her coat.

"Beth *Ann?*" The frail voice was even more panicked.

Christian watched the display unfold before him, feeling rather like a guest on a rambunctious talk show. Bernie was spread-eagle on the floor, screaming as if she were being tortured. Beth Ann was trying to get her to stand up, and Iris was across the hall wailing in distress.

"Cavalry is here!" a cheerful voice announced as the door banged open.

"Glenn!" Beth Ann looked up in relief, and

Christian felt a small twinge of jealousy, as her face relaxed into a smile welcoming the new guest.

"*Beth Ann!*"

"Garrrdennn!"

The tall, handsome man, with classic features and a smile that would make any woman's heart throb, brought that green twinge up several notches as he gave Beth Ann an affectionate smooch on the cheek, then turned toward Bernie with a playful growl. "And who's this doing all the screaming?" He swooped down and picked up Bernie who stopped midcry as her world spun crazily around her.

He hung her upside down, then placed exaggerated kisses all over her face until she giggled with laughter.

"Oh, Pop-pop!" she said with such adult exasperation that everyone laughed.

Two more notches on the green scale.

"*Beth Ann!*" The wail came again.

"Excuse me," Beth Ann said hurriedly.

"Looks like I came at the right time, sweetheart," Glenn said with certain affection.

Off the charts. The green scale no longer was an adequate measure of the envy Christian felt. He stared at the tall man, nearly the same height as himself, and grudgingly admitted that some women might find him attractive, if they liked the blond ski instructor type. With Bernie propped on his right arm and his left hand massaging the nape of Beth Ann's neck, Glenn looked like a welcome member of this little family. Glenn gave Beth Ann a quick kiss on the top of her curls. "Go to your charge. I'll take care of this rug rat." Glenn renewed his tickling of Bernie who screamed with laughter.

Beth Ann looked at Bernie and Glenn, then at Christian. "I'll be right back. Help yourself to the coffee." She gestured toward Christian. "Oh, by the way. This is my friend, Glenn. Glenn, that's Christian Elliott, Carrie's husband."

And then she was gone, her escape seeming well-timed.

CHAPTER THREE

BETH ANN could have kissed Glenn. On an average day, Beth Ann felt as if she were coming apart at each joint in her body. Now, she realized it was tension alone that held her together. If Glenn hadn't come when he had, she wasn't sure what she would have done. She didn't want Christian's software company, his contracts, his presence. She didn't want any ties to Carrie's other life, any reminders that would make Bernie wonder when she was older why she wasn't good enough for Carrie or for Carrie's husband.

Beth Ann was covered by a cold sweat. Asking questions that were uncomfortably dangerous, Carrie's husband was too threatening to her insulated world. She had tried to make herself believe that if the adoption were finalized, she would be able to greet Carrie's husband with the hospitality he deserved. But she knew that wasn't the case. Carrie had made things too difficult for Beth Ann to be honest, much less hospitable. Put on top of that the unthinkable—Bernie inheriting a software company! It gave Beth Ann a headache just considering all the implications.

"Beth Ann? Is that you?"

"Yes, Grans. It's me." Beth Ann pasted on a smile and then walked in to Iris's bedroom, still the same after twenty-some-odd years. Beth Ann remembered the first time she'd seen the room. She and Carrie had been there just a day, dropped off hastily by Carrie's father, her stepfather. She'd thought it the most beautiful room she had ever seen. It smelled like fresh lavender, and the nightstand and vanity were draped in delicate lace. She had been ten then, Carrie just six. She had stood in the door and admired Iris's bed, a dark mahogany four-poster, also draped in an intricately crocheted spread.

"Not tired?" asked Iris, old even then.

A ten-year-old Beth Ann wordlessly shook her head.

"Is Caroline sleeping?"

"We call her Carrie," Beth Ann corrected her.

"Then I will call her Carrie, too," Iris said softly. "It's been a long day."

"I'm not tired," Beth Ann replied politely.

"Well, I am. Why don't you sit on the bed with me and keep me company, while I finish this little drawing for your mother."

Beth Ann reluctantly climbed up to sit stiffly on the bed. Her hand traced the pattern on the bedspread.

"Do you like it?" Iris held up a pen-and-ink drawing of a wildflower.

"It's pretty."

"I can teach you how to do it."

"My mom's the best artist in the world. She said she would teach me."

Iris nodded. Then she stated gently, "Your mom's pretty sick."

"She's going to get better," Beth Ann said defen-

sively. "*She promised she would. We're only going to be here for a little bit.*"

Iris nodded. "*That's right. A little bit.*"

A little bit turned out to be forever. After her mother had died, her stepfather had visited just once to let his mother know he didn't want the children, not even Carrie, his own blood. As Carrie slept, Beth Ann cried silently, leaning up against the door, her chest aching, listening to him argue with Iris. He was the only father she had ever known. The next morning, he was gone and Iris never spoke his name again.

Beth Ann took a deep breath. Bernie would never, ever wonder whether she was loved. Ever.

"I hear voices," Iris said plaintively.

"Yes. Glenn is here. Remember, I told you he was coming to keep an eye on Bernie so I could get back to painting." She hoped. It had been a long time since she'd painted, really worked at it, rather than merely dabbling with interesting techniques and calling it work. When she'd stopped painting, neither Glenn nor his life partner, Fred, who was a highly regarded art dealer, had condemned her. Even when she didn't follow through on several projects, Fred did his best to cover for her, simply telling her to let him know when she was ready.

Two months earlier she had thought she was ready. So, believing the effort would spur her back into painting more regularly, she'd sent some slides of her older work to a hotel in Merced that wanted to use their lobby to showcase local artists. It had cost her a big gulp in pride. Before Bernie, she'd been accepted to some of the most prestigious Bay Area galleries. Way beyond showing in a local hotel.

Still when the white envelope bearing the hotel's logo had arrived a few days ago, she couldn't even open it. She didn't know what she feared most: the rejection or the acceptance.

Iris frowned, then brightened. "Has Carrie come to visit?"

Beth Ann shook her head. "No, sweetie. Carrie's dead. Remember?"

Iris looked away puzzled. "Why did I think Carrie was here?"

"Carrie's husband is here," Beth Ann said after a moment's hesitation. "Remember the man that stopped you on the road?" Damn near ran her down.

"Carrie's husband?" She looked puzzled. "When did she marry?"

"Years ago."

Iris's forehead wrinkled. "Did we go to the wedding?"

Beth Ann shook her head. "No, sweetie. They got married kind of quickly." She started straightening Iris's covers. "Do you want to get up? I can fix your hair and put in your diamond tiara before I take Bernie to the garden."

Iris sunk back down into the pillows. She closed her eyes. "No. I feel tired. I don't want to wear my tiara today."

Beth Ann kissed her on the head, wondering if she should take her to the doctor later in the afternoon. "Sleep well, Grans." Before she left, she switched on the portable baby monitor, then quietly closed the door.

When Beth Ann got to the kitchen, she found that it was completely deserted, but she heard screams of excitement outside. Despite its gray start, the day had turned out to be beautiful. Not yet noon and the sun shone brightly. She saw Bernie, bundled in her coat, scrambling wildly through a pile of decaying leaves as Glenn chased her from behind. Christian leaned against the old oak, watching intently, the collar of his leather jacket turned up as he nursed a mug of coffee.

Bernie lifted something and gave it to Glenn. Then she turned and gave whatever it was to Christian. Both men thanked her with enthusiastic nods of their heads. Suddenly aware that she had a moment of peace, Beth Ann was reluctant to open the door and join them. If Carrie's husband would just go away— It made no difference that Bernie was an heiress. As far as she was concerned, his money, his software company, his silver Jaguar and expensive shoes only made it heartwrenchingly clear that Carrie had chosen *things* over her own daughter. Beth Ann would not give him the chance to make the same choice. Bernie would not be rejected twice.

CHRISTIAN IGNORED the persistent ache behind his left ear and watched Bernie who dug furiously into the ground with a toy shovel and then chortled with glee when she found a huge beetle that raced to get out of the way. She reached to pick it up with two fingers, but it scurried past her and she followed, her little face pinched with her efforts to coordinate her eyes with her hands.

"Bug!" she declared and looked straight up at Christian. His heart jerked. Caroline. His fist tightened and he felt the sharp rock jab into his skin. He opened his hand. Glenn had long since discarded his, but Christian examined the garden rock, really an oversize piece of amber gravel, that Bernie had so judiciously bestowed upon him. Bernie shrieked with excitement, chattering away as she continued to doggedly pursue the bug, trying alternately to step on and grab it until it managed to squeeze its body through a small hole and out of reach.

Having been eluded, Bernie walked around in aimless circles. Her mind already searching for her next adventure. The steaming pile of compost looked promising.

"Oh, no, you don't, Bern-Bern," Glenn said as he intercepted her, pulling her up against him, then giving her a big affectionate squeeze and a wet smacking kiss on her cheek.

Christian felt slightly satisfied when Bernie screamed her protest and wriggled violently to be let down. Glenn obliged. Her mind now fixated on trying to move a small boulder, Bernie began to push.

The two men stood awkwardly, both watching Bernie, who got tired of pushing and decided to defeat the rock by sitting on it.

"I'm sorry about Carrie," Glenn said finally.

"Thank you," Christian replied and took a sip of coffee. It was cold now and it still tasted awful. The second cup was worse than the first. No wonder Beth Ann put so much sugar in it.

Glenn laughed.

"What?"

"She makes terrible coffee, doesn't she?"

"Is that why you didn't take any?" Christian raised an eyebrow.

"Yes," Glenn admitted. "I let her keep one or two of her illusions. One is that it's coffee in general that tastes so bad—not her coffee in particular."

"I think she might have an idea."

Glenn smiled. "Maybe, but that hasn't made her want to learn how to make better coffee. She just adds more sugar and cream."

They fell silent again.

After a moment, Christian asked, "Have you been friends long?"

Glenn shrugged. "Depends on what you think is long. We've known each other since graduate school."

"Graduate school?" Christian felt an unflattering wave of guilt at his surprise. He would never have imagined Beth Ann would have gone to college much less received a higher degree. Caroline had no degrees he knew of.

Glenn shot him a speculative look, then said, "Don't know much about her, do you?"

"Well—" Christian felt his face grow hot. Why was he so reluctant to admit he knew absolutely nothing?

Glenn nodded. "She paints, teaches when she has to, but mostly holds together her little family single-handedly."

"Single-handedly?" Christian asked, a flare of something coming up from under his ribs. "She's not married?"

Glenn called out to Bernie who was now lying on the rock, her head lolled backward, the tips of her curls brushing the dirt. She sat up quickly and then toppled over sideways. She chortled, babbling at them unintelligibly, clearly emphasizing the last syllable, as if she were scolding them. She placed her hands on her hips to make her point.

"No, she's not married."

"Divorced?" Christian tried to make his voice casual.

"Nope. Never married."

"So Iris has lived here all her life?" Christian looked around.

Glenn shook his head. "No. From what I understand, she was a botany professor, a science artist. She came here from U.C. Berkeley to retire. Taught Beth Ann most everything she knows about art."

"Are you Bernadette's father?" The question came out much more baldly than Christian had planned.

Glenn took a long time to answer. He looked at Christian, his eyes guarded, and Christian knew he was being thoroughly surveyed. Finally, Glenn asked, "What would make you think that?"

Christian felt as if he was negotiating one of the trickiest liaisons known to man. Then he shrugged and observed bluntly, "Bernadette called you Poppop."

"A nickname," Glenn replied, his eyes watching Bernie's progress, as she tried to balance on the rock, her baby gibberish supplying background noise.

"What is she saying?" Christian couldn't help asking when Glenn said something back to her.

"I have no idea," Glenn replied with an honest smile. "But we're sure it's something important and Beth Ann is a stickler for responses."

"Bernadette seems to talk well for someone her age."

"We think so." Glenn laughed. "But then we also think she's a genius."

"Did you know Caroline?" Christian asked,

abruptly changing the subject. He wondered if Caroline would have found Glenn attractive. She had a way of fluttering from one handsome man to the next. She was very flirtatious, but he'd never thought to doubt her fidelity.

Glenn glanced away and hedged. "I met her a couple of times. I wouldn't say I knew her."

"Mommy!" Bernie squealed and ran to meet Beth Ann.

"Bernie-Bern-Bern. What have you been up to?"

"Gar-*den*," Bernie said and then jumped up and said something rapidly before shouting "Bugs" and wandering off. She pressed her face against another rock, which left a dark smudge of dirt on her cheek.

"You know you're in charge of the cleanup," Beth Ann told Glenn. "I just gave her a bath last night."

"It's only dirt, sweetheart. It'll wash off. So go paint. I've got things covered."

"Thank you." She handed him a baby monitor. "Iris is sleeping for now. But she's had a tough day. She's going to be really hungry when she wakes up, so be sure to get to the kitchen before she does. She had all four burners going with empty pots on them last weekend."

"Again?" Glenn asked with sharp surprise.

Beth Ann's face tightened imperceptibly and she concentrated on staring at Bernie. "It's not again," she denied. Christian watched her turn away from Glenn and again wondered about their relationship.

"Didn't something similar just happen?" Glenn asked.

"No. It was a mistake. More my fault than hers," Beth Ann said dismissively.

"Beth Ann, she's nearly ninety."

"I don't want to talk about it."

Christian, an intensely private individual, had never seen a soul close up as fast as she did. It was as if she wasn't even present anymore.

"So," she said, her voice cheerful, changing the subject. "What's in the box in the hall?"

"Mostly samples. Fred got a whole case of new paints. It's a start-up brand, and he thought you might be feeling experimental. He wants a report on how the colors compare to the old faithfuls."

Beth Ann laughed. "My whole life is an experiment. I'll call him tonight and thank him. You don't know how much that helps. I didn't know how much more I could squeeze out of a dry tube." She glanced at Christian. "Watercolors," she said briefly, filling him in.

"Of course." He nodded as if he knew what she was talking about.

"Mommy, Mommy, Mommy," Bernie said insistently.

"Just a minute, Bern. I'm talking with Pop-pop."

Bernie was quiet for a quick second and then said more loudly, "Mommy, mommy, mommy, mommy—"

Beth Ann shot Christian another glance. He was amazed she remembered he was there, and his heart thumped louder as she gave him a rueful smile. "And I was the one who couldn't wait until she said 'mommy.' Teaching her to talk seemed like a good idea then." She chuckled, then turned to Glenn. "Can you get them lunch? I want to get as much done as I can before you take off."

"Will do."

"And…"

"And?"

Beth Ann looked around quizzically, past Christian, as if she had forgotten what it was she had say.

"I'm having an Iris moment," she laughed, and then slapped her forehead. "Oh, yes. There's plenty of food. Make sandwiches—don't cut the crust off for Bernie even though she'll want you to. Give her turkey instead of peanut butter. I'm seeing if she's allergic. Your choice of canned soup. Potato chips—"

"Above the fridge."

"Only a handful after Bern's eaten most of her sandwich or she'll just eat potato chips and no sandwich or soup. And applesauce."

"Yes, sir." Glenn saluted.

Beth Ann made a face at him.

Christian watched the exchange silently. It wasn't as if she were being overly rude. After all, she had a life, and he had the eerie sensation of being plopped in the middle of it. She afforded him no special treatment. He frowned into the coffee cup. And he wasn't certain if he liked that. He had always commanded attention, even as a young man. But of course, having Elliott as a last name didn't hurt, and three generations of money probably helped. But here, none of that seemed to matter.

Unlike most people who would immediately be trying to capitalize on the fact they had just been given a multimillion dollar software company, Beth Ann acted as if he had offered her a dead cockroach. So different from Caroline, who'd made it very clear from the very first moment they'd met that she was acutely, intimately aware of his existence.

They'd met through Max, who had been introduced to Caroline at an exclusive private party. She was the love of his life, Max had declared, but then graciously bowed out when it became apparent that Caroline only had eyes for Christian. He'd been drawn to how earthy, and even rather naive, she was. He found her a refreshing change from bored debutantes. She was so eager to learn about what he was interested in, listening for hours as he talked about the company, the business.

The next thing he knew, he was introducing her to his mother, and the two of them bonded quickly. His mother always liked projects and Caroline had no qualms about becoming one. Caroline relished, polished, and upheld her role as the future Mrs. Christian Elliott. Maybe a little too much. Still when Christian persuaded Caroline to elope, forgoing the large wedding that his mother was planning, she seemed almost relieved. He now realized why.

He also knew that he had no idea what earthy was. If Caroline was earthy, Beth Ann was the magma that formed the earth. When he saw Beth Ann turn back to the house, he realized she was leaving and there was going to be no further discussion of the software company, of Caroline, of anything.

"I need to talk with you." Christian stepped forward and grabbed her arm to halt her.

Beth Ann looked at him, then down at the hand that closed around her elbow. "Maybe later," she said shortly, and tugged at her arm. He released her, understanding that she didn't have to talk to him if she didn't want to. He wasn't even related. His resentment began to close his throat. Part of being married meant getting to know your spouse's family, and he felt unrealistically that Caroline, by her secrecy, had robbed him of that. Here was a family unit, perhaps more unconventional than any he had ever experienced, but he greatly disliked the fact that he was categorically placed outside the inner circle.

If he hadn't felt so desperate, he would have laughed at the irony. His *sister-in-law* seemed reluctant to acknowledge his existence. Usually, Christian Elliott was begged to participate in the most exclusive of the exclusive, his family an integral spoke of the most prestigious circles in Southern California. Yet here he was, his feelings battered because some farmgirl artist person would barely look at him.

"How much later?" he asked, forcing his voice to be casual.

Beth Ann shrugged noncommittally. "I have to paint. I don't often get the luxury of an undisturbed stretch of time. Glenn's here until—" She looked at Glenn inquiringly.

"I've got to be in Fresno by noon tomorrow to meet with a client."

"Glenn paints, too," Beth Ann informed Christian.

"So when can we talk?"

Beth Ann glanced around. "I don't know. How long are you here for?"

He'd planned to be on his way to the Napa Valley twenty minutes ago, the documents signed and ready for express shipping to his attorney.

"Indefinitely," he answered.

"Indefinitely?" Her voice squeaked. He saw that he'd rattled her and wondered why. She backed away from him, her eyes just barely shuttering abject anxiety. She shook her head. "You know, I can't really think about this now—"

With an abrupt turn she started to walk away. Christian followed her, giving a quick glance at Glenn who stood watchfully by, ready to insert himself if need be.

"Give me a time and place. I'll be there," he said insistently.

She was quiet and then stopped. Beth Ann looked back at Glenn who shrugged. She stared so hard at Christian's shoulder he thought he might have dandruff. Then she heaved a big sigh. "Tonight. Los Amigos on Pacheco Boulevard. Seven o'clock," she said wearily. "I'll give you enough time for a dinner and coffee. Will you leave us alone then?"

"Los Amigos at seven," Christian agreed and held up the coffee mug in his hand.

Beth Ann took it from him, peering into it. "You drank it," she said in surprise.

"Los Amigos at seven," Christian repeated, not understanding the feeling of hope welling through him. "I'll be there."

EVEN THOUGH her head was throbbing, Beth Ann worked for the rest of the morning. She took a small break for lunch and then went back to her attic for more. Really, what she spent most of her time doing was procrastinating. She straightened her files of reference photos. She organized the slides of her previous works. She studied them and looked around at the stuff she had been sporadically working on. Then she noticed the dust on the desk and decided to clean her work area.

As the light faded into dusk, she had not picked up her paintbrush at all. She swallowed her frustration, closing her eyes to the throbbing in her sinuses. Lack of sleep, she excused herself, not to mention the events of the morning. She had been up for the past several nights with Iris, making sure she wasn't wandering around the kitchen trying to roast marshmallows on the gas stove. Between that and Bernie's advanced mobility and ever increasing curiosity, Beth Ann's watercolors, which at one time had been a refuge, had been reduced to another source of anxiety.

When Fred had called in March with the news that the Merced hotel was opening up its lobby to new artists, she had been less than enthusiastic because she had very little new work. Okay, she had no new work. But she'd promised Fred she would try, at least make a start back into the art world, as small as her local region was.

The only thing she'd managed to do was discover how good she was at avoiding painting. Between family crises and sporadically teaching weekend classes for the city's parks and rec department, there didn't seem to be time. Now, as she looked at the half-finished paintings that hung around her, a few damp only because she'd accidentally spilt water when she was cleaning, she knew she couldn't blame Bernie or Iris or the lack of paints anymore. She turned on the light, realizing suddenly how dim it had gotten. A single tap on the door gave her an excuse to formally stop.

"Come in," she called, trying to make her voice stronger, in case it was Iris.

"Done yet?" Glenn poked his handsome head in.

"Yeah. No light. My eyes are shot," Beth Ann said guiltily, allowing the fatigue to creep back into her voice. She ran the water in the attached sink. Fred had run the plumbing up to the attic so she could do her work here. She pretended to wash out her brushes, and her water cans. "What time is it?"

Glenn glanced at her big clock that read eleven twenty-four.

"Battery died. I haven't changed it yet," she confessed.

"It's just after six-thirty. You've got a date at seven."

Beth Ann pulled a face. "I can't even imagine what he wants. If I weren't so tired, I'd have a talk about it with you."

"Talk about it with me anyway." Glenn sat down. "I'm dying to find out how things went. What did he say?"

"Where are Bernie and Iris?" Beth Ann asked.

"Bernie's still zonked out and Iris is in her room looking at her pictures."

Beth Ann nodded. That sometimes absorbed Iris for nearly an hour. "Any crises?"

Glenn shook his head. "Nope. Everyone seemed to be on their best behavior." He looked at her piercingly. "So. That was Carrie's husband?"

Beth Ann stared out the round picture window that overlooked the garden and the big oak, another improvement courtesy of Fred. She watched the horizon scatter brilliant reds and oranges from end-to-end. She studied the color of the sky, a perfect French ultramarine blue, and watched the lights of an airplane track across it.

"Yes," she answered slowly. "That was Carrie's husband. Did he stay long?"

Glenn shook his head. "Nope. As soon as you left, he left, too." He gave her a sly smile. "Though he did ask what kind of flowers you were partial to."

Beth Ann made a face. "You're kidding."

"Would I kid about flowers? I think he wants to get on your good side."

Beth Ann was silent.

"So, Bethy, why is he here?" Glenn probed. At her exasperated look, he admitted freely, "Yes. I'm under strict orders from Fred to report to him as soon as I know anything."

She stared at her old friend, feeling his empathy emanate toward her. They had been comrades for too many years for her to hide anything from him. She had met both Glenn and Fred in graduate school, the three of them quickly befriending each other, eventually sharing a three-bedroom house. Iris had expressed concern about her granddaughter living with two men, but Beth Ann had assured her they were just friends. Besides, Fred was gay and Glenn had a girlfriend. When Iris met the two for the first time, Beth Ann had been relieved when Iris squeezed her hand, approving the friendship.

Their relationship didn't end with graduation. When she moved back to California, she was pleasantly surprised to find that within a few months, both Fred and Glenn had found a place together in San Jose. After they'd popped the champagne for their housewarming, the two men had exchanged glances with each other and gently told her they were intimately involved.

Beth Ann had been stunned only because she'd had no idea that Glenn was gay. Once she'd closed her mouth, she'd hugged them both fiercely, her blessing genuine. Her unreserved joy for them had only deepened their friendship, especially after Glenn's family had reacted terribly to his announcement. Fred, originally from the Midwest, had long established a cordial if not enthusiastic relationship with his parents, exchanging cards at birthdays and Christmas but not much else. However, after their commitment ceremony, Fred's mother had started sending Glenn birthday cards as well.

Just friends. Beth Ann shook her head. No, just family.

Conventional or not, Glenn and Fred were as much her family as Bernie and Iris. They'd turned the attic into her studio. They'd stood by her side when Carrie abandoned Bernie. They'd come at anytime of the day or night, driving the hour and a half to baby- and grandmother-sit when Beth Ann couldn't stand it anymore. They were present for every important event in her life—from the rise and fall of her short art career to the death of her sister to Bernie's first steps to the mental decline of her grandmother.

But she remained silent, feeling like she wanted to be a color. If she were that perfect French ultramarine blue, she wouldn't have to think about Carrie or Carrie's husband or his reasons for being in Mercy Springs.

CHAPTER FOUR

BETH ANN FINALLY looked back at Glenn, who waited patiently for her to answer, one ear cocked for any sounds of disturbance downstairs.

"I can't imagine why Carrie's husband is here," she said slowly.

"Really?" Glenn's speculative look made her turn her back to him, knowing he could read her like a book.

She shook her head and then guilt pulsated in her stomach. She didn't want to lie to her dearest friend. She concentrated on rewashing her unused paint-brushes and then said, "He might have mentioned something about Bernie owning a software com-pany, but that didn't seem to be the reason he's here. He damn near ran Iris down."

"He said something about what?" Glenn asked, his voice incredulous.

"A software company," Beth Ann whispered with a grimace.

"A software company?"

"Yeah, uh, one called DirectTech."

Glenn was silent for so long that Beth Ann looked up. His handsome, dear face was extraordinarily pensive.

Eventually he said slowly, "That's not good, is it?"

Beth Ann blinked back tears that had somehow filled her eyes. It was that damned headache. "It can't be good."

"Does he want Bernie?"

Beth Ann shrugged and then turned the water on full blast, scrubbing her wash brush. "He can't have her. I'm going to tell him what he can do with his software company."

"He didn't seem particularly interested in her."

"Do you think he knows?"

Glenn thought for a minute before saying, "I don't think he does. And if he doesn't, you probably should tell him."

"Are you nuts?" Beth Ann whirled around, spraying Glenn with residual water. She promptly burst into tears, the thought of exposing Bernie to Christian sending terrible waves of dread down her back. What if he wanted her? She'd never be able to fight him in court. With his money, his clout, he'd cream her. Then another thought swept through her. What if he didn't want Bernie? What if Bernie was no more important to him than she was to Carrie? Once the papers were signed, Bernie would be forever tied to the Elliotts, but only as some sort of awkward addendum.

Glenn swiftly crossed the room and enveloped her in a warm hug. Beth Ann buried her face in his chest, feeling as if Glenn's comforting squeeze was the only thing keeping her from exploding into tiny pieces of emotional debris. Glenn was indeed a good friend.

"I know you don't want to hear this, but you need to tell him, Bethy," Glenn whispered. "He's got to know. Tell him now while you've got nothing to lose."

Beth Ann pulled away and sniffed loudly. "I have everything to lose. I could lose Bernie."

"You might," Glenn admitted frankly. "But, you'll lose her anyway when he finds out. And he will find out. He's on some kind of mission and I'm not even sure he knows exactly what it is. He doesn't know who Bernie is, but I saw him stare at her. I'm sure he sees the resemblance to Carrie."

"We're sisters."

"Half sisters. You two don't even look alike. Carrie was the spitting image of her father."

Beth Ann gave Glenn an annoyed stare. "I hate it when you play Jiminy Cricket."

Glenn laughed. "That's why I'm here." He glanced at the work that appeared to be drying around the studio. Beth Ann bit her lip as she watched him examine the painting, not realizing she was holding her breath. Glenn was an enormously talented and highly productive muralist, who traveled the globe painting both interior and exterior walls. So talented and so sought after, he was booked several years in advance. Unless he developed some artist's block, his next ten years would be filled with interesting projects, different places. But Beth Ann couldn't be jealous of his success. He deserved it.

Glenn studied the backdrop of a grove of newly pruned almond trees. "I like that."

"Party Girls."

"What?"

"I'm going to call that *Party Girls,*" Beth Ann ad-libbed, feeling like the biggest fraud of the century. "Don't they look as if they're dressing in their pink blossoms, as if they're going to an afternoon cotillion or something?"

"Nice."

"Too much burnt sienna?"

Glenn studied it. "No. Shades that hillside, nicely. Good job with the light." He looked closer. "Though you might want to play with the value on the right. Seems too dark, you need something else sort of dancing back there."

Beth Ann peered with him, then nodded her agreement. "I see what you mean."

"But very nice. I like the direction you're taking."

Beth Ann frowned in concentration, staring at her palette of colors.

"The photo came out a little dark and I haven't found a way to lighten the whole scene." It was amazing how she could sound as if she had just painted that yesterday, rather than over a year ago.

"Did you hear from the hotel about the show?"

Beth Ann felt her cheeks burn as she lied to her good friend. "No, not yet." She just couldn't admit to Glenn that she was afraid to open the envelope. Glenn had no experience with not painting, hating painting, having painting torture his very soul. Glenn *always* painted so he never lost the ability.

"Funny." Glenn shot her a quick glance. "Fred said they'd told him they mailed out the results last week. Should've arrived by now."

"Maybe this week," Beth Ann replied, annoyed that her voice was so chirpy.

"So Carrie's husband only came to deliver the news that Bernie inherited DirectTech?"

Beth Ann shrugged. "That's what he said."

"Nothing else?"

She shook her head and took a deep breath. "No."

"And are you going to tell him about Bernie?"

Beth Ann gave him a look and her chin started to quiver.

"You've got to tell him."

"Well, I'm not going to be dishonest—if he asks me straight out," Beth Ann said, placating herself. "However, if the topic doesn't come up, why in the world would I want to tell him? It can't be for anyone's good—"

"Least of all yours," Glenn inserted.

"She's mine," Beth Ann said stubbornly. "In two months the adoption will be finalized and she'll be mine."

"But if he's the father—"

"He's not the father," Beth Ann interrupted. "If he were, wouldn't Carrie just have told him?"

"She never told you who the father was," Glenn said. "Maybe she simply didn't want to have any kids."

"Then she should've had an abortion."

There was a stunned silence between them.

"You don't mean that, Bethy," Glenn said with reproof.

Beth Ann had the grace to look abashed and replied, "You're right, I don't." She then said fiercely, "Bernie is mine. What Christian Elliott doesn't know, won't hurt him." She wiped her hands on her jeans. "I've got to change."

ON THE WAY TO Los Amigos, Beth Ann felt terrible. She hated squabbling with Glenn. He and Fred were the kind of friends who took it upon themselves to be like annoying older brothers—never letting well enough alone. If she had answered that lawyer and claimed DirectTech for Bernie, then Christian Elliott wouldn't be sitting at Los Amigos, waiting for her, wanting something from her she didn't know she could give him.

She glanced at her watch. She'd be a few minutes late. And her eyes were red. One look at her and he'd know she'd been crying. When she got out of the car, she saw with dismay that he was waiting for her. His back was toward her as he faced the horizon, his hands shoved into his pockets, a bouquet of flowers tucked under one arm. But he wasn't impatient, which surprised her. Rather than checking his watch every few seconds, he actually seemed to be enjoying the coolness of the evening, gazing at the sky as if he needed to see every last remnant of color fade.

Deliberately, she slowed her walk, just to give him a moment to absorb the changing light and color, offering him plenty of space to immerse himself in the wonder of the night sky, the brightness of the stars that appeared from nowhere. He looked oddly alone, almost sad, standing there in his tailored clothes, his figure darkened by the onset of night. Beth Ann shook herself. Christian Elliott had access to one of the most spectacular evening views in California. His office overlooked the San Diego harbor, after all. What made her think he never really saw the stars?

"Hello," she called.

When he turned, her heart beat harder, apparently

not understanding this wasn't that kind of dinner. But, Lord, he was handsome. His face was perfectly proportioned, sharpened by the austere demeanor that seemed to be second nature. Her eyes were drawn to the most vulnerable part of his face, the curve of his bottom lip, held rigid even though he appeared relaxed. She felt her cheeks grow hot when she realized she was staring, fantasizing almost, about whether the tight lines of his lips would soften under a kiss. She shifted her eyes to the rest of him. He was wearing the same clothes he'd worn that morning, but it looked as if he'd had them pressed.

"Hi," he said and opened the door to the small restaurant for her.

"Sorry to keep you waiting," she began.

He dismissed her apology. "It doesn't look like there's going to be a big crowd."

"Well, it's Tuesday," she said in explanation.

He nodded, then, remembering the roses, thrust them at her.

"For you."

This was awkward. She told her heart to slow down as she accepted the beautiful apricot and pink bouquet. They weren't for her. They were just a means to get her signature so he could close this chapter of his life.

"Well, thank you," she said and sniffed. "Did you have any problems finding the place?"

"No. I passed it on the way back to the hotel. I just remembered that it was close to the propane store."

"That's Mercy Springs." Beth Ann chuckled, surprised when he helped her off with her coat and then pulled her seat out for her. "Thank you."

She watched him as he carefully pushed her chair in and then draped her coat over the unoccupied seat.

It was an odd sensation being out. It was an even odder sensation being out with a person who had such manners. Well-bred manners. She just wished the occasion was real, that she was out on a real date with a man who looked like Christian and who wasn't her dead sister's husband. She felt a pulse in the base of her throat throb and squelched the niggle of anticipation. It irritated her that this acute, uncomfortable awareness had decided to rear its dormant head right now.

"Hey, there, Beth Ann. How's it going?" The waitress came up and handed them well-used menus.

"Hey, Claudia. The same old, same old," Beth Ann replied, welcoming the distraction.

"Who's your friend here?" Claudia gave Christian a speculative glance, then saw the flowers and grinned broadly.

Beth Ann blushed.

"Christian Elliott, Claudia Ramirez. Claudia, Christian. Claudia's family has run the Los Amigos for two generations."

"Ricky'll be the third," Claudia said proudly.

"Ricky's Claudia's son. How old is he now?"

"Nearly seventeen."

Beth Ann shook her head, *tsk tsking*. "Time flies, doesn't it?" She turned to Christian. "We went to school together."

"Mercy Springs High."

"Go Gophers," they said in unison before Claudia asked, "You guys know what you want?"

"Give us a minute."

"Sure thing. It was nice meeting you." Claudia gave Christian a quick wink and walked away.

They lapsed into silence as they studied the menus.

"What's good?" Christian asked.

"Depends on what you want," Beth Ann replied, trying very hard not to look at him, not to feel drawn to him. "If you like fried food, they make excellent chimichangas. The enchiladas are good. The burritos are huge."

"Caroline hated fried food."

"Carrie had a thing about getting fat," Beth Ann corrected him. "She loved fried food."

Christian fixed his silver gaze on her, and she felt a flush creep up her neck. Then he asked quietly, "How do you know?"

"She was my sister."

"She was my wife."

"Are you ready to order?" a just-returning Claudia asked with a chirp in her voice.

After ordering, the silence continued. Christian stared at the paper-lace placemat, attempting to control the emotions churning through him. He didn't have much experience with people like his sister-in-law, but he still couldn't figure out where her animosity came from. Surely, she didn't think he was responsible for the fact that Caroline had never visited? An even more pressing question gnawed at him.

Why had Caroline left DirectTech to her niece in the first place?

It wasn't as if Caroline had really been interested in the company. She sat on the board but never attended the meetings. She simply collected the dividends. By the end, he wasn't sure Caroline was aware she owned anything. Her financial needs were so great he'd had to channel several other funding sources into her account.

"I'm here," Beth Ann reminded him.

Christian looked up, his eyes falling on the top of her curls, reminding him again how short Caroline's sister was. It took Christian a split second to figure out she was teasing him, an irreverence he found very attractive, almost comforting. As they waited for their order, Beth Ann nursed an unseasonal melon margarita. After a few minutes, Christian realized she wasn't going to initiate the conversation. She glanced at him and then looked intently at the table. So different from Caroline's almost nonstop chatter. The same thing that had stirred inside him earlier—when she'd been torn between Bernie and Iris—stirred again. He cleared his throat and searched for a neutral topic.

"So how old is Bernadette?" he ventured, and wondered at the guarded look that came into her eyes.

Beth Ann answered carefully, "Twenty-three months. She'll be two in June."

"Is it normal to be potty training this early?"

Beth Ann shrugged. "It's less about age and more about readiness. She started showing signs she was ready about six weeks ago, so I decided to try it. We take it easy. I still let her wear a diaper most of the time. I just put her on the potty in the mornings and after meals when I know she usually has something to do."

"She's quite a character."

"Yes, she is."

Another silence fell and lengthened until Claudia came back with steaming plates of food. Christian eyed what Claudia set before Beth Ann. She'd ordered the special combo, which consisted of a taco, chicken enchilada, beef tamale with rice, beans and salad. He doubted he could eat that much. And while he wasn't consciously comparing Beth Ann to Caroline, he couldn't imagine that Caroline would have even attempted such a meal. His plate looked anemic in comparison, even though he had ordered a burrito grande.

He stared at his dinner and then looked around in puzzlement, wishing he had ordered something that could be eaten more conventionally. How did one eat a dish that resembled a small torpedo?

"It doesn't matter," Beth Ann said in a conspiratorial whisper.

"What?"

"It doesn't matter how you eat it. You can either pick it up or cut it with your fork or knife. Anyway, nobody cares."

Christian glanced around him again. She was absolutely right. No one did care. No one was staring at him, trying to figure out which wine he'd decided to drink, what he'd ordered. Around him were a half a dozen family groups, and not one person was even looking at him, except a small baby who had no choice because of the way she was propped up on her mother's shoulder. She belched loudly and then gurgled.

"You want to know what I'd do?" Beth Ann asked, as she swallowed, a curiously attractive glimmer in her dark eyes.

"What?"

"I'd do both. Cut it in half and then pick it up. The best foods are the ones that use fingers. Burritos, barbecue ribs, cold fried chicken legs. Don't you think?"

Christian paused and nodded absently, still strategically studying the burrito. He remembered those things from the years he'd spent in boarding school. They'd always had a big barbecue on the last day of spring semester. The chicken legs were made by Max's mother. She always made extra for him. Max was one of the lucky boarding school kids who saw his amicably divorced parents often and went home for every holiday and got lots of care packages during the in-between times.

"Yes, I do think," Christian said suddenly.

"What?" Beth Ann looked up midbite. She seemed startled by his sudden return to the conversation.

He stared at her plate, amazed she had already worked her way through the taco and tamale and was embarking on the enchilada. Half of the beans and rice were gone. The salad was decimated.

"Are you going to eat all that?" he asked curiously.

Beth Ann glanced down at her plate in surprise. "Yes, I think I am. Do you want some? This is very good." She proceeded to separate a portion of her enchilada. "Burritos are nice, but they're not the same as the gooey cheesy stuff." She lifted her plate and slid half her enchilada next to his burrito. She indicated the burrito, still untouched. "You should eat. Just cut it in half and pick it up. Here."

She reached over and sawed it in half, then

wrapped the bottom with a paper napkin and presented it to him. "Problem solved."

Christian was stunned. In his thirty-six years, no one had ever assaulted his food in such a way. Years of training made him take it graciously, and the growl of hunger in his stomach made him take a bite.

It was delicious.

He took another bite and realized he was very hungry. They worked their way through the rest of the meal in silence. Between bites of his burrito, he studied Beth Ann as she ate, unable to pinpoint why his heart seemed to be beating a little faster. She wasn't beautiful. Not like Caroline was beautiful.

In fact, it would never occur to him to date someone like Beth Ann. But it was more than politeness that had prompted him to visit the only two florists in Mercy Springs to find the exact roses he imagined. And despite the fact their conversation seemed to alternate between territorial skirmishes and almost intimate teasing, there was something that made the silence between them comfortable. That was only one of the things Christian found unique about her.

Her appetite was another.

He had never seen another woman put away so much food. The women he knew usually picked like birds. Salads, cucumber sandwiches. He couldn't remember Caroline eating anything with her fingers. Beth Ann looked delicate, but ate like a horse.

When their meal was done and coffee ordered, Christian decided it was safe to broach the topic again.

"So I need some kind of confirmation from you about Bernadette's inheritance."

"We don't want it," Beth Ann replied simply.

It was such an easy solution! Beth Ann wondered why she hadn't thought of it earlier. Good old denial. By refusing DirectTech, they could go back to the way things were. He'd probably be relieved because he could keep the company and his family would make more money. It was a truly perfect answer to what seemed to be a complicated problem.

"What?"

Beth Ann met Christian's stare as directly as she could.

"We don't want it," she repeated and took a sip of coffee. She tore open three packets of sugar at one time and dumped them all in.

"You mean you don't want it," he corrected her, his voice very low and flat.

Beth Ann felt a small chill run along the inside of her shoulder blades. Why did his voice sound so menacing, when he looked perfectly civilized, even slightly smiling at her with very square, straight, white teeth?

"No," she replied. "We don't want it." Then, she said hurriedly, "I'm sure your family will be relieved you get to keep the company. Of course, I'll sign any papers that need to be signed to make it happen."

"The company isn't yours," Christian said quietly.

Beth Ann flushed at his observation.

"Don't you think you ought to give Bernadette the chance—"

"Bernie," Beth Ann interrupted him.

"What?"

"Bernie. We call her Bernie. We never call her

Bernadette. Just like Carrie. Carrie was always Carrie. She wasn't Caroline."

Christian was silent for a long time, his eyes unreadable. His voice was very controlled when he spoke. "I never knew Caroline as Carrie. She never let me know she preferred Carrie."

"Oh, she didn't prefer Carrie. She wanted to be Caroline. But she *was* Carrie," Beth Ann said for emphasis. "My mother called her Carrie, her father called her Carrie. I called her Carrie. She was Carrie. She became Caroline. She made up Caroline. Bernie's going to be Bernie. Not Bernadette, even if she does own a software company. She's not going to have to reinvent herself to find happiness."

"Is that what you think Caroli—er, Carrie did?"

Beth Ann nodded. "I know that's what she did. She was very unhappy living in a town this small. She loved reading magazines about the rich and famous and was forever telling me some day she'd be part of that world." Beth Ann gave him an assessing stare. "I guess she did that."

"Through me, you mean."

"Yes."

"I loved her."

Beth Ann turned away, feelings about Carrie and Christian and Bernie churning inside her. Or maybe it was just the taco, tamale and half an enchilada with rice and beans and salad.

"I don't know anything about that."

"I know you don't. Which is why I'm telling you. I loved her."

"Then why'd you let her die?"

"I didn't *let* her die."

"Sure you did. You let her do anything she wanted, even if it was bad for her."

Christian stared at Beth Ann in disbelief. How dare she talk to him like he had something to do with Caroline's death? He felt a sting of guilt, even though he understood her words were spoken from the pain of losing her sister. He met her dark eyes, black tonight in the low light of the restaurant and saw the grief and the loss—felt the sensations as acutely as when Max had come to tell him.

It was interesting that Max was the one to tell him about Caroline's death and not the police. That hadn't occurred to him before. At the time he had thought it meant that Max believed the news would be easier to hear coming from him rather than an officer. Now, he wondered why Max had known before him. Had the police contacted Max first? Then he remembered. Max was at the party with Caroline. But he took no comfort from that thought. He focused his attention on the woman before him and spoke succinctly. "I was not Caroline's father. I was her husband."

"And as her husband, maybe you should have said enough is enough."

"What do you mean by that?" He couldn't help the sharp tone in his voice.

"You weren't at the party where she died, were you?"

"I had to work."

Beth Ann threw him an appraising look. "Did you go to any of the parties with her?"

How would she know? He refused to answer.

She nodded. "Did you go on those cruises?"

He stayed silent.

She nodded again. "Then how in the world would you have ever known what your wife was doing?"

"Maybe that's what she ran away from," he said smoothly, turning the tables on her, and was satisfied when Beth Ann blushed.

"Maybe she lived in a place with a sister so controlling she couldn't breathe and all she wanted was a little freedom."

"Maybe," Beth Ann conceded.

"And maybe that sister is doing the exact same thing with her daughter and Caroline knew it and willed her niece the company so Berna—uh, Bernie at least had a fighting chance."

"A fighting chance at *what?*" Her eyes grew big at his implication.

"At life." There. He had got her.

His triumph faded abruptly when Beth Ann did not look defeated. Instead, she was silently shaking her head. When she met his eyes, he saw a completely different woman. This one was educated, cultured. Her voice lowered an octave, as she said, "I guess that depends on what you call life. In this life, what matters is what's being nurtured in that tiny body and head of Bernie's. She's got no need for a software company. She's fed, she's loved, she's given every bit of attention I can give her—"

"She looks like a boy."

Beth Ann shrugged. "She doesn't know that. When it makes a difference, I'll find appropriate clothes for her."

"At a garage sale or secondhand store." He couldn't keep the derision out of his voice.

"Repair, reuse, recycle. Things don't have to be new to be valuable." Beth Ann's eyes flicked over him. "But I guess you wouldn't understand that, would you?"

"All our companies adhere to the very strictest of environmental standards," he said stiffly.

"I'm sure they do." Beth Ann looked at the check and picked it up. "I think I'm ready to go now."

Christian took the check from her. "I'll get it."

Beth Ann paused for a minute and said graciously, "Thank you."

As they walked out, the night air just starting to have the hint of summer to it, he informed her, "This still isn't over."

She flashed him a brilliant smile. "Sure it is. Have your lawyer draw up whatever document we need to return the company back to your family. You can let me deal with the fallout when Bernie turns twenty-one and discovers I gave away her inheritance. Thanks for the flowers."

Christian shook his head. "Sorry, no can do. You just need to be a little more open-minded. It's Bernie's company. You don't really have a choice. Anyway—" he couldn't resist adding "—it seems as if you could really use a couple of months of dividends."

Beth Ann's smile died. "Why would you say that?"

There was no way to put it tactfully, so he said, "It's obvious you need the money."

Beth Ann didn't flinch as he'd expected.

She nodded in thoughtful agreement. "We do need the money. But we don't need it this way."

"What do you mean *this* way?"

She shrugged. "Through intimidation. You're

rich and we're poor. You have everything and we have nothing. For some reason, we're supposed to take money or software companies at whatever the cost." She poked a slender finger gently into his chest. "I'm going to keep the flowers, because they're so beautiful and because I believe you gave them to me sincerely. I don't want the software company because somehow I think the cost is going to be too great. Bernie's just going to get hurt."

"Bernie?" Christian softened his voice.

She looked away too quickly.

"Or you?"

"I don't know what you're t-talking about." For the first time since they'd started this conversation, Beth Ann sounded vulnerable.

Christian didn't know what he was talking about either. He was merely fishing. But years of business training told him Beth Ann's reasons for not signing the papers had less to do with the welfare of her daughter and more to do with herself.

"I think you do," he said shortly. "And I think you're hiding something."

CHAPTER FIVE

BETH ANN REGARDED the stranger who had been married to her sister for seven years and saw something behind those silver eyes, something that stopped her from flinging the truth at him in the middle of the parking lot. Even though he was obviously trying to provoke her, playing her like she was some complicated business deal, she saw in Christian Elliott a man unraveling. She was struck by the realization that they all had paid enormously for the secrets Carrie had kept.

How misguided he was. Money didn't get rid of the bags under the eyes. It didn't heal grief. It didn't make bad marriages better, even in retrospect. It didn't do anything but pay the bills and put clothes on the back and a roof over the head and he didn't seem to understand that.

Or maybe he did.

She stared at him for a long time. She understood what Glenn had been telling her and took a deep breath. Even though she believed she was making one of the worst mistakes in her life, she said, "I'll tell you what. I made some banana bread yesterday. Why don't you come over for dessert? There are a couple of things I think you need to know, but not here."

Just by looking at him, she had no way of knowing whether or not she should regret her words. His face was unreadable, made impassive by what was probably years of training. She thought she saw a flicker of light, but then that was gone as well.

"We'll talk about transferring DirectTech to Bernie?" he asked.

Beth Ann nodded and said, "But you may want to wait until after we talk."

Satisfied, Christian got into his car, feeling as if he had just pulled off one of the biggest coups ever. He'd thought he'd lost any chance with Beth Ann after he'd pushed so hard.

He followed Beth Ann, the short drive back to her house seeming interminably long. He didn't know what he thought he was hoping to find but he had an idea that whatever it was it needed to be found. Somehow. He parked the car to the side and kept his headlights on so she could see her way to the front door even though the porch light gleamed into the night, like a lighthouse beckoning to lost sailors. He then turned off his lights and strolled to meet her. He was waiting a step down as she jiggled the key in the lock, when the door swung open.

"Bethy!" Glenn poked his head out and Christian's spirits fell just slightly. He had forgotten about Glenn, his blond good looks and his familiar relationship with Beth Ann and her daughter. The reasonable side of his mind kicked in. Beth Ann had been able to meet him tonight because Glenn had stayed with Bernie. He felt a little better.

"Hi, there," she said cheerfully as she walked in the house. Christian hesitated slightly. He nodded at Glenn, but the other man missed the nod because he was staring affectionately at Bernie.

"Mommy!" Bernie, dressed for bed in her yellow duck pj's, squealed with two-year-old abandon and ran in place in her excitement. She then twirled around, crumbs from a fig bar flying everywhere. Her hair was a puffy brown cotton ball of curls with as many tangles. She spun even faster, the grip on her cookie tight.

"Bernie, Bernie, Bernie." Beth Ann crouched down and swung her daughter up. Bernie gave her a big wet kiss, smearing half-masticated fig filling over Beth Ann's cheek. "Can Mommy have a bite, please?"

Christian watched, the same spark of envy he'd felt that morning flaring.

"Bite, please?" Bernie asked teasingly, holding the cookie away from Beth Ann who was pretending to eat her way up Bernie's fat arm.

"Bite, please," Beth Ann repeated with chomping noises. Bernie chortled with laughter, her chins jiggling, and then generously gave Beth Ann a bite.

Glenn took the flowers from Beth Ann. "Nice," he commented.

"Fowers," Bernie said.

Christian stood on the threshold of this beacon of a house, not wanting to intrude on the scene. He was transfixed by the concept that in back of him was stark darkness but in front were the shining lights of home and hearth. He suddenly didn't see the house as old or in need of repair. It actually exuded a freshness that many of the homes he stayed in never did.

"Please, come on in," Beth Ann invited, as if she'd only just remembered him. Glenn looked his way in surprise. Christian gave him another curt nod. Beth Ann looked at the toys scattered around the living room with a resigned humor. "Watch your step. Don't worry about breaking anything but your ankle."

Glenn took Bernie out of Beth Ann's arms and Beth Ann took the flowers back.

"You're just in time," Glenn said. Christian watched them exchange a silent comment with their eyes. Glenn continued, "I was wondering how I was going to get a brush through her hair."

The detangler stuff, Christian remembered, the stuff in the blue bottle.

"Oh, there's a blue spray bottle of detangler on the kitchen counter," Beth Ann called as she walked down the hall. She turned to Christian. "Make yourself at home. I'm going to put these in water."

Picking up a Barbie arm from the couch, Christian sat down, placed the limb on the coffee table and prepared to wait. Despite the toddler clutter, Christian now observed that Beth Ann's home was almost hedonistically feminine. It smelled like an odd combination of baby shampoo and lavender. Flowers, fresh and representations thereof, were displayed on top of white lace generously draped across the many shelves and mantles. Small, well-cared for objects were interspersed among the flowers, along with dozens of meticulously framed photos all high enough and secure enough to be out of the reach of an exploring child.

At Bernie's level, he noticed dozens of children's books and watercolor magazines and an onslaught of toys and toy parts. From the looks of it, Bernie had had a busy night. A brown bear caught his eye. Fluff was uncomfortably wedged between the back leg of a thick leather armchair, the wall and the floor lamp. Christian glanced around self-consciously, and when he didn't see anyone, he got on his hands and knees to take a closer look, intent on retrieving the beloved bear.

"Ah, that's how I like a man," a voice said good-naturedly, behind his raised backside. Mortified, Christian grabbed the bear and stood hastily, dusting off Fluff, unable to control the flush that crept into his face. Beth Ann beamed up at him, her dark eyes dancing. Christian's heart jerked to a stop. Her whole face was lit, brown eyes wrinkling with fun, the corners of her wide mouth tilted up into two perfect points. And dimples. When was the last time he'd seen dimples? Especially ones so deeply embedded that they enticed him into her world.

"I saw him under the chair and thought that Bernie would probably be looking for him sooner or later," he explained awkwardly as she regarded him through now-serious eyes. He handed her the bear.

Beth Ann pulled it close to her in a hug, her dark eyes still searching his face. "Thank you. Bernie will definitely be screaming for Fluff when she goes to bed. Which—" she glanced at the clock "—should be any time now. Do you want some coffee to go with the banana bread?"

Christian didn't feel like he should ingest any more caffeine, especially the kind she served, but he heard his voice say politely, "Yes, please."

She nodded and then indicated that he should follow her.

In the kitchen, he found Glenn wrestling with Bernie's hair.

"There's got to be a better way," Glenn complained.

"You want coffee, Glenn?" Beth Ann asked.

"Nope. Too late." He gave Christian a wink. "Are you going to have some?"

"Sure." Her tone was offhand. "Where's Grans?"

"In bed," Glenn replied and Christian watched as he awkwardly tried to tame Bernie's curls into a pigtail. Bernie stood between his knees, waiting patiently, as if she were used to the drill. When he finished, Bernie's fat hand came up and patted the puff.

"Done?" Bernie asked, her tiny voice raised in an exaggerated question.

"No. One more to do," Glenn said.

"Cookie?"

"No more cookies tonight," Beth Ann answered for him.

Bernie frowned and Christian braced himself for a squall. But surprisingly Bernie didn't blink.

"It's because she had a long nap," Beth Ann whispered, as she set before him a generous slice of banana bread. "If she'd had a lot of excitement and no nap, you'd see the demon baby's head-spin right now." She addressed Glenn, concern clouding her voice. "You said Grans was in bed? This early?"

Glenn nodded. "She looked at her pictures until dinner, ate and then said she was tired, so I helped her get ready for bed. I just checked on her and she's out like a light."

"I'm going to peek in on her," Beth Ann *tut-tutted*. "I hope she's not coming down with something. That last bug really wiped her out. She couldn't get out of bed for a week.''

Christian watched her leave the room and was surprised at her constant movement. She had that in common with Caroline. One of the things that had attracted him to Caroline was her energy.

''Pop-pop done?'' Bernie inquired again. She tugged her head away from him.

''Almost.'' Glenn looked at Christian quizzically. ''You don't happen to know how to do this? I can't get this one for some reason.''

Surprised, Christian shook his head and answered carefully, not understanding why his hands were itching to try. ''Never done that in my life.''

Glenn laughed. ''Two grown men felled by one pigtail.''

''I'll take a whack at it,'' Christian suddenly volunteered. After a look at Bernie, he added, ''That is if she'll let me.''

''Bernie, do you want to get this done?'' Glenn asked.

Bernie nodded vigorously.

''Then will you let Uncle Christian do this for you?''

Bernie's suspicious blue eyes turned on him and he held his breath. He smiled at her and tried not to look intimidating. After a moment, she nodded less vigorously. Still it gave Christian the feeling he had just gotten permission from the Queen of England to kiss her hand.

Christian took the small, well-used brush and small rubber band. He saw the problem immediately. The tiny rubber band was too small for an adult male to even open. It barely stretched around the tip of his forefinger, but would have to be wrapped twice around Bernie's baby fine hair. He studied the problem and then laid a gentle hand on her hair. He couldn't remember any silk gossamer feeling as soft.

BETH ANN pushed open the door to Iris's room, relieved when Iris stirred. Beth Ann crept closer, pulling the covers up over the frail woman. She felt her forehead. Seemed fine. She brushed back the older woman's silver hair and then gently kissed her cheek. "Sleep well." She pushed away any feeling of dread. Of course, Grans had to die sometime. After all she was almost ninety, but Beth Ann couldn't think of life without her. Most of the time, Iris was good company, giving her conversation she couldn't get from Bernie, keeping her laughing with familiar stories and jokes. With Grans gone, she and Bernie would be alone.

She quietly walked out and into the kitchen, surprised to find Bernie sitting on Christian's lap as he secured the second pigtail.

"Group effort?" Beth Ann asked overly brightly, a small pain in her chest as she saw his gentleness. Why had Caroline told her Christian didn't want children? She shook her head because she knew the answer. Caroline didn't want children. She didn't want Bernie and she didn't want Christian to know about Bernie.

He seemed perfectly content to keep Bernie on his lap, his face softening as Bernie at the end of her day, leaned back against his broad, flat chest. Reaching across her, he gave her Fluff, and she pressed her face into the bear. Beth Ann knew how to read the signs. "She need a new diaper?" Beth Ann asked Glenn.

Glenn shook his head. "She shouldn't. We went in Mrs. Potty after her bath. I haven't given her anything to drink."

Christian checked in the back. He'd seen that enough on television. "Nope. Dry as bone."

"Then I think it's time for someone to go to bed."

Bernie yawned as if on cue.

Beth Ann bent to retrieve her, and was surprised when Christian said quietly, his deep voice resonating with tenderness, "I've got her. Just lead the way." He rose carefully, awkwardly propping up a quickly fading Bernie.

Beth Ann walked down the hall to Bernie's room. She bit her lip. It probably wasn't the kind of nursery Christian was used to, but Glenn had painted a lovely mural of parading baby elephants, giraffes and blue and pink bears, and she had refinished the recycled crib. She saw him glance at the daybed on the side. She flushed. That's where Caroline had slept for the five months she'd stayed and that's where she, herself, slept, when Fred or Glenn or both came to visit.

Christian carefully lowered Bernie into the crib and Beth Ann got a new appreciation of his physical strength. He obviously kept fit. His biceps tensed with Bernie's weight, but he handled her as if she weighed no more than a feather. Beth Ann carried her every day. Bernie was a good deal heavier than a feather. Bernie looked up at him with a flutter of her dark lashes and then they closed. She was fast asleep clutching Fluff.

"No book?" Christian asked.

"Usually," Beth Ann said with surprise. She came close to him, feeling the body heat emanate from him as she leaned across to pull the covers over Bernie. He smelled good. Some spicy fragrance. "But I guess she's really tired. Sometimes she does this. Other times, it's easier to wrestle dragons than put her to bed."

"She's beautiful." Christian's voice had an odd undertone to it.

Beth Ann looked at him. He was handsome, almost as if some prince had stepped into her ordinary life, but as he gazed at Bernie, his eyes studying every detail of her now cherub-like face, she saw a depth of emotion that she'd never expected to see. She stepped away from him, her heart beating rapidly. Something very much like physical attraction seeped through her. Beth Ann squashed it. It couldn't be. She and Caroline never liked the same kind of men.

"Yes. She is," Beth Ann agreed, not able to control the huskiness in her voice. "How about some of that banana bread? The coffee should be done about now."

Glenn was washing dishes when they entered the kitchen. "We trashed the kitchen," he said apologetically.

"Thanks for all you've done today, sweetie," Beth Ann came up behind him and circled her arms around his waist to give him a squeeze. "I'll take care of the rest," Beth Ann said. "Come sit with us."

Glenn finished rinsing a bowl. He wiped his hands

on the dishtowel and looked between her and Christian.

"No. I already brushed my teeth. I don't want to do it again. I'm beat. Did you know that two baby hours are like fifteen adult?" He glanced at his watch and said, "I've put in a seventy-five-hour day and I'm ready for bed. Christian, it was nice meeting you."

"You, too." Christian watched him disappear through the swinging door into the living room and wondered whether Glenn was going to sleep on the couch or if he was heading toward the bedroom in the front.

Beth Ann placed a cup of steaming coffee before him.

"You sure you don't want cream or sugar?"

Christian nodded and took a sip. It still tasted awful. He took a bite of banana bread. It tasted like ambrosia.

"This is excellent," he said as he took another swallow of coffee, then a corner of the bread, which cut the bitter aftertaste immediately.

Beth Ann settled across from him, looking very different than she had that morning. Had it just been that morning?

She cleared her throat. "I'm not exactly sure how to tell you this."

"Why don't you start anywhere?"

"Can I ask you a couple questions about Carrie first?" she asked.

Christian blinked. "Depends."

"Were you two close?"

He felt her eyes boring in to him.

"We were married," he replied.

"But were you close?"

Christian shifted uncomfortably. "I'm not sure what this has to do with you accepting DirectTech for Bernie."

"This morning you asked me why Carrie left her company to her sister's child."

"Yes. I remember." Christian felt a wave of suspicion run through him.

"How well did you know your wife?" Beth Ann asked. She looked as if the conversation was causing her much emotional turmoil.

Christian was tempted to lie, but then realized the sharp eyes studying him would probably see right through him. It was an interesting experience. Usually people were so afraid of him and the power he wielded they never looked at him that way. Even Caroline had never looked at him so intently. "By the end, I hardly saw her," Christian admitted.

"Whose fault was that?"

Christian didn't like the tone of her voice. After a moment, he said imperiously, acutely aware of how defensive he sounded, "It wasn't anyone's fault. We just had different interests."

"Different interests?"

"Caroline preferred to travel. I didn't like it as much."

"Ahh." Beth Ann nodded and was silent.

Christian wasn't quite sure what "ahh" meant.

A beat later, Beth Ann said frankly, "Carrie always wanted to be someplace she wasn't. If we were here, she wanted to be somewhere else. One year Grans took us to Disneyland. Grans was pretty poor then, so we couldn't stay in one of the nicer hotels. Of course, Caroline wanted to be in a better hotel.

Once we got to the park, she wanted to be on every ride but the one she was standing in line for. She was so busy looking ahead, she never got a chance to enjoy where she was.''

Christian had noticed that himself, when he was on those first cruises with Caroline. Once aboard a cruise, she was always flipping through brochures for others, speculating with her friends about better, bigger, more exclusive cruises. Rather than enjoy the view or the scenery or the food, she compared it to what she *could* do in the next three months, almost as if she couldn't wait for the one she was on to finish fast enough. As her cruises got longer, so did the stops in between, as she visited the latest spas. When she died, she had just come back from a monster cruise, customized specifically for her and a few of her friends.

Interestingly, Christian only now realized that his wife had spent their entire marriage and a considerable amount of money chasing after distant rainbows. Maybe it wasn't boredom that kept him from going on the cruises with her, but his impatience with her planning and her cluster of friends who relished the planning more than the actual trip itself. Everything had to be rated, the food, the room, the bedspreads, the carpet, the soap, the service and then reconfigured into the next ultimate trip.

He grunted, pushing away those thoughts and turned his attention back to Beth Ann. ''I think you should tell me what it is you wanted to tell me.''

Beth Ann took a deep breath. This was it. She'd worry about custody, about all the details that would have to be fought over, ironed out, and set in stone later. Now, she was going to make right what Carrie should have over two years ago.

"Carrie left DirectTech to Bernie because Bernie is her daughter," Beth Ann said baldly. There was no other way of telling him. She stared down at her coffee mug, bracing herself for his reaction.

But none came.

She expected a hot denial or a spark of anger or contemptuous disbelief, but she saw nothing in the handsome lines of his face and that scared her. Earlier she had thought she'd seen him opening up, that she could see fleeting emotions pass over his face when he gazed at Bernie, but she couldn't now. His silver eyes and well-molded mouth gave away nothing. He appeared two-dimensionally handsome, like the flat page of a *GQ* magazine cover, not at all like the man who had so tenderly carried Bernie to bed.

"Is that so?" he said finally, his voice carefully modulated.

Beth Ann nodded.

"She calls you Mommy." Christian sounded very much like a man shrouded in authority, clearly used to people bending to him. He set the half-eaten bread down on the table and pushed his coffee cup toward her.

Beth Ann refused to feel like an employee.

"I've raised her." Ignoring his cup, Beth Ann got up and dumped the rest of her coffee down the sink. Her stomach churned. Telling him had been a dreadful mistake.

"Since when?"

"Since she was ten days old."

"When did Caroline allegedly have this child?" His voice was crisp. He could have been talking about the weather or a bank robbery or whether a fish was fresh at the market for all the emotion he showed.

"June 27. Bernie'll be two at the end of June."

"Uh-huh." Christian gave her a pleasant smile that she didn't trust for one minute. "So you don't think I would know if my wife were pregnant?"

"That's why I asked if you were close." Beth Ann took a deep breath and said, "Look. Don't stare at me as if I were somehow concocting a huge scam—"

"So DirectTech wasn't enough, is that it?"

Beth Ann felt as if he'd slapped her. She stared at him in shock.

"How much do you want?"

"What?" Beth Ann found her voice.

"How much do you want?"

"Nothing. I don't want any—" She stared in horror as he whipped his checkbook from his jacket pocket.

Christian felt the cool Italian leather of his checkbook cover and was reassured. He couldn't comprehend what she was saying to him, yet his parents' words flashed through his mind. He was different. They were different. They had to hold themselves to different standards. Money could pretty much buy anything. It could buy him out of even having to think of the fact that this woman with the open gamine face had just told him Bernie was Caroline's daughter.

Impossible.

If he paid her enough, he wouldn't have to think about the fact that she hadn't told him Bernie was his daughter as well. He searched for his Mont Blanc pen and felt the familiar weight. The specialized highly polished resin gleamed in the stark light of the kitchen.

"How much do you want?" He gave her his most imperious gaze, which made even Max back away.

Beth Ann didn't budge an inch. She just looked at him as if he had lost his mind. If what she said were indeed true, then he had lost his mind, because how could Caroline have been pregnant—given birth!—and he not even know it?

"Please leave," were her only words.

"If you don't give me an amount, I'll just— Ah, what the hell," he scribbled an arbitrary number on the check followed by several zeros. His pen ripped through the fine paper because of the force with which he wrote. He tore the check out and put his pen and checkbook away. "Is this enough?" he asked crudely, pushing it toward her.

Beth Ann didn't even glance at the check. "If you don't leave, I'm going to get Glenn."

Christian rose to his full height, another intimidation tactic. But she wasn't intimidated. She just walked away, taking his coffee cup and his plate of half-eaten banana bread to the sink.

Beth Ann was shaking. This was a terrible, terrible mistake. Did he think he'd just bought Bernie? That money could compensate for everything that had happened? Beth Ann realized she was shaking not from fear but from anger. She had raised Carrie's child for two years and all he could do was pull out a checkbook. His money couldn't replace a career that had taken a nosedive because she'd spent five sleepless nights by Bernie's hospital bed, holding her little hand, begging her to breathe. His money couldn't make Bernie feel more wanted when she was old enough to ask about her real mother and father.

"Arggghhh!" Beth Ann whirled.

She snatched the check up from the table where he'd left it, crumpled it into a ball and smashed it with as much force as she could into his chest. His rock solid chest. He didn't even flinch, but her shoulder felt the jolt as he grabbed her wrist and pushed it back toward her. She could feel his restraint but felt no fear.

They both watched the check fall to the floor.

"Let go," she said.

He let go.

As she rubbed her shoulder, Beth Ann searched to find any emotion in his face, even smoldering anger, but his pale eyes were blank.

"You're more foolish than I thought," he said quietly and nudged the paper ball with the toe of his Italian leather shoe.

Suddenly, her anger was gone and she felt sorry for this man who wouldn't, couldn't allow himself to feel anything.

"I'm not the fool." Beth Ann smiled sadly. "I'm not the one who thinks he has to pay for the sins of his wife."

That did it.

His eyes flashed and then with a sharp turn that reminded Beth Ann of a military maneuver, he stalked out of the kitchen through the swinging door. Seconds later, she heard the front door open and then close.

She slumped down into a chair, her heart thumping and stared at the check for a full minute. She blinked back her tears, feeling no satisfaction that she had finally hit a nerve. The little paper ball had been flattened by his expensive leather sole.

CHRISTIAN JAMMED the key card into the door handle at his hotel. He was staying at the nicest place in Mercy Springs, but he hardly noticed because his mind was spinning. He entered the sparse room, and threw his jacket on the bed, turned on the television and cranked up the volume. He needed something to cut through the thoughts running through his head.

He quickly punched the autodial on his cell phone and flipped to find a news channel. He eyed the stock market report and waited impatiently for his call to be answered.

"Yes." The voice on the other end of the line was clearly irritated.

Christian didn't care that he was probably interrupting one of Max's many liaisons.

"Max."

"Christian." His friend's voice changed considerably and Christian could hear him sitting up. "Where the hell are you?"

"In Mercy Springs."

"Did you find the sister?"

"Yes."

There was a long pause.

"So?"

"Is there someone there with you?"

"Yes."

"Get rid of her. I need to talk to you." Christian had no patience to be cordial. But then Max didn't care.

"Do you know how long I've worked—" He sounded exasperated. "Can't we talk in the morning?"

"Get rid of her."

"Okay, okay. I'll call you back. Are you on your cell phone?"

"Yes."

"Later then."

Christian closed his phone and went to the bathroom, running the water. That baby couldn't be Caroline's. There was no way. When would she have had time to have it? Why wouldn't he have noticed?

He knew the answers and his guilt stabbed at him even more. He just didn't know what project he'd been working on or what body of water Caroline had been floating on. All her trips had merged together. He began to count backward. Caroline had died eighteen months ago—that would put Bernie at about six months old. Caroline had just come back from a long trip that had started as an Alaskan cruise and ended as a stay at a health resort in Alberta. She'd been gone for almost a year. He took a deep breath and tried to control the implications of what he was thinking. That was plenty of time to have a baby. He shook his head to try and clear it, but one burning certainty remained. Caroline had lied to him. Then another certainty fought its way through to his consciousness.

Bernie—adorable, chubby Bernie—wasn't his.

CHAPTER SIX

CHRISTIAN ANSWERED his cell phone on the first ring, his hair still wet. Splashing cold water on his face hadn't helped. In fact it had only made him damp and angry.

"So what's the big deal?" Max asked, irritation clearly evident in his voice. Christian didn't feel sorry for his friend. It was only by the luck of the draw that Max didn't have half a dozen women with half a dozen offspring suing him for paternity. In the era of safe sex, Max's practices were downright dangerous. Christian had probably just saved some ingenue from certain heartbreak and a lifetime of responsibility.

"Do you know if Caroline was ever pregnant?"

"Pregnant?" Max snorted, his disbelief obvious. "Of course she wasn't. When would she have had time to be pregnant? She hated getting fat and had no maternal instincts whatsoever."

Christian agreed, but he was finding it difficult to doubt Beth Ann. "Her sister is saying the child is Caroline's."

"That's a load of bull," Max dismissed. He added, "Don't you think you would have noticed whether or not your wife had had a baby?"

Christian hoped so, but there was still that knot of guilt gnawing at him. He didn't know. If she'd left when she was a few months pregnant, she could have had the baby while she was away and he'd be none the wiser. Caroline was obviously skilled at keeping secrets. Lots of them.

"Christian, you there?" Max asked impatiently.

"Yes." Christian didn't know what was making his voice short.

"I think it's highly unlikely the child could be—"

"I don't know. She was away a lot."

"How old's the kid?"

"Two."

Max was silent for only a split second. Then— the good old boy tone evident in his voice—he suggested, "I think the sister's trying to run some scam on you. Maybe get you to pay child support or something. Hell, I didn't even know Caroline *had* a sister until you told me."

"Do me a favor."

"Sure thing."

"Have Mrs. Murphy send me my appointment books for the past three years." Christian rattled off the address of the hotel.

"I thought you had a date with a cozy chalet in the wine country tonight," Max asked, his voice casual.

"Not until this is taken care of." Christian couldn't get the image of Beth Ann's stricken face out of his memory.

"What's there to take care of? Give her some money and call it a day."

"I tried and she seemed mortally offended."

"Good actress. Maybe she's holding out for more. You can't possibly be thinking about turning over D-Tech to her?"

"She won't take it."

"Good. Get her to put it in writing. Give her a check and go get some R and R."

"That's just it." Christian shook his head. Why wouldn't she take DirectTech? What was the big deal?

"What?"

"Nothing." Even though Max had been his friend forever, there were some things he did not confide in him. This would be one of them. More and more it seemed as if Max would be happier out in front of his own business. He'd practically pushed Christian out the door when the doctor had told Mrs. Murphy that Christian needed a three-month hiatus from work. Christian didn't question Max's loyalty, not because of his faith in their friendship, but because he knew that Max would have a hell of a time duplicating the salary, benefits and perks the conglomerate afforded him.

"Tell me you have more for me to do than that. I just didn't get rid of the date of the century for some sister that Caroline didn't want to admit she had."

"No, sorry," Christian said, forcing humor into his voice. "Maybe you can call her again."

"She did give me her pager number."

"Call it."

"We done?"

"Yep. Just get the message to Mrs. Murphy."

After Christian hung up, he lay down on the bed, his head pounding, wanting nothing more than a stiff drink. The doctor had said that alcohol at night would only aggravate his insomnia, much like caffeine. He remembered Beth Ann's terrible coffee.

According to his doctor this was exactly the kind of excitement he should be avoiding. He'd coped with the grief of Caroline's death in the same way he coped with everything. Keep a tight rein on any potential emotional problems and throw himself into work. That was what he'd learned in military school. The more trouble he got in, the harder they worked him, until he'd taught himself not to feel or be angry and to work so hard that at night he would just fall asleep in a dead stupor.

The only problem now was that he couldn't sleep. For Christian, sleep did not simply elude him—it viciously fought him, ravaged him, taunted him with the spite of a scorned lover. Even when his head ached terribly and he was bone weary, the closest he got to sleep was an uneasy doze, where he would fade in and out of this and a bleary dreamworld. Since Caroline had died, he'd spent more time thinking why, why, why. Although he worked harder than he ever had before, eventually, he had to lie down and then the thoughts would come. Tonight, he couldn't even doze—his eyes remained open, his head hurting, until the dawn cracked through the window of the hotel and he was allowed a reprieve from the darkness.

He glanced at the clock. Six-thirty. And he felt like hell. He took a shower, which helped considerably, and tried to formulate a plan of action that would be more successful than the one he'd had last night. He didn't know what Beth Ann's game was, but he'd find out today.

BETH ANN awoke to squeals of laughter and the clattering of dishes in the kitchen. She groaned and rolled over. What time was it? Nearly seven. She leapt out of bed, forgetting she was in Bernie's room, and stubbed her toe on the cast-iron leg of the daybed, scared to death of what Iris was doing with Bernie.

"Ow!" Hopping on one foot, she pulled on her robe and hurried to the kitchen, almost skidding to a halt when she saw Glenn strapping Bernie into her high chair. Standing in the doorway, she smiled at the scene. Iris was reading the paper and she could hear and smell Glenn's famous pancakes sizzling on the griddle.

"Bethy!" He gave her a cheerful greeting. "I'd hoped you'd sleep in."

"Mommy!" Bernie chortled. "Pop-pop. Pancakes."

"Yes. I smell them. Pop-pop's making you pancakes. Yum, yum."

"Yum, yum," Bernie echoed.

Beth Ann yawned and gave Iris a kiss. "Good morning, Grans. You have a good sleep?"

Iris looked up from the paper, her brown eyes alert. "I did indeed, Beth Ann. What a surprise to wake up and find young Glenn here. You didn't tell me he was coming."

Beth Ann smiled sadly. "He surprised us last night."

"You know," Iris said reflectively. "I also had the oddest dream that Carrie was here for a visit." She sighed deeply. "But that's impossible."

Beth Ann poured herself a cup of coffee and exchanged a glance with Glenn as he placed a small plate of cut up pancakes in front of Bernie.

"Well, Grans, Caroline didn't come for a visit, but her husband did."

"Her husband?" Iris frowned.

"Remember? Christian Elliott."

"I don't think I've met him."

"Yes, you did, Grans. At Carrie's funeral."

Iris nodded but Beth Ann could tell she didn't remember.

"Why did he come?" Iris asked.

Beth Ann took a deep breath. She needed to take advantage of Iris's better moments to glean as much advice as she could.

"He came to give Bernie a software company."

CHRISTIAN DROVE down the road, no fog in sight. The sun was inviting, filtering across the empty fields, promising a very warm day. At Beth Ann's, he hesitated to pull into the driveway and opted to park on the side of the road, pausing for a minute to take a deep breath. After his behavior last night, she had every reason not to want to speak to him or see him again. But he couldn't stay away. He thought about Max's advice to just get Beth Ann's refusal of the company in writing and then he sighed. He hadn't done much for Caroline while she was alive. The least he could do was make sure that Bernie got what she was entitled to.

He didn't feel any remorse at losing the company. For too long, his whole life had just been about the money, keeping it, making it, securing it. Even if they lost all their companies, the Elliott fortune was so vast and so deep, it would almost take the collapse of the entire world market to make them even skip a step. His grandfather had taken care of that.

His grandfather had taken care of a lot. His father never really was into the business, and when Christian graduated from Yale, his grandfather had a position ready for him and, at Christian's request, for Max. The next four years had been spent learning everything about the company. His grandfather had needed to know that Christian could handle the responsibility and could continue to support his parents in the style they were accustomed to.

His grandfather had died about six months before Christian had met Caroline and at the time he'd been sure his grandfather would have approved. Now, as his eyes focused on the small bungalow, he wondered if that were true. His grandfather had had a deep respect for hard work, for family—even though his own wasn't all that functional.

Christian got out of the car and walked purposely across the driveway and up the short steps. Just as he was about to knock, he heard laughter drift through the door and felt as if he was being stabbed by a thousand tiny daggers. It was ironic really. He had everything and anything money could buy, but he couldn't laugh. Not like the laughter that was coming from Beth Ann's house.

He rapped sharply on the screen door.

"HEAVENS!" Beth Ann looked up. "Who could that be?"

Glenn peeked out the kitchen window. "I see a silver Jaguar on the side of the road."

The knock came again. This time louder and more demanding.

"Impatient, isn't he?" Beth Ann muttered, pulling her robe tighter around her, then running a hand through her curls. She must look terrible.

"You want me to get it?" Glenn asked between mouthfuls.

Since she had already finished her pancakes, she shook her head. "You eat. I'll get it."

"Who owns a silver Jaguar?" Iris asked.

"Carrie's husband, Christian." Beth Ann heard Glenn answer her. She went to the door, her heart pounding in her throat, and opened it just a crack.

"Hello?" she asked, and took a deep breath in surprise. If she had been bracing herself to resist a charming, polished businessman bent on shoving money down her throat, she was sorely mistaken. The man before her looked awful, so awful he didn't even appear handsome anymore. Christian Elliott looked as if he'd been to hell and back and had tried to take a quick shower to wash off all the singe marks.

"We need to talk," he said abruptly, his voice gravelly, making her think he hadn't spoken at all that morning.

"Have you eaten?" Beth Ann asked. For some reason, her heart ached for him. And she was reminded again, that even with all the money in the world, this man couldn't buy a decent night's sleep. And she could see from the paleness of his skin and the dark bags under his eyes that he could sorely use a decent night's sleep.

He looked at her, surprise etched in his face. She also noticed how the black rims around his gray eyes seemed to have darkened, making his gaze that much more compelling.

"We need to talk," he repeated.

"Have you eaten?" she asked again.

After a long moment, he shook his head and admitted, "No."

Beth Ann opened the door wider and stepped to the side. "Why don't you come and have some breakfast? After that, we can talk."

When Christian stepped over the threshold, he felt like Alice in Wonderland. Except his life was the crazy one and this little yellow bungalow was a place of sanity. The smell of freshly made pancakes and coffee, no matter how bad it was, made a strong imprint on his mind. As he entered the kitchen, he was assaulted by the life he saw around him. Iris was at the table, a section of the newspaper in front of her, the rest scattered on the floor by her feet. Bernie, in the same pj's as the night before, was sitting almost sideways in her chair, and Glenn was seated next to her, finishing up what looked like a hearty stack of pancakes. His eyes were drawn to the roses he had given her last night, set in a place of honor by the sunny window.

"Glenn, are there more pancakes?" Beth Ann asked behind him. "We have one more for breakfast."

"Plenty. You just have to turn the griddle on."

"Have a seat, Christian," Beth Ann offered and then said with an odd look in her eye, "You haven't met my grandmother, and Bernie's great-grandmother, Iris Curtis. Grans, this is Carrie's husband who has come all the way from er, San Diego—"

Christian nodded in surprise.

"—just to visit us."

"Well, hello there," Iris said brightly. She held out her hand.

At Beth Ann's pleading look, Christian gently shook Iris's hand.

"Glad to meet you. I'm sorry we weren't able to meet before this."

"When Carrie was alive," Iris said bluntly. She nodded sadly. "But I know how busy she was. My goodness, she certainly enjoyed all that traveling." She patted the seat next to hers. "Why don't you sit down? Would you like some coffee?"

Christian exchanged a glance with Glenn who grinned.

"Yes," he said without hesitation. "I would love some coffee."

"Glenn made it this morning," Beth Ann volunteered.

Christian was slightly relieved. After the night he'd had, he didn't think he could fake enjoying another cup of her coffee. Iris brought it to him with steady hands. She peered at him.

"My, you certainly are a handsome one. Beth Ann, doesn't he look like one of those models whose pictures Carrie used to have hanging around her room?"

Even though she might have made the same assessment yesterday, now Beth Ann didn't think he looked anything like a model. He looked like an ordinary man struggling to stay sane in extraordinary circumstances. As she waited for the griddle to reheat, she asked, "Do you want a couple of eggs to go with that?"

"Sure," Christian said, looking up from his conversation with Iris.

"How would you like them?"

"Scrambled, please."

Beth Ann nodded. "Scrambled soft or hard?"

"Hard."

"*Deggs!*" Bernie suddenly demanded.

"Eggs?" Beth Ann looked at the toddler. She had already eaten two small pancakes and half an apple. "Are you still hungry?"

"Deggs," Bernie insisted with a vigorous nod.

"Well, I don't know, sweetie. You can't eat a whole egg."

"She can have some of mine," Christian said suddenly.

Beth Ann felt her cheeks warm. "It's not that we don't have eggs," she said hurriedly.

"No. I know," he said. "If she just wants a bite or two, you don't have to fix her a whole egg, she can have some of mine."

"That's nice of you but—"

"*Deggs!*"

"You heard her, Bethy," Glenn put in. "The princess wants deggs. And she should have deggs." He leaned over to Bernie and coached her. "You also need to say, 'right now!'"

"*Glenn!*" Beth Ann couldn't keep the laughter out of her voice, though she knew she would have a heck of a time getting those words out of Bernie's vocabulary.

"Wight *now!*" Bernie added with an imperious note in her voice.

Christian took a deep breath. Even with the baby lisp, she had Caroline's intonation. With her blue eyes sparkling at the new concept of control, her face had an expression he had seen often on Caroline, especially when she was speaking to one of the servants.

"Bernie," Beth Ann said sternly. "Pop-pop is wrong. You don't say, 'right now!' You say 'please' if someone is going to do something nice for you. And you say thank you to Uncle Christian for sharing his eggs with you."

"Peas, Mommy?" Bernie said sweetly, her face wrinkling in smiles.

"And thank you to Uncle Christian for sharing his eggs with you."

Bernie ignored that and hunted down a stray piece of apple on her tray.

Christian watched Beth Ann pour the batter onto the griddle, finding her efficient movements surprisingly attractive. She looked like she had done it a million times. She rummaged through the refrigerator for eggs and pulled out two. After she cracked them in the bowl, he noticed she discarded the shells not in the garbage but in a large container next to the sink that overflowed with vegetable and other organic refuse obviously headed for a compost pile. The flattened check, a sharp reminder of the night before, poked out from under a heap of green strawberry tops. Christian felt a small twinge. It was probably where it belonged.

With his senses of sight, hearing and smell all heightened, Christian felt the pleasant atmosphere of this kitchen soothe away the torture of the night before. He found his mouth watering as he waited. Soon, Beth Ann pushed toward him a plate of eggs and an impressive stack of pancakes. Glenn passed him a bowl of fruit salad.

"Deggs!" Bernie reminded him, her blue eyes fixed on his eggs.

Christian looked at his plate, not quite certain what he should do.

"Just give her a corner."

He cut off a corner and put it on her tray.

"Tank you," Bernie said to him with a flutter of her dark lashes.

Christian was touched.

"She is adorable, isn't she?" Glenn commented.

"The most brilliant baby in the world," Christian agreed.

Iris laughed. "I knew we liked him."

"Careful," Beth Ann said to Bernie. "It's hot."

Bernie poked a tiny finger at the eggs. "Ott." She waited a millisecond and poked it again. "Not ott."

"Okay. If it's not hot, then you can eat it. Christian, do you need anything?" She pushed two bottles toward him and plopped a tub of butter next to him. "This one's maple syrup and the other is wild raspberry syrup."

Glenn added, "She makes the stuff herself from raspberries as big as walnuts."

"The butter's fresh, too, from the dairy down the road," Iris said proudly.

Christian slowly took his first bite of pancakes with homemade raspberry syrup and real butter. He closed his eyes. Culinary heaven. Taste was a wonderful sense, he thought reflectively as he took another bite. He watched as Beth Ann scooped out a generous portion of the fruit salad, mostly strawberries, peaches and apricots.

"Cantaloupes don't ripen until the end of the month," she said apologetically. "Eat up!"

Christian ate ravenously, not having realized how very hungry he was. It felt like the first meal he had ever eaten.

"You want more?" she asked once he'd cleaned his plate. "There's more batter for pancakes."

"No, thank you. That was enough." It was more than enough. If last night had robbed his soul of whatever reality he'd thought he'd shared with Caroline, this breakfast of homemade pancakes and fresh plump fruit, accompanied by genuine laughter and affection, fed him something more precious than food.

Beth Ann felt a wave of contentment wash through her. This was her idea of a perfect morning. Iris was in full control of her faculties, Bernie was sweet and happy, Glenn provided his usual wit and even Christian sat at her kitchen table as if he had done it his entire life, as if the tension that had crackled between them last night had never existed. She stood up and started to clear the table, watching her daughter carefully.

Bernie had worked her way through almost half of Christian's eggs, and Beth Ann noticed tenderly, that he didn't eat the rest. Instead, he cut them in small pieces and let Bernie reach out and take the bits from his plate. Yet another bad habit Beth Ann would need to monitor.

Caroline had been so wrong about him. What had made her think Christian wouldn't give this child his name? Beth Ann frowned, cautioning herself. She didn't know for sure whether he was even the biological father. If he was, Caroline certainly wouldn't have gone through all the trouble and secrecy to keep a pregnancy from him, would she?

She started when Christian came up behind her, bearing a stack of plates.

"Oh, you don't need to do that," she said hastily.

"I don't mind," he said, rolling up the sleeves on his fine silk shirt. As he began to rinse the dishes, he glanced around for a dishwasher.

"You're looking at her," Beth Ann laughed.

"Move over. I'll wash, you can dry." Christian gently bumped her out of the way.

Beth Ann felt her heart accelerate. It was a small movement, just a soft bump, hip to hip. Glenn bumped her all the time, but she'd never felt this strong attraction to him. When she looked up, she found Christian staring down at her, his gray eyes unreadable, the lines of his face softening. She squelched the emotions that warmed her chest and throat, grabbing a towel to wipe her hands.

This was Carrie's husband.

She shouldn't be having feelings for or anything else intimate with Carrie's husband. If Carrie were still alive, he would be Beth Ann's brother-in-law. Since Carrie hated doing dishes, she no doubt would be avoiding the chore, and her husband would simply be covering for her. Beth Ann resisted the impulse to run her hand down his back and feel the heat of his skin through the thin fabric of his shirt.

"You do that like a pro," she commented.

"Military school. Had to do a lot of dishes. Bathrooms, too."

"Just because?" She hadn't been wrong about the military turn. That bit of information explained the rigid control he had over his expressions and emotions.

But the control was not evident now.

"No." He gave her a mischievous grin and a quick wink and her heart fluttered. "I got into a lot of trouble, which was exacerbated by a really hard head. Spent many an afternoon peeling potatoes or scrubbing out the latrines. Those skills come in handy once in a while. If you're impressed with this, I do a great toilet."

Beth Ann laughed appreciatively, ducking her head, her ears hot. She couldn't believe she was flirting. "You're hired." She looked over her shoulder and noticed the only person remaining in the kitchen was Bernie, who looked at her inquiringly.

"Yes, it's time to sit on Mrs. Potty." Beth Ann was relieved to move away from him, his clean smell.

"Mrs. Potty," Bernie repeated.

After wiping down Bernie's face and stripping off her pajamas, Beth Ann sat Bernie down on the small potty with Fluff and a book. Bernie looked at the pictures for about two minutes and then said, "I done."

Beth Ann gave her a skeptical glance. "Already?"

Bernie nodded. "I done."

Beth Ann went over, surprised to find Bernie was indeed done. "Wow, Bernie-Bern-Bern. That was quick."

"Kik." Bernie looked up and smiled. "Go garden?"

"We'll see. First we have to find out when Poppop has to leave. Then, we'll open that letter and see if Mommy has a show."

Christian was finishing up the last of the dishes

and couldn't help eavesdropping. "You have a show?"

Beth Ann made a face as she put a clean diaper on Bernie. "Maybe. I've sent slides. I got a letter a few days ago." She left the room with the potty and Bernie trailing behind her.

"Bye, bye, poo-poo," he heard Bernie say. Then the toilet flushed. They appeared a few minutes later. The potty cleaned, their hands washed.

"And you didn't rip it open immediately?" Christian asked curiously.

"What?" Beth Ann asked.

"The letter."

Beth Ann looked away, her face flushing. "No. I've been busy." She looked at Bernie. "Go get your clothes, sweetie. On your box."

Christian watched in amazement as Bernie toddled off. "She understands you, doesn't she?"

Beth Ann nodded. "Very much so. Just because she's not articulate, doesn't mean she doesn't understand."

"Are you going to open it?"

Beth Ann looked stressed at the idea. "It's not that important. I haven't been in it for a while."

"It?"

She nodded. "The art circuit. This isn't much. Just five spaces in a hotel lobby." She made another face.

Christian thought he understood. "But that's a good start, isn't it?" He was thinking about his mother's connections to some galleries in San Diego and then caught himself. He didn't even know if she had any talent.

Beth Ann said noncommittally, "I guess."

"So where is the letter?" Christian pressed on.

Beth Ann went to the china cabinet and dug through the mail. "Here." She held up the slender envelope. Bernie came back with two pair of pants. "I need a shirt, too, Bernie. Go get a shirt."

Christian watched as Bernie ran off, her little feet pounding on the hardwood. A second or two later, she reappeared, this time clutching a red San Francisco Giants T-shirt.

"So open it."

Beth Ann sighed and ripped it open, her dark eyes quickly scanning the short letter, a frown creasing her forehead. Christian wondered what he could do to smooth that frown away. She looked up at him and said, "Well, that was fun."

Christian watched Beth Ann's expressive face. In just the few hours he'd spent with her, he'd seen the range of emotions she was capable of. Now, she pressed her lips together and was apparently fighting the urge to cry.

"What'd it say?" he asked cautiously.

Beth Ann looked up as if she had forgotten he was in the room.

"Bad news?" He didn't want her to get bad news. He wanted her to get good news, so that her face would light up and she'd flash him those dimples.

Beth Ann blinked rapidly to hold back her tears. Obviously, she didn't want him to see her like this. "Not good." She laughed, but there was no humor in it. Throwing the letter in the garbage, she turned her attention to Bernie who waited patiently. "Let's get the Bern-Bern dressed." She crouched down to Bernie's level.

"Not good? About your paintings?"

"I think the word they used was tired."

"Ouch," Christian winced. She was clearly hurt. "So does this mean your paintings don't get shown?"

"Well, no," she admitted reluctantly. She pulled the letter out of the garbage and read it again as Bernie pulled up her pants. "Not exactly."

"What does not exactly mean?"

"They hated the paintings."

She thrust the letter at him and he took it and read it.

"Yes," Christian agreed. He winced. They were blunt in their criticism, but there was a spark of hope. "But it says if you can get them some more slides by July first they'll give you another chance. Something fresh. That sounds like good news. It's over a month from now."

"Good news?" Beth Ann laughed weakly. "That's only good news if you have something *fresh* to send."

"You don't?"

Beth Ann's face closed up again. "I don't want to talk about this anymore." She took the letter back, put it in the garbage again, then started to pull Bernie's shirt over her head. After several fierce tugs, the shirt still wouldn't go on and Beth Ann yanked it off in frustration.

"I'm surprised."

"What?" she asked distractedly. "Bernie, you grew too big. We need another shirt. Go get one in the basket."

Christian watched Bernie take off down the hall and then lowered his voice. "I'm surprised you're not even going to try."

"I don't have anything new and I don't have child care. I don't have time." Her voice was flat.

"Glenn?" Christian glanced down the hall.

"Glenn's working on a mural. I can't ask him to give up his career so I can jump-start mine—" Then she whispered fiercely, "And I don't want him to know about this."

She crossed the room and Christian saw the tightness in her shoulders. There must be a solution. He spotted the check in the compost pile, but did he dare?

"Do you need money for child care?" he asked abruptly, controlling the urge to duck when her eyes spit fire at him.

"You don't understand, do you?"

"Why don't you tell me?"

"I need two kinds of care. For Bernie and Grans. Even if I had all the money in the world, there's no one who's willing to take on both." She tightened the tie on her robe.

There was someone. Christian's heart beat faster. Was he out of his mind? In the next few days, he was supposed to be in Napa or at least, heading in that direction. Besides, he couldn't—she wouldn't let him.

"Well, there is another option," he offered anyway.

Beth Ann looked at him skeptically. She raised a doubtful eyebrow. "Really?"

"Sure." Christian's voice was very casual.

"What?"

There was a long silence. Beth Ann wasn't sure she wanted to hear what he had to say. She already felt guilty enough. If she had painted yesterday instead of cleaning, she might be able to say she would have something new to send. But she didn't. She had no one else to blame but herself and she didn't want Carrie's husband looking at her with such compassion.

"I can stay," he said reasonably.

Beth Ann shook her head. "You've got a company to run. Don't you have an important meeting in Napa?"

Christian was silent for a minute and confessed. "Actually... Well, I'm under orders not to go back to work for three months."

Beth Ann digested this new piece of information.

"I've been overworked," he explained.

"Surely, you must have other plans."

"Nothing that can't be canceled."

"But—" Beth Ann looked down, thinking furiously. She should just say no. "What about your family and your friends? I'm sure they'll think you've dropped off the face of the earth."

"I only have one friend and he knows how to get in contact with me," Christian said placidly.

"Your parents," she tried.

"The last I heard they were off the coast of Greece and wouldn't be back until Thanksgiving."

"You can't."

"Yes, I can. I'll look after Iris and Bernie."

"Have you ever taken care of a two-year-old?" Christian shook his head.

"A senile ninety—"

"She's perfectly fine now."

"Today, yes." Even though her heart was telling her to think about it, Beth Ann stated, "I don't think you can do it."

"I wouldn't have offered if I didn't think I could." He spoke with such confidence that Beth Ann actually believed him.

"I can't offer you any compensation."

"Sure you can," Christian said deliberately. "You can agree to sign Bernie's papers when I leave."

Beth Ann was distracted by a tug on the robe.

"Mommy, mommy, mommy."

She had forgotten about Bernie, who had returned with another shirt. "Bernie! I'm sorry, sweetie," Beth Ann said hurriedly, and pulled the shirt over Bernie's head. "Last wear on this one, too. You're getting too big."

"Too big," Bernie singsonged.

Christian clicked his tongue impatiently. "So what do you think?" he asked.

Finally, she looked up at him, feeling tears of helplessness gather in the back of her throat. What did she think? She was too exhausted to think. "You're a stranger. I have no idea why you're here or what your motives are." She turned her head away, as the tears slipped from her eyes. She dashed them away angrily.

"Mommy, okay?" Bernie asked, patting Beth Ann's face.

"Yes, Bernie. Mommy's okay," Beth Ann reassured her.

"Mommy, sure?"

"Mommy's sure. Thank you."

"Welcome." Bernie smiled and gave her a big hug.

Beth Ann looked up and saw Christian staring at

them intently, and she thought she could tangibly *feel* the longing in his eyes.

She said roughly, clearing her throat, ''Thanks for not letting on to Iris that you met her yesterday.''

He shrugged. ''No problem.''

''Bernie, why don't you go find your brush? I think I saw it on the coffee table.'' Beth Ann took a deep breath and shook her head resolutely. ''We can't impose on you.''

''It wouldn't be an imposition,'' Christian said firmly. ''The doctor said I had to rest—''

''Then this isn't the place to be.'' She tried to smile. ''Thank you very much for the kind offer but this is something I need to work out by myself. This is my doing, it's my choice.''

''Seems like it was Caroline's,'' Christian observed.

Beth Ann stopped what she was doing, surprised at how much his words stung. She might have hit a nerve last night, but he'd found one all his own. She wouldn't give up Bernie for all the time in the world—but Bernie wasn't her mistake. She was Carrie's. It had been Carrie's choice to leave her daughter and it was Beth Ann's choice to raise her. Just as it was Beth Ann's choice to care for Iris. Carrie obviously hadn't felt any compunction about leaving either. Just like her stepfather.

''We owe you,'' Christian said quietly.

''You don't owe me anything,'' Beth Ann said shortly. To be fair, not painting had nothing to do with Carrie at all.

''Caroline was my wife.''

''Carrie was my sister.''

She stared at him and watched his face grow

closed before it relaxed and he gave her a small smile, the clench of his hand belying his calm.

"Let me have the chance to get to know Bernie."

"You can't have her." Beth Ann felt a chill shimmy down her spine. "And you'd crush me in court."

He took a deep breath and looked at her again, and Beth Ann saw pure raw pain in his eyes. He said quietly, "I know you have absolutely no reason to trust me on this, but I wouldn't dream of taking her from you. I just want to know Caroline's daughter. So what do you say?"

"You won't tell Glenn about the—" Beth Ann said, jerking her head toward the letter in the garbage.

"Won't tell me what?" Glenn asked as he walked through the swinging door carrying Bernie.

CHAPTER SEVEN

"CHRISTIAN'S OFFERED to Bernie- and Iris-sit,"
Beth Ann informed Glenn, but she stared into Christian's face, wondering if she could trust him about
something as small as the letter from the hotel.

He gave her a nearly imperceptible nod and Beth
Ann felt a tiny rush of relief flood through her.

"Really?" His eyebrow raised up. "When did
this happen?"

"Just now," Christian said easily.

Beth Ann watched Christian position himself between them. Surprisingly, she didn't find his show
of authority overbearing, but rather oddly endearing.
Almost as if he was trying to reassure Glenn he
would take good care of them while Glenn was
gone.

Beth Ann hoped Glenn would grasp the complexity of the situation and just accept it rather than become the protective big brother.

Beth Ann said, her voice perky, "He wants some
time with Bernie."

Glenn nodded his head, his eyes still on her. *You
sure, Bethy?*

Beth Ann nodded.

He made a clicking sound with his tongue.
"Okay. Then I'm outta here. Come give Pop-pop a
kiss goodbye, Bernzie."

Bernie's eyebrows puckered. "No! Garden!"

"Pop-pop's got to go to work."

"No werk. Garden."

"We'll go to the garden when I come back."

"No go bye-bye, Pop-pop." Bernie's little bottom lip quavered as she slung her arms around Glenn's leg and wailed.

Christian watched enviously and wondered if Bernie would ever wrap her arms around him to prevent him from leaving. Beth Ann gently extricated her daughter and lifted her up. The wails subsided to whimpers.

"She has a problem with separation," she explained.

"No go bye-bye," Bernie moaned.

"I'll see you soon, Bern-bern," Glenn assured her with a kiss on her cheek.

"No go bye-bye."

"Breaks my heart," Glenn said with a glance at Christian.

Beth Ann gave Glenn a quick kiss. "Time to make your escape."

"Noooo!" Bernie sobbed as if her heart was breaking when Glenn slipped out the front door.

Christian watched helplessly.

Beth Ann smiled at his discomfiture and said, "She'll be over it in a minute. Her sadness rarely lasts very long." She paused, midrock, her hand rubbing Bernie's back and added, "You don't have to do this. There'll always be another show."

Christian couldn't stop staring at the two of them. Bernie laying her head on Beth Ann's shoulder, her finger in her mouth, the residual hiccups of her distress racking her small body.

"I need to do this."

"Well," Beth Ann said a tad gruffly. "I guess you should probably go get your stuff. It doesn't make a lot of sense for you to pay for a hotel when we have plenty of space here."

WITH CHRISTIAN GONE, Beth Ann took Iris and Bernie to tend the garden. She stood with them, thinking about the implications of what had just happened. What in the world had possessed her to ask him to stay? Wasn't she inviting some sort of disaster on herself? On Bernie?

"Look me, Mommy! Look me!"

Beth Ann looked up and gasped, as Bernie, quick as lightning, had made her way through the beans and was trying to climb through a small hole in the shed.

"Bernie, come on, sweetie. We need to help Nana with weeding."

"Weeding. Weeding." She wriggled and came out of the hole, butt first, then tripped. Beth Ann's heart was in her throat, especially as Bernie's head came dangerously close to smacking the corner of the shovel propped up against the shed.

"Bernie!"

"I okay. I okay." Bernie chortled and immediately got up and toddled toward Iris.

Beth Ann watched Iris teach Bernie the right way to weed the furrows of beans, laughing when Bernie ignored her and pulled on the tender stalks, taking with her the entire plant. Iris praised Bernie's effort and directed her to another patch of weeds, which Bernie proceeded to clear with vigorous hands, most of the leaves landing on the ground rather than in Iris's refuse basket.

Beth Ann suddenly wanted to capture what she was seeing. And even though she primarily focused on landscapes, the urge to depict this moment was powerful. Much more compelling than the landscapes she ignored in the attic. It was odd because this would require her to do two things she wasn't very good at—drawing people and capturing a scene live, not from a reference photo. As Iris and Bernie conversed, Beth Ann took the opportunity to run up to the attic and snatch her sketchbook, making sure she only left Iris and Bernie for a few seconds.

Although Iris was having a good day, it wasn't wise to rely on her for any period of time. Beth Ann rushed back, laden with a terrible sense of dread that the small indiscretion of leaving the two would result in a fall by Iris or Bernie. The dread was only reinforced by the horror stories of toddlers drowning in two inches of water or the elderly lost for days wandering up and down roads. It was impossible, but Beth Ann knew in her heart of hearts the only safe thing was to keep an eye on both of them twenty-four hours a day, seven days a week.

When she returned, her worst fears were not confirmed. Her two charges had moved on to weed around the adolescent tomato plants, Iris pointing out the new flowers and the small fruit just beginning to grow. Bernie pulled off the flowers she saw and chuckled as Iris scolded, telling her there would be no tomatoes if there were no flowers. Iris was forever a teacher.

Beth Ann smiled, as she tried to capture the arc of Iris's back and the movement of Bernie's stubby legs. She felt a little sadness that Carrie wasn't here to see this. She shook herself. But then, Carrie wouldn't have found the same joy in what she saw. Her hand moved rapidly, trying to define the differences between Iris and Bernie. The end of life and the beginning of life.

She frowned, and where was she?

Caught in the middle, not middle-aged, but feeling as if her life wasn't hers anymore. No life to call her own, no place to process the awareness of how physically arid she'd really become. Christian's masculinity nearly overwhelmed her, his size, the depth of his voice, the shuttered emotion and hurt behind his cool eyes. She wanted to run from him and at the same time, she wanted to embrace him, to be as close to him as she could get. She shook off the sense of a small, newly heard cry of wanting. She concentrated on the lines that she sketched. All her time belonged to the two precious individuals before her, who were giggling at some shared joke. The wanting would have to wait.

She drew Bernie in profile. After her depressing attempt at art yesterday, it surprised her that she even felt compelled to pick up the sketchpad and realized with a small tinge of guilt that she was looking forward more to Christian's company than the opportunity to immerse herself in painting. *Don't count on it.* She didn't even know whether Christian would be able to stick it out.

Beth Ann reflected on Christian. He seemed to be as thoughtful as Carrie was thoughtless. More careful, more prone to study detail. More like herself. Carrie's flamboyance was contagious, but she was a hard individual to know. She kept things locked away, selfishly guarding the most secret parts of herself. As she'd grown older, Carrie had become even more closed. Beth Ann thought that was why her sister had relished cruising so much. During her pregnancy, she'd talked nonstop about the wonder of being in a different place every night, at how, even when she was sleeping, she was never in the same place. But what it really meant—Beth Ann realized—was that no one was ever around long enough to discover the truth about Carrie.

After Carrie had graduated from high school, she'd left, never intending to come back. Staying in Mercy Springs when she was pregnant ate away at her patience. Beth Ann suspected it was not simply the sameness that scraped at Carrie's nerves; it was being trapped in the cage she'd thought she'd escaped from.

"Pitty," Bernie said, bringing her a weed with a blue flower on it.

"Thank you. It's very pretty."

"The weeds are just springing up," Iris said, walking slowly with the heavy basket.

Beth Ann hurried to take the basket and then dump it in the garbage. Weeds didn't compost well. They all started back to the house, Bernie running ahead to climb the stairs and try to open the screen door.

"Is Glenn coming back?" Iris asked.

Beth Ann shook her head. "No, Glenn's gone to Fresno. But..."

"But?"

"But Christian offered to stay with Bernie, so I can paint. What do you think about that?"

Iris looked at her serenely. "A better question is what do you think about it?"

"It's okay. Bernie seems to like him well enough." She bit her lip and looked away. "What about you? Do you like him?"

Iris was silent a long time. "I like him very much."

"How can you know that? You only met him this morning," *as far as you remember,* Beth Ann added silently.

"I see it in his eyes. He's looking for Carrie and he's hoping he'll find her here."

Beth Ann shook her head. "He's not going to find her here. She left a long time ago."

Iris nodded in agreement. "She left him a long time ago, too."

IT TOOK CHRISTIAN a little longer than he expected to gather up his things and check out of the hotel. He got caught in a cryptic conversation with Max who wanted to the know the details about Caroline's child. Max was persistent when he wanted to be and Christian had learned to be equally evasive. After all, they'd known each other since they were seven, when the smaller Max, brand new to their boarding school, had challenged Christian, by then a veteran, to a fist fight. The fight hadn't lasted long enough to determine a victor, but their subsequent posteri-oral discomfort, compliments of the headmaster, ce-mented their grudging respect. They became uneasy friends, an intimidating pair of, well, bullies, until Christian was transferred to military school.

They rediscovered the benefits of collaboration at Yale, this time in conquering not boys smaller or

less skilled than they, but women. Christian and
Max were almost opposites, although equally handsome, equally charismatic. Christian was dark with
silver eyes, Max, fair, with eyes the color of a rich
malt brew. Christian was silent, controlled and rich
as Midas. Max was affable, boyishly attractive and
had a flattering nature that seduced more than a few
women. Together, they made a formidable team,
neither feeling any qualms about capitalizing on
their combined charm. Both broke several dozen
hearts by the time they graduated.

Max's strength was in investments, but he had
agreed to be Christian's right-hand man when Christian's grandfather had decided it was time to retire.
Their success with the company—moving it from
an era of typewriters and dictaphones into the age
of computers, faxes and the World Wide Web—had
reaped them both great rewards. Greater wealth
hadn't changed Max, nor his attitude about women.
He still was essentially the same Maximilian Riley,
thirsty for the thrills of the romantic chase, bored
within days of the capture.

When they'd met Caroline, Christian had long
outgrown the need to accumulate women like tro-
phies. He'd admitted that for the most part he and
Max had acted like pigs and that much of their
friendship was based on a mutual understanding that
women were nice distractions, but not very essential.
That fact hadn't really changed—Christian had simply grown weary of the amount of work necessary
to meet new women and had settled on Caroline.
He'd loved her in his own way and she'd certainly
benefited from their marriage.

But this situation with Beth Ann and Bernie and

Iris felt different. He didn't feel like talking to Max, allowing Beth Ann's household to be a target for Max's biting wit. As succinctly as he could, Christian had let Max know it was going to take a little longer to iron out this deal than he had anticipated. He'd then promised to call in about a month and let him know what had happened.

When Christian arrived at the house, it was unusually silent, but the front door was wide open. He peered into the house and then tapped on the door lightly. "Hello?" he called.

"I'm in the back," Beth Ann called in response.

He placed his luggage inside the front door, then walked around the back. Beth Ann was in the middle of hanging the laundry on two wires that ran between the old oak tree and the house.

"Hi," he greeted her.

She smiled and he noticed she looked really tired.

"Where is everybody?" he asked.

"Napping." She glanced at her watch. "They should be out for another hour or two. I'm just taking the opportunity to get some laundry done. These are your sheets and towels." She whipped the bottom sheet out and Christian automatically caught it. It seemed as if it were the most natural thing in the world to help her. He felt the damp sheets, smelled the clean smell of freshly washed laundry. He reached into the bag that hung across her shoulder and fished out two clothespins.

"Dryer broken?" he asked, with nothing better to say. For some reason, his ability to come up with scintillating conversation had deserted him entirely. He was too distracted by her graceful movements, as she worked at her mundane task.

She shook her head. "No. Too hot. If I dry something, it heats up the whole house. Good for winter time, but miserable in the spring and supermiserable in the summer. It's warm today so these should dry in no time."

She gave him the end of the flat sheet and together, they hung it up. Then they hung a series of Bernie's T-shirts and sweats. He reached for another pile and Beth Ann said hastily, "Thanks, but I'll do those."

"You'll get done a lot quicker," he commented and picked up a few of the articles.

She snatched them away from him. "That's okay. I'll hang them. You can go unpack your stuff."

He looked at her strangely, but as her face turned bright red, he nodded and walked toward the house.

"Take my bedroom," she called. "It's the one on the right when you walk in. The bottom drawer is empty, so if you want you can put a few things there."

Christian raised a hand and then discreetly looked over his shoulder as he walked into the house. He realized with a smile that she was old-fashioned enough not to let a man hang her underwear.

He picked up his bags and walked to her room, suddenly wondering if she and Glenn were lovers, then surprising himself by how much he didn't want that to be true. He ventured in, slightly uncomfortable. Like the living room, her bedroom was purely feminine. She'd chosen pinks and yellows, but it wasn't a little girl's room. It was a woman's room, with a woman's taste evident in the wallpaper and wall hangings. Her four-poster bed was antique cherry, hand carved and high. A pale pink matelassé

coverlet lay smooshed to one side, the bed bare of
sheets. He imagined that during the fall and winter
months, she would replace the coverlet with blankets
and perhaps a quilt that was much more substantial.
Christian grinned when he saw well-used cherry
wooden steps. If she didn't have steps she would
have to pole-vault into the bed each night.

He studied the photographs she had artfully hung
around the room and a large watercolor that was
visually appealing if not very sophisticated. He
picked up a photo of Beth Ann and Glenn with another man, all three smiling. It looked as if it was
taken in college. Behind them, her old truck was
piled high with furniture and whatnot. Maybe art
supplies. Christian couldn't tell. Putting the photo
down, he turned his attention to the other objects in
the room. There was some more of Bernie's art, a
piece of jewelry here and there. He opened the bottom drawer and the stiff smell of cedar washed toward him from the small blocks scattered on the
bottom. He quickly unpacked his few possessions,
going to the closet to see if there would be any
chance of hanging up a few pairs of slacks and
shirts. If she was anything like her sister, all the
closet space would be completely used. Eventually,
Caroline had needed another closet down the hall.

To his surprise, Beth Ann's closet was relatively
empty, though he did spy a pile of dirty laundry
hiding inconspicuously in the corner. He counted
four dresses and two very nice, very tailored suits.
She also seemed to have just two pairs of dress
shoes. He hung his shirts and slacks next to hers,
liking the way they looked together. Side-by-side.
As if that was the way they were supposed to be.

When he finished and went to the living room, Beth Ann was there, too, flipping through a trade magazine for watercolorists.

She looked up when he walked in and put the magazine aside.

"I want to thank you again for doing this. You don't have to."

"I know I don't have to. But it would be nice to get to know Caroline's family. Hey, that looks good—"

Beth Ann glanced at the iced tea in her hands. She rose hurriedly. "I'm sorry. I should have asked if you wanted some."

"Sit down," Christian ordered her. "If I'm going to be watching Bernie and Iris, I should at least be able to fix myself a glass of iced tea."

Beth Ann sipped at her tea, and listened to him walk around, trying to get used to his light step. He walked quietly, gracefully for a man so tall. She heard three or four cupboards creaking before she heard him open the freezer for ice and then the refrigerator. A moment later, he was back.

"Is now a good time to talk?" he asked directly.

Beth Ann nodded. They would have to have this talk sooner or later. At least she was sitting at home on her couch, in a safe place. She didn't know about him. "As good a time as any."

"Do you have proof that Caroline is Bernie's mother?" he asked, his neutral face back. He sounded like a businessman doing research rather than a man discussing his wife.

Beth Ann nodded. "I have lots of proof. Birth certificate. Photos of Carrie pregnant. If it makes you feel any better, she had a lousy pregnancy. She fought it all the way and wasn't a glowing mother-to-be."

Christian didn't blink and Beth Ann wondered if that was any surprise to him.

"I don't understand why she would keep it a secret," he muttered almost more to himself than her.

Beth Ann's heart went out to him as she watched him struggle to process the information.

"Maybe she didn't want to be a mother," Beth Ann said simply. *Or you're not the father.* She resisted the urge to touch him, to try and comfort him.

Christian must have been thinking the exact same thing, because he was silent. His next question came out of nowhere.

"How close are you and Glenn?"

Beth Ann was too surprised to be offended.

"Very close," she said frankly.

"Bernadette seems attached."

"She is."

"Are you thinking about making Glenn her father?"

Beth Ann choked back a cough, then shook her head solemnly. "Don't think so."

"Why not?" Christian's eyes were hard to read.

"Because," Beth Ann said placidly, "he's already married. And Fred would be very disappointed if I took his husband away."

She watched Christian's face until it became clear that he'd absorbed the full meaning of what she'd said.

"Ah." Christian nodded with new understanding. "I'm embarrassed."

"Why? How could you have known?"

"So Glenn sleeps in your room—"

''And I sleep in the daybed in Bernie's room. Just like now. You'll sleep in the front. I'll sleep in the back.'' Beth Ann spoke practically, but now she wondered if that was enough space between them. He seemed to be sitting awfully close.

''Did Caroline ever see Bernie?''

Their small conversational reprieve was over. Beth Ann swallowed hard. ''Not after she left.''

''I know you mentioned it before but how old was Bernie when she left?''

''Ten days.''

''Ten days.'' Christian nodded. She could see he was thinking, making calculations. ''So if Bernie was born in June—''

''June 27.''

''Caroline would have left at the beginning of July.''

Beth Ann nodded. ''I think she went straight to San Francisco and caught a three-month Alaskan cruise, so she would have been home the beginning of October. I kept thinking she was going to come back and pick Bernie up, that she just needed to get away for a time—postpartum depression and all.''

''But she never did.'' Christian's voice was flat and hard.

Beth Ann wanted to cry for him.

Christian clenched his stomach and regulated his breathing. He was trying every trick he'd learned, but nothing seemed to keep the feelings down. He had tried to intellectualize the situation. Here they were having a perfectly rational conversation about his wife and the baby his wife had abandoned. But he just felt like his guts had been blown out.

He avoided looking at Beth Ann, her dark, dark

eyes, so expressive. He felt his throat close and he sat straighter to take a long swig of the iced tea. He knew she was still staring at him, just as she had in the parking lot of Los Amigos, and he felt that if he looked at her, she would see how terribly he was dealing with the entire situation.

Christian took a deep breath. He could do this. He had negotiated deals worth millions of dollars. He had saved his grandfather's company from hostile takeovers and stared down lawyers and reporters during verbal assassinations of his family name and reputation. He had even managed to maintain a level of corporate decency through a period when all his peers were cutting loyal employees loose to save their bottom lines. So why couldn't he manage to look in those espresso-brown eyes?

Because, despite all his training, despite all the control that he had managed the past thirty-six years of his life, he couldn't stop the pain that was beginning to pulse right under his sternum. And with every expression of concern she gave him, the hurt pulsated even harder.

"How do you do it?" he asked.

"Do what?" Suddenly, her eyes were wary.

"Raise someone who isn't yours."

She laughed. "I'm just returning the favor. Iris raised me and I wasn't hers. Carrie was her granddaughter by blood. I was barely a granddaughter by marriage—Carrie's father never even adopted me. But that didn't make any difference to Iris. I was her granddaughter." She continued, her voice fierce. "Besides, you can't tell me that Bernie isn't mine. She is my daughter."

"Have you adopted her?" Christian asked, wondering if he would have any say in the matter, given that he was Caroline's husband.

"I'm in the process right now. But it's long." She cleared her throat. "Probably, I would have needed to get in touch with you for something in the end."

"I'd do anything to guarantee that Bernie got to stay right here." Christian's statement was flat.

Beth Ann looked at him in surprise. "You'd want to help?"

"Why wouldn't I?"

She shrugged. "I just thought— Well, it occurred to me—"

"That I'd want custody?"

"Well, maybe."

"Is there any chance that I'm her father?" Christian asked, his voice light.

From the pain in his eyes and the tight set of his handsome lips, Beth Ann knew he wasn't joking at all. She wanted to be able to tell him that Carrie had told her he was the father and that she loved him desperately, but Carrie had only referred to his money, rarely the man. This time Beth Ann didn't resist the urge to touch him. She caught his hand and squeezed.

"I don't know."

"You don't know?"

She shook her head. "She never said."

"But surely if I—"

"Carrie was complicated. I've long given up trying to figure out how she could have walked away from Bernie. I know I couldn't."

"I wouldn't walk away," Christian said.

Beth Ann regarded him for a long time, tenderness welling up in her as she realized she believed him. She took a deep breath, not daring to contemplate a permanent relationship between Christian and Bernie. And maybe herself. When she realized that she was still holding his hand, liking the feel of his fingers entwined with hers, she hastily pulled her hand away. He seemed reluctant to let her go.

"How did Carrie die?" Beth Ann asked, changing the subject, taking a large gulp of tea. She could still feel his touch.

This time he didn't do anything to hide the pain.

Beth Ann added carefully, "The person who called said she was in an accident. I thought you would call."

Christian looked at her in surprise, then replied, "I didn't know how to get in contact with you. If you remember we didn't even really meet. I didn't know you existed until the day you showed up at the office."

Beth Ann shook her head in disbelief. "No. I know Carrie was distant, but I don't think she'd— No, she wouldn't—"

"Caroline told us she had no family," Christian said flatly.

Beth Ann was not prepared for the pain his words caused. She swallowed hard. "Well, technically, I suppose that's true."

"When you showed up that time in San Diego, I felt terrible about your reception," Christian said. "But I was in the middle of one of the biggest contractual agreements I'd ever negotiated and I couldn't stop what I was doing."

"I waited three days for Carrie to call me." Beth Ann couldn't keep the reproach out of her voice.

"The next day, after the deal was signed, I asked

Caroline about inviting you over to the house, but she said you were only in town for the day.''

"You mean she lied?''

Christian didn't say anything. This time he grasped her hand. They stared at each other in silence, Carrie's lies looming between them.

He said quietly, "After she died, I remembered you but I didn't remember your name. I didn't know how to contact you. My lawyers hired an investigator to find you. By then, I didn't want to be the one to tell you your sister was dead. I thought it would be better coming from my lawyer.'' He hesitated. "But maybe I was wrong.''

Beth Ann moved closer to him on the couch, so her shoulder touched his and shook her head. "No. I'm sorry. I'm glad we were told in enough time to attend the funeral. I know it was an overwhelming time for you.'' After a long pause, she asked again, "So how did she die?''

He began in a halting voice, "She was in an accident. She was coming home from a party and she crashed her car into a tree. The police said there weren't even tire marks, which means she didn't even brake, she just ran into the tree at full speed.''

"Is that all?''

Christian was silent for a long time, then nodded, his eyes rimmed. "I wish it were more complicated than that.''

"No drugs or alcohol?''

"No. They did an autopsy.''

"No reason?''

"No.''

Beth Ann wondered what he was hiding. His whole body tensed and he shifted away from her.

"I know Carrie was my sister, but I don't think she ever knew how to be a sister."

Christian gave a strangled laugh. "Funny. I was just thinking she didn't know how to be a wife. But then again, maybe I didn't know how to be a husband. Or the kind of husband she needed."

When his eyes met hers, Beth Ann saw his soul. She saw the torture that Carrie had caused him and knew it was unfair. Beth Ann wasn't sure what kind of man Christian was, but whatever he'd done, he didn't deserve to suffer like this. She stared at the hand that still clasped hers tightly and lifted it to her mouth.

CHAPTER EIGHT

CHRISTIAN FELT Beth Ann's soft lips on the back of his hand and a warmth suddenly spread through him, engulfing the hurt, washing it away.

"Why did you do that?" he asked, his voice barely above a whisper.

Beth Ann shook her head, her dark eyes seeing into him and he never felt safer.

She was so close. He could feel the heat of her shoulder against his and he released his hand so that he could cup her face. Then, he kissed her, gently, his lips feeling hers experimentally. They were softer than he imagined, plumper, their landscape so different from Caroline's. Their tentative response evoked a whole wave of conflicting emotions, and he pulled away as an onslaught of feelings swept through him.

"I'm sorry," he said.

"For what?" Beth Ann looked confused by his apology.

"For kissing you. I didn't mean—"

"I liked it." Her eyes spoke of something deeper, more primal than he expected of her. "I'm not sorry."

"I didn't mean— It won't happen again," he promised, his voice stiff.

Her face flushed, Beth Ann jumped up quickly.

"Beth Ann—" Christian caught her wrist.

"I'm going to start getting dinner ready," she said as she gently extricated herself from his hold. She walked toward the swinging door, her voice overly perky. "If I don't have something planned by the time Iris wakes up, she wants to experiment in the kitchen. It's too hot for experiments."

"Beth Ann." He followed her into the kitchen.

She whirled around, her eyes wide, her lips slightly parted. "Don't," she instructed him. "It never happened, okay?"

"Mommy, I wake. I wake," a small, groggy voice called.

Beth Ann answered over her shoulder, "Hey, there sweetie." She looked up at him, all traces of vulnerability gone, and asked with a quick smile, "You want to go get her?"

Christian hesitated. "Do you think she'll let me?"

"She better let you." Beth Ann grinned, her dimples flashing at him, making him want to kiss her all over again. "You're going to be keeping her for the next month. Two-year-olds require routines. So ask her if she had a good sleep and about her dreams. When you pick her up, hug her really close, because even though she thinks she's awake, she's still coming out of it." She fixed her smile on him. "Think about how it was when you were just waking up—how your mother would give you a big smile and welcome you to the real world."

Christian nodded, not knowing there could be a transition between the dreamworld and the real world. He never remembered his mother once giving him a big smile and cradling him close when he woke up. Never once.

"So are you game?" Beth Ann tossed him a fun look. She lifted an eyebrow and added, "I double-dare you."

Double-dare you. The incantations of a child's game he rarely got the chance to play.

"I could never resist a dare." Christian chuckled, then added as he ventured down the hall, "If she's unhappy, it's your fault." Beth Ann's laughter erased the tension caused by his kiss and he was grateful.

"Mommy, I wake. I wake," Bernie called again as Christian pushed open the door.

He glued on his most charming smile, pushing away the feelings of panic when Bernie's little mouth turned down. He said in a gentle voice, "Hi, Bernie. Did you have a good sleep?"

"Mommy?" Bernie looked skeptical, but was too blurry from sleep to really object.

"I'm going to take you to Mommy right now. She's in the kitchen. Did you have a good sleep?" Christian picked her up, surprised when she offered him no resistance. Beth Ann was right; Bernie was still half-asleep. She rubbed her face into his shirt.

"Good sleep," Bernie said and yawned. She clutched his sleeve and then snuggled into his chest.

"Did you have good dreams?" he asked softly, trying to imagine how she was feeling tucked close in his arms. A little girl raised with such security. Had his father ever tucked Christian in his arms, greeted him after a nap? He sought his first memories, trying to find his father and came up without one that was even close to tender. Instead, he remembered his father rebuttoning his little blazer when he was first going to boarding school because

Here's a **HOT** offer for you!

Get set for a sizzling summer read...

with **2 FREE ROMANCE BOOKS** and a **FREE MYSTERY GIFT!**

NO CATCH! NO OBLIGATION TO BUY!

Simply complete and return this card and you'll get **2 FREE BOOKS** and **A FREE GIFT** – yours to keep!

Visit us online at www.eHarlequin.com

- 🌀 The first shipment is yours to keep, **absolutely free!**

- 🌀 Enjoy the convenience of Harlequin Superromance® books delivered right to your door, before they're available in stores!

- 🌀 Take advantage of special low pricing for **Reader Service Members only!**

- 🌀 After receiving your free books we hope you'll want to remain a subscriber. But the choice is always yours—to continue or cancel, any time at all! So why not take us up on this fabulous invitation, with no risk of any kind. You'll be glad you did!

336 HDL C26D

135 HDL C253
(H-SR-OS-06/00)

▼ DETACH HERE AND MAIL CARD TODAY! ▼

Name:	
(Please Print)	
Address:	Apt.#:
City:	
State/Prov.:	Zip/ Postal Code:

The Harlequin Reader Service® —Here's how it works:

Accepting your 2 free books and gift places you under no obligation to buy anything. You may keep the books and gift and return the shipping statement marked "cancel." If you do not cancel, about a month later we'll send you 6 additional novels and bill you just $3.80 each in the U.S., or $4.21 each in Canada, plus 25¢ delivery per book and applicable taxes if any.* That's the complete price and — compared to cover prices of $4.50 each in the U.S. and $5.25 each in Canada — it's quite a bargain! You may cancel at any time, but if you choose to continue, every month we'll send you 6 more books, which you may either purchase at the discount price or return to us and cancel your subscription.

*Terms and prices subject to change without notice. Sales tax applicable in N.Y. Canadian residents will be charged applicable provincial taxes and GST.

he'd done it wrong. He'd been so young. His mother had lied, telling the school he had turned five, when in reality, he had just turned four.

Be a man now. You're a man now. Don't cry. Be a man.

Christian swallowed hard, not understanding why that memory leapt to his mind. He had forgotten all about it.

"Good dreams," Bernie murmured.

He kissed the top of her head. Her curls were so soft and smelled so clean. "Good dreams. What did you dream about, sweetheart?"

Bernie looked up at him and tilted her head in thought and then said loudly, "Bang!"

"Bang? You dreamed about bangs?"

She nodded and then started talking gibberish, each sentence ending with bang and boom and bang, bang, bang.

Christian nodded, asking her questions as they made their way to the kitchen.

"Mommy!" Bernie held out her arms to Beth Ann, who took her and gave her a big kiss.

"You woke up."

"Woked up."

"You want some juice?"

"I'll get it," Christian volunteered quickly. His arms felt empty without Bernie's weight and he wanted to do something. "What kind of juice do you want, Bernie?"

Bernie suddenly turned shy, burying her face into Beth Ann's shoulder, then peering at him with one eye.

"What kind of juice do you want, Bern-Bern? Apple or grape?"

"Grape."

"You sure that you want grape? It's purple."

"No purppo, appo."

"Apple juice is the brown juice."

"Appo."

Beth Ann gave Christian a smile. "I think she wants apple juice. But just pour a little and see if she likes it. There's a sipper cup in that cabinet."

"Sipper cup?"

"The plastic cup with the lid and lip."

"Oh." Christian was looking hard. "I've got it."

"Only a little. Sometimes, she thinks she wants grape but she gets the words confused. Believe me, you don't want to be wearing a shirt covered in grape juice because she really wanted apple. That's why I always tell her which is which, just to make sure she knows what she's getting."

Christian nodded, making a mental note, wondering for the briefest of moments if he had gotten himself in over his head. It seemed there was enough to do with just Bernie. He hadn't even begun to learn about Iris's needs.

"It's not that hard," Beth Ann said, almost reading his mind. "You can feel free to back out. We won't be any worse off."

"But then you can't paint."

Beth Ann shrugged. "What it means is that I can't paint now. I've got a whole life ahead of me to paint. I'd prefer to give Bernie and Iris a stable, happy home than be the most successful watercolorist out there."

"Did you do the mural in Bernie's room?" Christian changed the subject and handed Bernie her sipper cup a quarter full of apple juice. She drank it all down and gave him an angelic smile.

"More peas?" she asked as she handed the sipper cup out to him.

"I think she wanted apple juice." Beth Ann laughed.

"Appo juice," Bernie echoed.

As he went for the juice, Beth Ann answered his question, "No. Glenn did that in water-based paints. When we finally realized Carrie wasn't going to come back, we wanted to do something to celebrate Bernie's place in our lives."

THE DAY WAS one of the most pleasant Christian had ever experienced. When Iris awoke from her nap, she was in cheerful spirits and she and Christian went out to collect the laundry, while Bernie played in the garden. He let Iris take down Beth Ann's underwear. When they walked in, Iris insisting on carrying her half of the basket, Beth Ann gave him an approving smile. Out of her sight, he sorted the laundry, taking special care to smooth out Beth Ann's simple cotton panties, amazed that something so basic and fundamental could be so darned sexy. He had seen some of the skimpiest, raciest of French lingerie, as well as the most expensive, and nothing seemed to be as touchable as these cotton panties with the tiny flowers scattered across them. While he was trying to imagine what they looked like on her—spectacular—Beth Ann walked in. He hastily covered the pile with a towel.

Together, he and Iris put the new linen on the bed. She insisted on hospital corners and placing the pillowcases with the ends tucked in like an old-fashioned sandwich bag without the zip. She didn't even resemble the disoriented woman of the day before. She was funny and lucid and obviously very much concerned with the welfare of her granddaughter.

"Beth Ann is a marvelous artist," Iris said as she sat down to rest in the big leather chair in the corner of Beth Ann's room and watched him unpack the rest of his belongings. He liked the fact that he and Beth Ann were sharing space. He put his cologne next to her atomizer. His comb next to her brush. His watch next to hers. He stared at his wedding ring and after a moment's hesitation, pulled it off as well.

"I haven't seen any of her work," he remarked.

"Sure you have. That's hers," she said, pointing to the large watercolor that was right across from the bed.

Christian remembered noticing it earlier.

"She did that when she was fourteen." The pride in Iris's voice was apparent.

Fourteen. Christian whistled. Amazing.

"Glenn said she went to art school?" he asked casually. Now that he fully understood Glenn's relationship with Beth Ann, he felt as if the other man was an ally.

"An M.F.A. program in Chicago. Very competitive. She was one of four that year."

"Wow."

"She's gained a lot of depth since that." Iris sighed as she indicated the painting on the wall. "She just doesn't do it as much as she should."

"No time?"

"Maybe. Maybe not." Iris suddenly appeared

weary. She smiled at him, her eyes far away in thought. "I think *she* would tell you it was time. Do you want to know what I think?"

Christian nodded, very much wanting to know what Iris thought.

Iris said carefully, "I think she worries about everything. And the worry keeps her from painting. If I weren't an old woman and could take care of Bernie—"

"From what I've heard, you've done more than your share of taking care of people."

Iris brightened at his words. "Did Carrie tell you that?"

Christian was at a loss for words. Then, he lied, "Yes, she did. She told me all about you. How you were a botanist before you retired. Did you paint as well?" He distinctly remembered Glenn referring to Iris's art.

"Well, I *liked* to paint," Iris said. "Until my eyes got too bad. But I was nowhere near Beth Ann's league. She and Glenn. Two very different kinds of painters, but still very much kindred spirits when it comes to art. Carrie on the other hand." She looked at him, as if she knew he had lied to her about Caroline, but forgave him. "Carrie and Beth Ann were never alike. Even when they were small."

"I'm realizing that."

"Were you happy with Carrie?" The question came out of nowhere.

Christian hesitated. She seemed too alert for him to lie outright. Then he said, "Caroline was always able to make people happy." He felt good about his hedge.

"But was she able to make you happy?" Iris's question was piercing.

"No," he answered honestly and then explained. "But I'm a pretty hard person to make happy. I think I'm one of those perpetual pessimists. The glass is always half-empty."

Iris nodded, then said, "I think Beth Ann could make anyone happy just by smiling at them."

Christian couldn't agree more.

THAT NIGHT, Christian lay in Beth Ann's bed, fully expecting to stay awake. So much had happened since the day before. He'd had no idea he would be sleeping in an antique cherry bed listening to the cows moan in the distance. So much to think about, to process. The least of which was that Caroline had based her entire marriage on lies.

The heaviness of the night began to weigh on his eyelids. He stared at the painting, almost glowing in the bright moonlight, studying the scene through Beth Ann's fourteen-year-old eyes. He rolled over, his face in the pillow, inhaling the clean scent of laundry soap and sunshine. The heat of the spring day had cooled and in addition to the rather noisy cows, he could hear the crickets chirping and the hum of the semi-trailer trucks rolling down the distant freeway. He felt as if he was a million miles away from anything real, anything unhappy....

Christian woke to a curdling scream.

Dragging his eyes open, he flung himself out of bed, wondering what it was as he stumbled in the direction of it. Highly disoriented, he banged his knee, but somehow managed to make it to the kitchen. Iris was standing frozen in the middle of the room with the flames of the gas stove flaring on all four burners. He quickly turned them off and turned the kitchen light on. Beth Ann, her hair tousled, came rushing in, her sleeveless nightgown askew at the shoulders. Christian couldn't help but notice how her small breasts pushed against the soft fabric, worn thin from years of wear.

"What's wrong?" she demanded, panic crowding her voice, clearly unaware of her state of undress.

"Nothing. Nothing. Go back to sleep," Christian assured her, trying the best he could to be a gentleman and look at her face and not the delicate outline of her nipple.

"Grans? What did you want?" Beth Ann asked.

"An egg."

"An egg, Grans?" Beth Ann's voice was soft. "What kind of an egg?"

"A fried egg."

Beth Ann looked at the stove and then looked at Christian.

He shrugged. "They were going full blast."

"I told you, Grans, if you want an egg, you can just wake me up and I'll fix it for you."

The confused look in Iris's eyes broke Christian's heart. How was it that after just two days with this family, he was so deeply entrenched in their lives that he felt all their breakdowns personally?

"I didn't want to wake you. You were sleeping." Iris looked to him for help.

"Why don't you go back to bed, Beth Ann?" Christian offered. "I'll fix Iris an egg. I could use an egg myself."

Uncertainly, Beth Ann studied the man before her, relaxing when he nodded. Even though he was only dressed in pajama bottoms, he looked every inch in charge of the situation. She let her gaze linger on his bare chest, then trail down his flat stomach to where a thin line of dark hair disappeared down into— Her heart fluttered in her throat.

"Are you sure?" she whispered. "You don't have to do this."

"Go back to sleep." His voice was gentle, like a deep caress.

She gave him a questioning look and when he nodded again, she kissed Iris on the forehead.

"Well, Grans, enjoy your egg. I hope Christian can make them sunny-side up."

"My specialty," Christian said cheerfully, and his gray eyes assured her that Iris would be fine.

Beth Ann had a hard time getting back to sleep. She could hear murmured conversation punctuated by quiet bursts of laughter. She had to admit that Carrie, whether she'd intended to or not, had married a wonderful man. The ache in her soul seemed to grow larger at the vivid memory of his kiss. Even if he regretted it, it was significant to her.

CHRISTIAN AWOKE to the sound of movement in the kitchen. He opened his eyes, slowly realizing he had been asleep. He looked at his clock in surprise, hardly daring to believe he had been asleep for four hours, the longest stretch of sleep he had had since Caroline's death. What was more amazing was the way he felt. Rested. Sort of. He peered out the window. Dawn was just breaking. A beautiful day. He pulled on a pair of comfortable jeans and a white shirt he didn't even bother to tuck in. He reached for his wedding ring and hesitated. He grabbed instead a small leather notebook that fit perfectly in his shirt pocket. He wouldn't be caught unprepared when Beth Ann gave him tips about Bernie and Iris. He walked across the living room and pushed open the swinging door, anticipation washing through him when he saw Beth Ann hard at work at the sink.

"Hello, there," he greeted. He couldn't stop his eyes from surveying her small breasts, chastely covered by an oversize T-shirt. His imagination supplied the image from the night before. "What're you doing?"

She looked up and her elfin smile with the perfect points filled him with relief. She wasn't going to hold the kiss against him. "Just finishing up the dishes from last night. The pan had to soak. You want to make the coffee?"

"Sure." He crossed the kitchen and looked around. "Where do you keep it?"

"In the freezer. There are two cans. You want to put one scoop from the can with the X on top and three scoops from the can without."

"Why?"

"Why?" Beth Ann stared at him in surprise.

"Yes," Christian asked. "What's the difference?"

"Oh, the can without the X has recycled grounds."

He laughed in disbelief. "You're kidding."

"No, I'm not," she said seriously. She vigorously scrubbed the pan.

"That's why your coffee is so bad."

"Did Glenn tell you my coffee was bad?"

"No, I figured that out myself," Christian said.

"Beth Ann, you can't recycle coffee grounds into the coffee you drink."

"Why not?"

"Because it doesn't taste good. Regular coffee shouldn't taste bitter. Trust me."

"Coffee is expensive," Beth Ann muttered.

"I'll buy you a lifetime supply of coffee," he said. "Please, let me use four scoops of the good grounds. You can recycle the used stuff in your compost heap."

Beth Ann thought for a minute and then said grudgingly, "Okay. Don't ever let Glenn tell you I don't compromise."

Christian laughed and put four scoops of the fresh coffee into the filter.

"How'd you sleep?" Beth Ann asked as she flashed him another friendly smile—one that sent a wave of comfort down his back.

Who but his physician had ever made that inquiry?

"Good," he answered honestly.

"Thank you for getting to Grans last night."

"Don't mention it. That's what I'm here for." He poured the water into the coffeemaker.

"Well. I didn't mean it to be trial by actual fire," she said ruefully.

"Have you ever thought about putting a lock on her door?"

Beth Ann frowned. "Glenn and Fred have talked to me about that. But I can't bear to lock Grans in her room."

"It's better than burning the house down."

"That's what Fred and Glenn say." She snorted. "You men all think alike. Is that your solution to everything? Lock 'em up. No wonder we have so many prisons.''

Christian backed down from the topic. Obviously a touchy subject.

"Mommy!"

Beth Ann instantly made a move to go get her but Christian stopped her.

"Stay and enjoy the peace, I'll get her. That's another thing I'm here for. Any special tricks?"

Beth Ann shook her head and put the pan upside down to drain. She started clearing away the clutter of toys on the floor. "Not anything you don't know already."

"Potty things?"

"We potty after we eat breakfast, because she's already gone in the night."

"So diaper change."

"Diaper change would be good," Beth Ann grinned. "You sure you want to do this?"

"Well, maybe you should do it once, while I look on."

"Why don't you go to her? I'll be there as soon as I finish picking up all Bernie's toys so she can have the joy of spreading them around the house again. Those diapers are so heavy-duty, she could wear one for three days and not feel wet."

Christian laughed and walked down the hall, already becoming familiar with the creaks of the floor.

"Mommy!" The cry was a little more insistent.

When Christian pushed open the door, he was greeted by an anxious Bernie who was standing on her tiptoes at the very corner of the crib. With another inch of height, she would be able to scale the side of the crib with no problem.

She smiled at him and Christian felt a tug at his heart. With her eyes filled with sleep and her smooth skin the color of peaches, she was adorable. "Mommy?"

"Mommy's in the kitchen."

"*Garden!*" She bounced a couple of times, then raised her arms for Christian to pick her up.

"So did you have a good sleep, sweetheart?" he asked, not being able to help himself as he planted a kiss on her cheek. With a gentle hand, he carefully plucked the sleepy goo from her eyes. She gave him a big hug.

"Garden!"

"Garden later, sweetie," Beth Ann said as she walked in the room. "You're going to take advantage of your Uncle Christian while he's here, I can tell." She indicated to Christian that he should put Bernie on the changing table.

"Unckiss!" Bernie held one arm out to him as she lay down.

Christian felt a small spurt of pleasure. His very own nickname.

"We're going to change you and then we can go have some breakfast," Beth Ann said cheerfully.

Christian noticed everything Beth Ann said around Bernie was upbeat, as if eating breakfast was the most fun thing in the world. He wanted to have breakfast just because of the way she said it.

"Diapers are here," she instructed him. "And if these run out, there's more in the closet. If that supply is down to one package, let me know and I'll make a trip to the store. Usually, I can find a sale before I run out."

He had learned to be an excellent student at the

military academy. He pulled out the notebook and began to scribble. "So you'll go paint after breakfast?" he asked, watching her as she wiped Bernie with quick efficient strokes.

"Use these wipes, too, if she goes poo in the potty." Beth Ann's lips quirked up as he took more notes. "But these don't flush like toilet paper."

"Mrs. Potty!" Bernie exclaimed with a wriggle.

"Yes. Mrs. Potty. But after breakfast." Beth Ann rubbed her nose into Bernie's bare tummy and Bernie chortled with glee. "Toilet paper's a little rough and she hates it."

"Then the diapers go back on." He made a note.

Beth Ann laughed.

"No Pull-Ups?" he asked. He watched television. He knew what was available.

Beth Ann made a face. "I don't know. I hear good things and bad things about those. I don't want to force anything on her. And she's used to using Mrs. Potty every morning and every night after her bath. Maybe in a few months. We'll see."

Christian nodded and realized with a sinking heart that he wouldn't be around to see that milestone. Instead of watching this little girl grow, he'd be back in San Diego, hurtling from one meeting to the next and at night, when he finally quit working for the day, he'd be alone in his private wing of the Elliott estate. He shook off the feelings, focusing on the fact he was here, not there.

When Beth Ann put Bernie down, she immediately went to grab Fluff from between the slats of the crib. Her grip on his ear was deathlike.

"Why don't you dress her?" Beth Ann asked. "We usually do that after breakfast—saves on two clothes changes in the morning—but we don't have to.''

"Why don't we wait? After breakfast, you can paint. And I'll dress her.''

"Grans will be up by then. She can help, too.''

Christian could hear Beth Ann's unspoken words. *If she's having a good day.*

"And Bernie and I will take care of her,'' Christian said a little more confidently than he felt. "After all, I know how she likes her eggs.''

THREE DAYS LATER, Beth Ann stared at the man who had taken over her household with the efficiency of a Marine Corps sergeant. Not that she was threatened by how easily everyone, especially Bernie and Iris seemed to have taken to him. Of course not. He was no threat. She could trust the judgment her family had shown. Children and the aged were by far the best judges of character. Breakfast, as usual, was a lively affair, but for some reason, even though she knew Bernie and Iris were in capable hands, Beth Ann didn't want to leave the fun. She didn't want to go upstairs to the attic and paint while Christian got to play with Bernie and talk philosophy with Iris.

"Go paint,'' he ordered her, as he started to rinse the dishes. Bernie banged on the table in her attempt to swat a fly. "What time do you want lunch?''

"About noon. Are you *sure* you can handle this? Maybe I should spend today with you—''

"Go paint. You've shown me everything you can and I think it's time that you took advantage of the fact that I'm here.''

She was reluctant to go.

"Go paint!" Bernie ordered her.

"Go paint!" Iris echoed with a sly smile.

"It's a conspiracy," Beth Ann grumbled, already dreading the climb to the attic. She grabbed the baby monitor. "I'll take this just in case."

Christian reached over and took it from her with a soapy hand. "If it's bad enough, you'll hear the screams. Otherwise, you should just go paint."

He stared at her for a long time and she felt as if she was getting lost in the stormy gray of his eyes. The transitions had been almost effortless. Iris was on a streak of good days and Christian had proved himself an adept student when it came to reading Bernie's moods. He knew that Bernie loved the garden, so since the days were so nice, they spent much of their time there.

"Trust me," he said now, with a slow smile that made her heart thud heavily.

"Okay," she whispered.

"I'll call you for lunch."

With a regretful look back, she turned and walked down the hall to the stairs.

Once inside her studio, she took stock of what needed to be done. Nothing but painting; she'd already done all the cleaning she could. She studied *Party Girls* and remembered what Glenn had said about the value in the corner. She'd fix that today—maybe. *Tired.* The response of the hotel jury rang in her head. And she saw what they saw. Even Glenn, when he was commenting on value, was trying to tell her something was missing.

She listened attentively at the door, hoping for the sounds of distress, so she wouldn't have to face the fact that her painting had become so dull. But there were no such sounds. She dug through her files and found some reference photos, hoping to become inspired. But this was no time to be experimental. Time had already ticked away, leaving her with just a month to produce something worth showing.

She couldn't use the excuse that she didn't have paints. The box Fred had sent, the new tubes gleaming, mocked her, and she almost cried with frustration. She took out her slides and studied what she had done before. What was missing?

Reluctantly, she dug through the box of new paints, squeezed half of the tubes onto a clean palette and authoritatively swirled her brush through the paints. She could at least create a color chart, something to talk to Fred about. He did want a comparison. She'd been making color charts her entire life. Start with a blob of color and keep adding water.

She looked at her colors and her mind rebelled. She wanted to be downstairs with Bernie, Iris and Christian. She wanted to be anywhere but where she was. She didn't want to do a color chart. She didn't want to paint. So she didn't. She covered her palette with plastic wrap and set it in the corner, feeling like a prisoner as she peered out of her window and watched Christian and Bernie play in the garden.

A knock on the door startled Beth Ann. She looked frantically around to find something to do.

"Can I come in?" Iris asked.

Beth Ann grabbed the palette and pulled off the plastic wrap, snagging three brushes from her paint can. "Sure," she called as she put a brush between her teeth as if she couldn't decide which one to use.

Iris walked in slowly. "I haven't been up here in so long."

"You shouldn't have taken those stairs," Beth Ann scolded, taking the brush out of her mouth. "I'll tell Christian about that at lunch."

Iris shook her head. "Don't do that. I needed the exercise. Bernie's a little fussy."

Beth Ann's head shot up. "She's fussy? Do you think she's sick?"

Iris laughed. "No, just fussy. She was denied a third fig bar, and now she wants lunch, figuring she can have a fig bar after."

Beth Ann laughed.

Iris looked at the blank piece of paper. "Hard at work?"

Beth Ann flushed. "I'm a little out of touch."

"Maybe if you put some paint on those brushes, you'd get better results," Iris observed.

Beth Ann looked away.

"You haven't lost it," Iris said quietly.

"I feel like I have. I don't want to paint."

"It's not that you don't want to paint. You're scared to paint."

"What do I have to be scared of?" Beth Ann didn't want to have this conversation with Iris.

"You're afraid that we've taken every little bit of creativity you had. That you have no reserve."

Beth Ann was silent. Finally when she spoke, her voice was raw. "What if it's gone?"

Iris gave Beth Ann a strong hug. "It's not gone. It's just changed. You can't go back to what you had. You have to forge ahead to things that are new. Movement. That's what this life is all about. Movement."

"Movement?"

"Movement." Iris fixed her faded eyes on Beth Ann and Beth Ann squirmed. "Movement."

"I don't really know what you're talking about."

Iris nodded, her eyes full of wisdom. "I think you do."

CHAPTER NINE

THE NEXT WEEK crawled by for Beth Ann, whose progress in the painting department was depressingly slow. She had at least made the color chart and discovered that this new brand wasn't inferior to her old ones. She'd had a lengthy conversation with Fred, which made her feel even more like a fraud. She could talk art, she could see art, she just couldn't produce art.

Christian, on the other hand, had no such difficulty. He was like a chameleon that changed colors with its surroundings, and after a few days, it was hard to remember what life was like before him. The switch of caretakers went so smoothly neither Bernie nor Iris seemed to show any distress when Beth Ann excused herself from the breakfast table to climb the stairs to her studio.

Midweek, after twenty minutes of *whir, beep, beep, beep, beep, whir, whir,* she heard a loud crack and was halfway down the stairs to intercede, when Christian told Bernie in an oh-so-sad voice that the toy—an annoying toy Beth Ann had declared unfixable several months earlier—was broken. It was then, as she stood frozen in the hall, that she realized Christian had his own way of doing things and it created a bevy of emotions inside of her.

"Boken?" Bernie asked, her tiny voice rising

with the inflection of her question, maybe her disbelief.

"Yes, broken. Can't be used. Died," Christian said rationally to her. Beth Ann felt a pleasant shiver run down her back at the deep resonances of his voice.

"Fix it!" Bernie suggested. Beth Ann imagined Bernie batting her dark eyelashes in Christian's direction. Who could resist that?

She heard a couple of rattles.

Then Christian confirmed his original diagnosis with the somber tone of an emergency room doctor, "No, it can't be fixed. It died and went to heaven."

"Oh, no!" Bernie's voice was filled with sorrow.

Then the sorrow turned into heartfelt tears, and Beth Ann could hear Christian say hurriedly, "Maybe I can fix it."

"Fix?" The tears were miraculously gone.

Beth Ann smothered laughter and knew that after Bernie was asleep, they would discuss her incredible powers of persuasion. She looked forward to the evenings, when both Bernie and Iris retired, and she and Christian sat in the kitchen or in the living room or most often, on the steps overlooking the garden and talked. About everything. About the death of her mother, about the desertion of her stepfather. About his experience in boarding school, then military school. His friend, Max. And Carrie. They always talked about Carrie. Carrie wove in and out of their conversations as if they both needed to resolve her life and her death.

If Beth Ann's days crept by like stale molasses, the evenings were gone in an instant. She enjoyed Christian's company so much that it was almost enough to keep her from being disappointed when he made no effort to kiss her again. Almost. As the nights turned hot, Beth Ann found herself tossing and turning restlessly in the daybed, wondering if he felt the physical tension between them or if she simply imagined it. In the mornings, when she was exhausted from her own thoughts, he looked well rested, happy, apparently oblivious to the fact that he was driving her crazy.

One afternoon while Bernie and Iris napped, she ventured down from the attic, on the pretense of taking a break, and found Christian out in the yard, stripped to the waist, clearing away some dead branches and vines. As she spied on him, admired his nice body, she yearned for the natural ability to draw people, to draw the fine, taut lines of his chest and shoulders, the bands of muscle that flexed as he bent to his tasks. She longed to capture his eyes, the eyes with the ever changing gray irises, that looked just like clouds moving across a stormy sky.

Iris must have instructed him on what she wanted done in the garden because he moved efficiently from one task to the next, stopping only occasionally for a break and a deep swig of lemonade. In his short stay, he had already rebuilt Iris's compost pile, constructing three boxes out of old lumber that had been rotting at the side of the house. He'd reinforced the shed, and retrained the out of control grapevines to create a small arbor across the shed. A perfect jungle for Bernie to play in.

He'd also managed to move a large pile of composted cow manure, a welcome and most significantly, free, gift from the Marquez family down the road. Abel often dumped a load from his tractor if he was passing by. Beth Ann still had to make a visit to thank him, and now, she had to thank Christian for moving the pile to where it would be more accessible.

The garden had never looked so good. The plants seemed to grow faster, their stalks straighter with all the attention, all the care he lavished on them. He'd even mixed up a special mash of alfalfa pellets, dairy compost and bonemeal that Iris liked to use for an early summer feed. Sometimes, if Christian came around to the other side of the house, she could watch him work from her attic window. She'd seen him wash his car and then her truck. He'd even found a can of polish and had managed to pull some shine from her twenty-year-old truck.

Now, she was captivated by the play of muscles across his bronzed back as he moved the debris to the compost. The sight made her pick up her sketchpad and start to draw, trying to capture his masculine grace on the page. His clean profile, those sensuous lips, his head cocking to one side as he kept an attentive ear to the baby monitor—propped in the crook of the cherry tree—occasionally glancing at it, telling her he must have heard a shift in Iris's room or Bernie babble in her sleep.

With excitement pounding in her chest, Beth Ann returned to the attic and stared at the sketches. Movement. This is what Iris had been talking about. Movement. Eagerly, Beth Ann started to draw, focusing on Christian in her mind's eye, seeing his lean frame bend to his work. With a confidence she had thought long gone, Beth Ann sketched on the watercolor paper and then began to paint, to put color on the white. She used the entire range of colors—from the bright alizarin crimson dots for the tomatoes beginning to ripen to vivid sap green for the vines. Soon the colors and the desire to capture what she'd seen filled her mind, replacing the paralyzing dread she'd come to associate with her attic workspace.

That night, when she flossed her teeth, her eyes bleary with fatigue, her brain still whirling with what she had accomplished in just that afternoon, she suddenly noticed the sparkling commode, a tile floor that gleamed to the very corners and grout so white that someone must have used bleach and a toothbrush. Her heart tender, Beth Ann basked in Christian's support. Because he did such a great toilet, because he took such good care of Bernie and Iris, she was able to rediscover a part of herself that she thought had died with Carrie. And she loved him for it.

ONE TUESDAY MORNING, exactly three weeks after Christian had first arrived, the commotion underneath her feet made her stop painting. It hadn't started out so bad. Some unfamiliar noises, the sound of trucks in front, the opening and closing of vehicle doors. She couldn't resist peeking out her window, but the trucks were parked in such a way she had no way of reading their side panels. Again, there was a great deal of noise and banging and loud men's voices, none of which she could identify. Not to mention Bernie's loud but happy shrieking.

As Beth Ann tried to pinpoint a precise shade of violet, another loud clank shook the bungalow. Unable to concentrate, Beth Ann pounded down the

stairs and found herself face-to-face with two of the
biggest men she had ever seen in her life.

"Howdy, ma'am," one said with a tip of his hat.

"Excuse us, ma'am," mumbled the other.

Beth Ann went to look for Christian. He was in
the living room, an impressive sight even in his casual T-shirt and jeans directing several other men
through a sea of gigantic cardboard boxes. Bernie
screamed with excitement as she tramped from one
box to another, screeching more loudly, if possible,
to hear the echo. Iris sat in the corner out of the
way, watching the action, grinning from ear-to-ear.

"Who are Tweedledee and Tweedledum?" Beth
Ann demanded in a low whisper, craning her neck
to glare at him, appreciating how tall he was, and
how good he smelled. A masculine, spicy scent. She
took a step back and bumped into a box. His hand
shot out to steady her and Beth Ann blinked at the
contact, especially when he didn't let go of her elbow once she was balanced. Instead, he pulled her
close to him in an almost intimate embrace and
whispered in her ear, his poker face on, "It's a surprise. Go back to work. Everything is taken care
of."

Beth Ann looked around and surveyed the mess,
her voice doubtful. "It doesn't look like everything
is taken care of."

"Go back to work."

It was as close as it could be to a command without being a command. Something that should have
caused Beth Ann to bristle yet didn't. She was having too much trouble focusing as the subtleties of
his cologne, his warm hand on her arm and his sensuous mouth, so close to her ear she could feel his

breath tickling her earlobe, penetrated her fuzzy brain. Why, oh, why wouldn't he just kiss her?

Beth Ann firmly pulled herself out of his grasp, took a step back and shook her head to clear it. "I can't with all this racket. What is going on?" She started to go toward the kitchen.

Christian caught her arm again, and she was suddenly aware how strong he was as he firmly but gently kept her from moving closer to the kitchen. "Do you trust me?" His eyes searched hers, his gaze keen.

"That you're not tearing down my house?" She reverted to sarcasm to keep her heart from pounding out of her chest. Three more men emerged from the kitchen, and she tried to see what was going on, but was thwarted when the swinging door closed. She hated having no sense of control over what used to be a fairly well-run household. Bernie was screaming, her living room was torn to shreds. Well, not really. But it *looked* torn to shreds. This was almost worse than when he'd told her Bernie had inherited DirectTech.

"That I'm doing something nice for you." There was reproach in his voice.

"Well, that depends on what that something nice is." She felt the subtle pressure of his hand and tried to think straight.

"I just got you a few things to make your life easier."

"TV!" Bernie yelled.

"A TV?" Beth Ann shot Christian a surprised glance and then looked behind him, only now noticing that he was standing in front of a fifty-inch color television set, the remote control balanced neatly on top of it. She pulled out of his grasp again, this time positioning herself well away from him as she asked in as calm a voice as she could muster, "Why in the world would you get us a TV the size of Maryland?"

"Well, actually, that's for me." He gave her a boyish grin. Beth Ann tried to be the immovable object to his irresistible force as he continued, "I'm going nuts not knowing what's going on in the world. I've got to at least have access to CNN."

"Well, the cable is very limited in this area," Beth Ann informed him. "We're really, really rural, you know."

"That's why I got the satellite dish, too."

"Satellite dish?" Beth Ann, as if in a dream, heard herself yelp.

"Just a little one. You know a fifteen-inch one. You'll never see it on the roof."

"I don't want Bernie watching TV twenty hours a day."

"Bernie won't be watching TV twenty hours a day," he assured her with a slight twinge of annoyance to his voice. He pointed out, "But it might be nice for Iris. They have lots of old movie channels and I thought it'd keep her mind occupied during, you know, those times."

Beth Ann felt as if her mind was imploding. How could he do this? Without even talking to her first. He couldn't say he didn't have the opportunity. Just last night, they'd talked until two. She shot the new television an angry glare. It was a monstrosity. Her antique walnut curio cabinet with all her precious collectibles was almost completely obliterated by the width of the screen framed in conventional television black. *Oh look, honey, a television with a little living room to go with it.* There went their evenings. No more talks.

Beth Ann swallowed her remorse and turned it into anger. "What in the world made you think—" She couldn't get the words out of her mouth.

"All done, sir. The dishwasher's hooked—"

"*Dishwasher?*" Beth Ann watched two men start to gather up all the boxes and toss them outside. To her relief, her living room reemerged. But that didn't make the television look any less obscene. Tweedledum reached for the final box, but found Bernie, legs and arms akimbo, glaring proprietarily at him from inside. He took a step back, said, "We'll leave that one, sir," and gave Beth Ann a wink. Beth Ann reluctantly smiled as Bernie sat down, rolled onto her back and worked her way through a variety of syllables just to hear the echo.

Christian thanked him and with a handshake, Beth Ann saw that he passed both of the big men neatly folded bills. Other men tramped out with toolboxes and loud calls to each other. She heard truck doors slam and motors start up.

Tweedledee looked down, his eyes lighting up at the denomination. "Thank you, sir. Thank you very much, sir. If you have any problems, sir, just give us a call. Ma'am." He tipped his hat to her again.

Christian nodded and saw them to the door.

"Dishwasher?" Beth Ann hissed. "What did he mean, dishwasher? We're not even plumbed for a dishwasher—"

A man wearing Joe's Plumbing across his chest came out of the kitchen. "That wasn't that hard. I just hooked the dishwasher up to the sink. I replaced that old garbage disposal like you asked and—''

''Garbage disposal.'' Beth Ann had to sit down. They hadn't had a working disposal since she was in high school. Bernie came out of her box to climb into Beth Ann's lap. Beth Ann pulled Bernie close, but traitorous Bernie hopped off the couch and back into the box. It was easy to see where her priorities lay.

''Hello, ma'am—'' the plumber nodded to her and continued explaining to Christian ''—replaced all the pipes. Good thing, too. They were ready to bust anyway. All as good as new.''

''Thank you,'' Christian said graciously, and gave him a generous tip as well.

''If you have any problems, any problems at all, just call and we'll send a man out immediately.''

''Thank you. I've got your number.''

''I'm hoping you won't have to use it.'' The plumber grinned and then *he* tipped his hat. ''Ma'am.''

Then, it was quiet.

The wind rustled the remaining box that Bernie sat in. The toddler was surprisingly quiet as she watched Christian and her mother. Beth Ann didn't speak, and Christian stared at Beth Ann, hoping she wasn't as angry as she appeared. He knew he should have consulted her. But he also knew that if he had asked, she would've refused. He didn't know what had moved him to do what he just had. He simply wanted to give to Beth Ann in the same manner she gave to him.

Hell. Most women would be delighted to find that all their old broken-down kitchen appliances had

been replaced or that a brand new TV and dishwasher had come into the family. Most women
would think he was the most wonderful man in the
world. But not this one. Christian couldn't suppress
his disappointment at her cool reaction to his efforts.

He also couldn't control how aware he had become of her every movement, her every smell, the
scent of her watercolors becoming more of an aph-
rodisiac than the most expensive perfume in Paris.
He didn't dare touch her, because that meant he
would have to kiss her, but it didn't keep him from
sitting on the back steps after Iris and Bernie went
to bed, hoping that she would sit close and talk to
him. And she always did.

Now, her natural friendliness had evaporated as
she pulled her arms tightly across her breasts. Jeez.
He had managed to bring them into the twenty-first
century, and she didn't look a bit appreciative. In
fact, Beth Ann looked as if he had committed some
cardinal sin of generosity. If espresso-brown eyes
could spray bullets, he'd be dragging himself to the
hospital with multiple gunshot wounds.

Christian tried again. "I'm not sure I'm understanding what the problem is."

The bullets again. He fought the reflex to duck.

"So I now have a television set, a satellite dish,
a dishwasher and a garbage disposal."

Christian hesitated and then added sheepishly,
"And a refrigerator, new gas range, a washer and
dryer."

"Any new wallpaper?" Her voice dripped with
sarcasm. He didn't exactly know what that meant,
and it made him cautious. Christian Elliott rarely got
caught with his pants down, but he was now think-

ing he didn't know her well enough to negotiate this transaction. Perhaps he should have discussed this with her before making it happen. Then he wondered why he was defending his actions. It wasn't as if he'd done something awful. Right? Except why didn't she look at him adoringly, then, as if he had done something heroic, rather than just twisted the head off her pet canary?

"I think all the new things are wonderful," Iris said overbrightly.

They both turned to look at her. He'd forgotten she was in the room.

Iris continued, "I'm glad he got a television big enough so I could see the screen. Now I can watch old movies."

Christian could have kissed Iris, as Beth Ann's face softened just a little. No bullets for Iris, but he knew he wasn't in the clear yet.

"Well, I guess it'll be a little while before the satellite dish works," she conceded. "We have a few more days before we let the real world in."

Christian shook his head again. "Well, no. Actually, it works now. They make it really easy."

"TV, TV, TV," Bernie chanted.

"I thought she could watch the children's channel and I had them deliver a couple of videos, too. The show about some purple dinosaur—"

Beth Ann couldn't contain herself any longer. She couldn't.

"Can I talk to you in the kitchen please?" She gritted her teeth, unable to really express how she felt in front of Iris and Bernie.

"Now, gee. Even though you ask so nice, I don't think I want to," Christian said warily, his silver eyes on her face. "Maybe later, when you don't look like you're seeking the death penalty."

Beth Ann would have laughed at his expression, as endearingly pleading as it was, if she weren't so darned mad at him. She turned on her heel and marched into the kitchen, fully expecting him to follow.

Behind her, she heard a heavy sigh and then his quiet footsteps.

"I still don't understand the problem," he said, his voice carefully modulated.

"I am not a client you need to negotiate with," she spit out.

"I know that."

"This is my family, my house, my life. You can't just come in here and change things because you can't live without CNN."

"It's not just that," he said reasonably.

"What is it?" she demanded. "Why didn't you talk to me about this?"

"Because I knew you'd refuse."

Beth Ann was at a loss for words. Of course, she would refuse. Any sane, reasonable person would refuse. Why she hardly knew the man. *You know him well enough to leave your most precious possessions with him.* She squelched that thought. It wasn't as if she really was leaving Bernie and Iris in his care. She was on the premises at all times. She glanced at her kitchen. It looked old compared to the shiny newness of the appliances—top of the line, superexpensive appliances. She could barely stand it.

Finally, she said flatly, "Take them back."

Christian's eyes narrowed in response to her im-

perious tone. "That would be a dumb thing to do."
There was no mistaking the insult in his voice.

She glanced at the appliances and secretly agreed
with him. It would be a dumb thing to do, but she
said instead, trying a different tactic, "We don't
need charity."

Christian's handsome mouth tightened with annoyance. He waited so long to answer, Beth Ann
actually thought he was counting backward from
ten. When he spoke, his voice was even. "You want
to know what started it?"

Beth Ann refused to be intimidated and took a
deep breath, crossing her arms, pressing them hard
against her rib cage. "Okay. Sure," she said shortly.
"Why don't you tell me?"

"Do you really want to know?"

She finally looked up at him surprised to find
something that resembled finely tuned irritation in
his smoky eyes. What in the world did he have to
be angry about? It was her house he was disrupting.

"Yes," she said more calmly, and relaxed the
death grip on her chest. "I really want to know."

"I was looking for a safe stove."

"A what?"

"Well, you didn't want to lock Iris in at night,
but on the other hand, Iris and the stove just aren't
a good combination and sooner or later, you'd be
standing outside in your see-through nightie while
the firemen sprayed water over what they could sal-
vage."

"You can see through my nightie?" Beth Ann
looked away, her face flushing. Why hadn't she realized he would have a good reason for his generosity? She hated the fact that Christian was right.

There was going to come a time when she wouldn't catch Iris trying to cook, when the house would go up in flames. And she hated him for pointing out to her that she'd better break down and buy a new nightgown.

"And so?" Her voice sounded very cold, even to her.

"And *so*," he replied matching her tone for tone, "I knew there must be a stove out there that was smart. That you could lock or something. That would only work when you wanted it to. And I found it. They make them in Germany."

"This came from Germany?" Could it get even more ridiculous? Christian Elliott had ordered a smart stove from Germany.

"It would've been here yesterday, but they had an airline delay," Christian said, his voice tight.

"Oh, an airline delay." Her eyes wandered to the refrigerator. "Is that smart, too?"

Christian nodded. "It's a set, along with the dishwasher."

"So you bought me a smart kitchen." She tried to smile. "Does it do the cooking, too?"

Christian laughed shortly, but there was no humor in his tone, "No. You still have to do that."

"I suppose. So tell me what that stove does." She really didn't want to know, because then she would have to swallow her pride and be forced to acknowledge the extent of his thoughtfulness.

"It's gas, but it's digitally wired. You need to punch in a code before it will start. You can change the code as often as you like. It keeps small children safe as well as older folk." As he spoke, he leaned against the wall, his hands jammed into his pockets.

If she didn't know better, she would swear that beneath his placid facade lurked some seriously hurt feelings. The clipped tone of his voice confirmed what she thought. "That way, you don't have to worry about Iris. She can get anything she wants from the fridge, but she can't turn on the stove without your code."

Beth Ann sat down hard and put her face in her hands. He had every reason to have hurt feelings. She felt awful. Awful and embarrassed. After a long moment, she ventured to look at him through her fingers. "And the dishwasher, garbage disposal, washer, dryer, television and satellite?" She made a special effort to make her voice more curious than condemning.

The hurt feelings seemingly buried, Christian grinned at her, his even teeth flashing, his tone wry. "I was on a roll. If you really hate the television, we can get you a smaller one. But I do think it would be good for Iris. You know how much she loves looking at her old family photos. Letting her watch old movies may help keep her mind agile. Might help keep her focused. I know that's what you want."

Beth Ann nodded and replied faintly, "Yes. That's what I want." She shot a quick look at him. "May I ask how much this all cost?"

Christian shrugged, his eyes shuttered. "You can ask, but I won't tell you."

"I'll try to pay you back." She looked away, tears of stress filling her eyes. "Maybe if I sell a couple of paintings, I can give you a down payment."

"No," Christian said impatiently, his lips tight. "It's not about the money."

Beth Ann gave a weak laugh. "Not for you maybe."

Christian crossed the space between them, and leaned toward her, his face close. She could smell the mint on his breath. "Listen to me. Bernie is my wife's daughter, not to mention, a very wealthy young lady. If you want to pay me back, we'll take it out of next year's dividends."

Beth Ann shook her head. "That won't work."

"Why not?"

"Because Bernie's not going to have DirectTech. I'm going to refuse it no matter what you say."

"And what if I won't let you?" His voice was dangerously calm.

"Then I'll sign it over to a good cause. If you don't want it back, then some charity's going to love you."

"It's not your company to sign away," he said decisively. "It's Bernie's."

Beth Ann didn't know if she should be insulted or pleased he cared so much about Bernie. Either way she could barely speak, her mind was so full of what was happening at that moment. For a lack of anything better to say, she asked, plain and baldly, her voice a lot sharper than she intended, "Why do you even care?"

Christian couldn't answer her question. Why did he care? If he had stayed with his original travel plans, he'd be sitting in an isolated chalet, sipping the finest wine in the world. He wouldn't be standing in a well-worn kitchen fighting with one of the most obstinate women he had ever met in his life.

He also wouldn't be trying to cajole a two-year-old to eat her applesauce or fixing an octogenarian a special egg, sunny-side up.

He'd be alone.

Just like he'd been all his life, even when he was married to Caroline. He cared because for the first time in his very privileged life, he wasn't treated as if he was privileged. It was as if Beth Ann didn't realize he was a man of enormous wealth. Or maybe she didn't care. Which was why, when he displayed such wealth, even in an act of generosity, she was outraged, insulted or something he couldn't even put a finger on.

Usually she treated him like an ordinary person and obviously, his money meant nothing to someone who hadn't started with much. He felt a twinge of guilt. Was that what all those appliances were about? Was he trying to buy her acceptance under the guise of giving her something she desperately needed? He stopped the self-analysis. She needed the appliances. She needed a new roof and real air-conditioning instead of an antique swamp cooler that wasn't going to make it through the rest of the summer.

He stared at Beth Ann who stared back at him, her full mouth tight with her disapproval and Christian just wanted to shake some sense into her, his frustration with her stubbornness at accepting help in any form even if it was hers to begin with at an all-time high. But somewhere beneath that frustration was a deep sense that never in his whole life had he ever met a woman like Beth Ann, someone so totally unimpressed with his wealth that he had to measure up as a person in order to be let into her private circle.

That was why he cared. But he couldn't tell her that. He said instead, "I just wanted to make your life a little easier."

"Why?"

Christian laughed. "I've taken care of Bernie for nearly three weeks now and, no offense, but she's frankly, er, challenging. I can't imagine the sacrifices you've made to raise her. No wonder your painting has suffered. Why wouldn't I want to help make your job easier?"

"Who said anything about sacrifice?" Her voice hard, Beth Ann looked ready to do battle and Christian had no idea what had triggered the change in her. "Or that my art has suffered. How would you know that?"

He answered as honestly as he could, hoping she would appreciate his straightforwardness, "All I have to do is look at you." And he realized it was true. All he had to do was see her to know that the activity of her mind, seeing, thinking, painting had revived parts of herself that had been dormant for the past two years. He could see that as clearly as if she had told him. Her art was the only thing she refused to talk about.

"Is that so?" Her voice was mildly curious, very low. "What makes you say that?"

Christian shrugged, though he knew he had to tread carefully. "I see someone who's afraid of taking the risks needed to paint. Someone who gets so much reward from being 'mommy' that she's forgotten she's anything else."

Beth Ann's face turned bright red at the points of

her cheeks and it took Christian a second to realize she was not embarrassed or impressed by his insight, but very, very, angry. However, nothing could have prepared him for the bitterness of her words.

"So why couldn't you do that with Carrie?" Her words were blunt and flat.

Christian felt as if he had been kicked in the stomach. He stared at her, not imagining so few words could stun him speechless. Her words hurt, not because of her tone, but because of the truth behind them. She had a valid question. Why *couldn't* he have done that with Caroline? Maybe if he had been able to read her as well as he could read Beth Ann, Caroline wouldn't have felt the need to go to all those parties, those cruises. Maybe she wouldn't be dead. In the past eighteen months, he had spent a lot of time wondering what he had done wrong.

He realized, in his short time here, that Caroline had been a hard person to know. Although outwardly more vivacious than Beth Ann, she'd been much more closed, more secretive. After seven years of marriage, he still hadn't been able to tell what she was thinking, what made her tick, except to come to some abstract conclusion that money and lots of it somehow soothed whatever demons chased her. Beth Ann on the other hand was as open as a book. After three weeks, Christian felt as if he could breathe for her, he was so in tune with her needs.

But obviously, she wasn't looking for anyone to breathe for her, or help lighten her load, or even share her load. She liked having those burdens all to herself, squarely on top of her slender shoulders. Knowing that didn't help. So Christian did what he had been trained to do all his life—even though he knew it frustrated the hell out of the people he did it to—rather than engage in battle, he walked away.

Beth Ann watched his silent departure and felt awful. And lonely. She hadn't meant to say what she'd said. It had just come out. She tried to make herself feel better by rationalizing that if he had talked to her first rather than played King Midas, they could have come to some reasonable compromise. *I knew you'd refuse.* She got up and studied the gas range.

"If you're so smart, why didn't you stop me before I said anything?" she asked it. She flipped through the owner's manual and then put it down, actually uncomfortable with the fact that she had crossed the line. She had broken their implicit agreement and had used his evening confidences against him. She knew he felt enormous guilt for not paying enough attention to Carrie and that was clearly not the case with her. He paid too much attention, knew her needs too well and that was scary as hell. Beth Ann took a deep breath. The frozen look on Christian's face was deeply, deeply troubling. She wandered over to the refrigerator, perfectly fit into the space allocated for it, vaguely aware that he must have had it special ordered. Her chest was tight, partly from shame and partly from— She couldn't possibly love him. Could she? Of course not. He was her sister's husband and a billionaire. Beth Ann sighed. When this babysitting job was done and over, he'd go to his chalet in the wine country and they'd never see him again. Or maybe he'd just drop them off an appliance every Christmas.

It was as if dumping DirectTech on them could ease his responsibility to Carrie and to Bernie. She ran the garbage disposal, and took a deep breath. She didn't like it one bit that he had replaced every appliance in her house, but she couldn't fault his motives. She opened the dishwasher, surprised at all the space. She spotted a few empty cups and put them in, just to test it out. She looked around the kitchen. She did need new wallpaper now—the new appliances made it look drab and faded. Exactly the way she felt, drab and faded.

She nodded, a brief flash of insight as to how Carrie must have felt when she'd been confined to this house for the duration of her pregnancy. She'd probably stared at the wallpaper and the old appliances and wished she were in a place where things were new and shiny.

CHAPTER TEN

FOR TWO DAYS, Christian and Beth Ann didn't speak. Well, Beth Ann thought, that wasn't technically true. They spoke about Bernie and Iris. They discussed the secret code that would make the stove work. They even exchanged polite chitchat about how clear the fifty-inch television screen was when they watched a nearly new movie without commercials or fuzz. They didn't sit next to each other anymore. In fact, he sat on one end of the couch and she sat on the other with Bernie and Iris as buffers in between.

It hadn't helped that Christian had been right.

After the inaugural load of laundry in the brand new washer, she saw how much cleaner their clothes were. Embarrassed by her reaction to Christian's generosity, Beth Ann didn't know how to apologize and with each day that passed, it was harder for her to do. While she still felt strongly that what he'd done was presumptuous, another part of her acknowledged the thoughtfulness behind the gifts. After all, these were *appliances* for goodness sake, not the crown jewels. But she had every reason to hate that television, especially when it so easily replaced their evening conversation.

So, they didn't speak of his hurt feelings or her sense of sorry. But when Christian casually mentioned at the dinner table his plans to leave a week from Saturday, Beth Ann was startled back to reality. As he talked about going on to Napa, his original destination, Beth Ann realized she'd never thought about him as a guest, but as a permanent fixture, like the new stove and refrigerator he'd had installed for life.

After his announcement, Beth Ann's appetite was gone. Was she so morose because Christian's leaving meant her freedom to paint would be gone? She watched Christian talk with Iris, saw Bernie's hand reach to grab *his* green beans, not the ones Beth Ann had put on her tray, and knew she would miss him, the deep-down achy kind of missing, the kind of missing that comes from loving someone and wanting them around forever. She would miss Christian's broad shoulders filling her doorways, his light footsteps down the hall, his laughter and Bernie's squealing infiltrating every nook, every corner, every bend of this old house that had never really had a permanent male resident.

It had always been a feminine household. Always. Even before she and Carrie moved in with Iris, whose husband had died before Beth Ann had even been born. Men passed through, like Glenn or Fred or her grandmother's dear friend, Henry, who had died more than a decade ago, but no one had ever stayed. Never before had she ever felt there was any need for a masculine presence. But now, having experienced a sense of completeness, like a circle finally joining at the ends, she missed Christian already.

Even though her heart was breaking, Beth Ann took advantage of the precious time remaining. She no longer dreaded her time in the attic, but climbed the stairs with anticipation. She was now confident that she had what she needed to preserve her five slots in the hotel lobby, and she had Christian to thank, which made her heart ache more. His blunt comments about her art had pushed her forward. As she painted, Christian's words pounded through her head. *I see someone who's afraid of taking the risks needed to paint.*

It was a risk branching so far away from what she was used to, when she had so much riding on getting into this small show. But she painted what she knew, what she felt in her soul. There was less need for landscapes than for faces as she tried to capture movement around the axis of the garden. Yes, it was risky, but there was no going back.

No way of getting back who she was. That artist, that person was gone—like Carrie. When she surveyed her work again, she was pleasantly surprised to see a freshness that hadn't existed in her painting in a long time. Maybe not being able to go back wasn't a bad thing.

WITH BERNIE DOWN for a badly needed nap, Christian sat in the living room and sweltered, despite the swamp cooler rattling so badly that it seemed to want to come through the roof. He regretted not having central air-conditioning installed while he was at it. The cool days of spring had not prepared him for the intense, constant heat of summer. Ninety was considered cool in the valley where the temperatures could soar past one hundred ten degrees.

The floorboards above him creaked. Even though it was her own stubbornness that brought it on,

Christian felt for Beth Ann. If it was eighty-five degrees where he was, it was easily ninety-five in the
attic. Christian reached for the Federal Express
package he had ordered from Mrs. Murphy nearly a
month earlier. For most of his stay, he'd been able
to ignore the appointment books that contained the
past three years of his life. His intimate conversations with Beth Ann had revealed much to him about
Caroline so he no longer felt the driving need to
track Caroline's travels.

But he was painfully aware that his departure date
from Mercy Springs was only a few days away. Beth
Ann's only reaction when he'd mentioned it was to
comment that Fred and Glenn were coming for Bernie's birthday party on the Saturday he planned to
leave. She didn't ask him to stay, but when he
hemmed and hawed and finally said, "Well, I guess
it'd be better if I left on Sunday," she didn't dis-
agree.

Now, he opened the black leather-bound books
more to track his own life than Caroline's, trying to
find out what he'd been doing on the day Bernie
was born. He studied the books, using Mrs. Murphy's small, neat script to jog his memory. He
started with the months prior to Bernie's birth. What
he learned was depressing. During the last few days
of Caroline's pregnancy, he was working on nego-
tiations he didn't dare send Max to. Instead, he himself had been in limousines and taxis, off to meet
with corporate heads, who'd been mostly suspicious
of his company's motives.

It had taken him hours to reassure them that they
would fare much better with his family's backing,
rather than flounder under the salivating jaws of a

less caring set of corporate wolves. On the day Caroline had pushed Bernie into the world, he'd sat in a board room pushing documents back and forth. Thanks to Mrs. Murphy's notes, he remembered the meeting clearly even down to the tuna fish sandwich that had given him indigestion. When Bernie was being born, he was making money for a conglomerate that had more revenue than they knew what to do with.

He heard the water running above him and Beth Ann's footsteps as she moved around in her attic workshop. Perhaps he had been hasty to announce he was leaving. He didn't *need* to leave. In fact, there was nothing for him to go to. It was a knee-jerk response to Beth Ann's reaction to the appliances. She had been so angry, the atmosphere around them so tense that he thought it would be better if he left.

Now he wasn't sure. The past week, he'd found Beth Ann reading the thick manuals for the appliances, fiddling with all the switches, programming the stove. If he was asked, or rather if Beth Ann asked him, he would readily stay another two months beyond Bernie's birthday festivities. Maybe even longer. After all she needed a good sitter so she could keep painting. They had both said things they didn't mean. Maybe it was something they should talk about. Maybe in some circumstances engagement *was* better than walking away.

"Are there any good movies on?"

Christian looked up and instinctively shut his appointment book.

Iris settled herself next to him on the couch.

"No nap this afternoon?" he asked.

Iris shook her head. "I'm tired, but not sleepy. I thought I'd try out this satellite dish of yours. Do you think you could find a Humphrey Bogart movie?"

Christian smiled and found the satellite directory he'd had express-mailed to him. He had also tacked on a three-year subscription to the monthly guide while he was at it, which he hadn't told Beth Ann about. By the time she discovered it, he'd be long gone.

"I'll see what they've got but you know, this television—it's yours now, not mine. I'm not going to take it with me when I leave."

"Oh, but that's not going to be for a while, right?" Iris asked.

"The Sunday after Bernie's birthday," Christian said, feeling a little twinge as he did. He had casually mentioned it again at dinner the night before, hoping Beth Ann would ask him to stay, but she had looked away and he took that as his cue. So Sunday it was. He scanned through the listing, looking for Humphrey Bogart.

"Will Cary Grant do?" he asked.

"I thought you'd stay," Iris commented instead.

"Stay?" Christian looked at her in surprise. His heart pounded a little bit harder. He shot her a hard look. "What would make you say that?"

"I thought you liked it here." There was the barest trace of reproach in her tone.

Christian was quiet and then admitted, "I love it here."

"Do you have to leave?"

"I don't think Beth Ann—"

"Do you like Beth Ann?" Iris interrupted bluntly.

Christian didn't know how to answer Iris. Beth Ann was very different, irreverent in ways that were wonderful. He admired the fierce nurturer in her, as well as the talented artist. When he saw her with Bernie or she gazed at him with those brown, brown eyes, he couldn't stop the rush of feelings that swept through him. Did he like Beth Ann? No. It was much more than like.

"I love her," came shooting out of his mouth. He felt his face flush.

Iris smiled broadly. "She's different from Carrie."

Christian was silent.

"They were always different," Iris continued. "Carrie couldn't wait to shake the dust of this town off her heels. Mercy Springs just wasn't, oh, I don't know, *enough* for her."

"May I ask you a question?" Christian found his voice.

Iris nodded, her eyes twinkling. "Can't guarantee I'll know the answer."

"Did it bother you that Caroline never came back?"

Iris looked at him puzzled. "But she did come back. She came back and gave us Bernie."

"But didn't you find that odd?"

"Odd? Why would that be odd?" Her question startled him.

"Because—" Christian tried to put it tactfully "—she never spoke of you or invited you to visit in San Diego. She never included you in her life."

"San Diego?" Iris looked at him blankly. "Who are you?"

Christian shook his head, not understanding. "Who am I?" He laughed. "I'm the babysitter."

"Where's Beth Ann? Where's Carrie? Does Beth Ann know you're here?"

Christian could hear the panic in Iris's voice and his smile faded.

"I'm Christian," he said slowly. "I'm Caroline's husband."

"What do you take me for? A fool? Carrie's too young to have a husband. The girls aren't even out of school yet. You should be ashamed for what you're trying to do to an old lady." Iris's voice shook with agitation and she got up, rapidly putting half the living room between them. "If you don't leave, I'm going to call the police."

"Iris." Christian rose and took a cautious step toward her, but Iris backed up against the side of the door, frozen with fright.

"How do you know my name?" she quavered. "Beth Ann! Carrie! Beth Ann!"

Christian heard the clatter of a tin can hitting the floor, then the sound of Beth Ann pounding down the stairs. She appeared in a flat minute, her hair disheveled as if she had been running her hands through it, her skin glistening with sweat from the heat in the attic. She skidded to a halt, as if forcing herself to slow down. Her shirt and shorts were splattered with paint. Green smudged her tanned legs. But she seemed unconcerned with her appearance as she walked calmly up to Iris and placed a reassuring hand on Iris's withered arm.

"Grans, I'm here," Beth Ann crooned.

"Who are you?" Iris demanded, a wild look in her eyes. She glanced back and forth between Chris-

tian and Beth Ann, pressing herself harder against
the wall. Her hands feeling behind her. As Beth Ann
stepped a little closer, Christian slid over to retrieve
a vase that was about to be tipped over by Iris's
panicked movements.

"I'm Beth Ann." Beth Ann had adopted a soothing, low, almost hypnotic voice.

"No, you're not," Iris denied frantically, slapping
Beth Ann's hands away. "Beth Ann just started high
school. You're too old. You can't fool me. Where
are my granddaughters? What have the two of you
done with them? Carrie! Beth Ann! *Run!*"

"No, honey, I was in high school a long time ago.
Carrie's gone. This is her husband, Christian." Beth
Ann put both hands on Iris's upper arms, gazing
straight into her eyes as if by mental will alone, she
would pull Iris back to the present.

"Liar! *Liar!*" Iris screamed, her arms starting to
flail. "Give me back my granddaughters!"

Christian watched helplessly, as Beth Ann ducked
her head away from the blows and enveloped Iris in
a big bear hug.

Beth Ann's heart pounded as she hung on to Iris,
her throat tight with adrenaline, as she tried to re-
strain the older woman without hurting her. But Iris
was strong and her kicks hurt.

Damn, she hated this.

She absolutely hated this.

The worst part was that she'd been almost lulled
into the belief that Iris's dementia was merely passing. The distance between Iris's spells always caught
her off guard. Most of the time, she could realisti-
cally believe that Iris was functioning in this world.
But each subsequent episode jerked Beth Ann rudely

back to the awareness that at these times, Iris didn't know what world she was in, and Beth Ann couldn't blame her for her terror as her normally agile mind regressed fifteen, twenty, sometimes forty years. Iris stopped struggling and Beth Ann eased her hold, relieved that it was over.

Iris's elbow jerked up, and pain burst in Beth Ann's eye. She tightened her grip again, catching Iris's arm before she got away. Iris struggled to free her arm. Beth Ann pulled her close, feeling sweat drip down the side of her face.

"Let me go!"

"Grans," Beth Ann pleaded. Her eye hurt like the dickens and it was swelling closed. "It's me. Beth Ann."

"Let go of me! I don't know who you are! What have you done with my family? *Carrie! Beth Ann!*"

Then Iris was gone, not because she escaped, but because Christian had come up from behind and pulled Iris against him, one strong forearm across the top of Iris's chest. Beth Ann saw him take a sharp jab in the ribs, but undaunted he moved with her toward the couch, finally pulling her down to sit on it.

"Listen!" he said in a voice so quiet and so serene that Beth Ann could have kissed him.

"No!" Iris still struggled, trying to stand, but she was effectively pinned between his arm and the couch.

Beth Ann watched him use one hand to turn up the volume loud, loud enough to startle Iris. The opening orchestral music to an old film filled the entire bungalow and Iris immediately looked in the direction of the television.

"What's that?" The frenzied look left Iris's eyes, curiosity getting the better of her. She relaxed slightly.

"I think it's Cary Grant," Christian replied evenly, as if this were an everyday occurrence. "Why don't we watch it?"

Beth Ann watched Iris stop struggling and stare at the actor, his face huge on the fifty-inch screen. Beth Ann couldn't have been more grateful for Christian's foresight. A smaller television would have fit her decor better, but the fifty-inch set was positively panoramic, riveting those who watched it.

"I always did like Bogie better," Iris said conversationally.

"Here," Christian offered and gently pulled his arm away from Iris. "Why don't you take this pillow?" He put a worn throw pillow in her lap and Iris immediately clutched it. Christian rose, remarking, "I'll make some popcorn."

"Where is this coming from?" Iris looked around the living room that she had lived in for more than forty years. "This isn't the Mercy Springs Playhouse."

"No, sweetie," Beth Ann said. "You're home now. And Christian bought us that television." She went to the kitchen and got a glass of water, a cookie and a bottle of small white pills. Her hands were shaking so badly she could barely open the child-proof top. She sat next to Iris and gave her the glass. "Why don't you take this?"

Christian watched Iris obediently swallow the pill and then eat the cookie, crumbs falling from her mouth. Beth Ann brushed Iris's lips with a paper towel and then left her, ducking past him with the empty water glass. He followed her into the kitchen. She had the faucet running full blast as her thin shoulders shook.

Christian did the only thing he could think of doing. He wrapped his arms around her. With her fists at her throat, her elbows pulled tightly against her body, Beth Ann sobbed and pressed her face into his shirt. Christian stroked her hair, surprised at the softness of her curls, deeply inhaling the smell of lavender and paint. The most natural thing to do was rest his chin on her head and tighten his hold, saying nothing.

The comfort of Christian's embrace was terrifying. Even though he was hot and sticky, he smelled of clean aftershave. She could feel his heart pounding against her cheek and she couldn't help but cry. All these years of being in control, of handling thousands of everyday crises had taken their toll. Not just on her painting, but on her sense of self.

Once she started bawling, she couldn't stop. Iris's episode had just reminded her how hard this was. She sniffled, the salt from her tears stinging her eyes. She rubbed one and it throbbed terribly. The only thing she could think of in her misery was that if this had been an ordinary day, she would be handling Iris by herself. Without Christian, there wouldn't be a television to sedate Iris. Without Christian, she would be alone and the prospect of returning to that was dismal.

She wiped her eyes, wincing at the sore one, and pulled herself back from him, embarrassed. Instead of focusing on his face, she stared at the perfect mother-of-pearl buttons, not really registering the bright red smeared on his pristine white shirt. She touched the damp stain and then gasped.

Blood. Her blood.

With disbelief, she touched it again, feeling the heat of his skin through the thin cotton and then touched her eye.

"I'm so sorry," she said, her voice rough with her dismay. "I didn't realize I was bleeding. I don't usually break down like that."

"Iris sure popped you one," he said, tilting up her chin to examine her eye. "Your eye's not that bad. It's mostly cosmetic."

Beth Ann touched her eye again and turned to search for a clean washcloth.

"You should wash the blood out of your shirt, or it will stain," she said hurriedly. "We should soak it. You should have told me."

"I think you had more pressing things on your mind." He smiled kindly at her. Beth Ann looked away, her throat swelling at the thought that he would be gone by Sunday. "Are you feeling better?"

"Yes, thank you." Beth Ann felt around her wound.

"We should take care of your eye."

"Your shirt."

"I have others," he observed and then dampened the washcloth, under the running the water. "Why don't you sit down?" He pointed to the chair.

Beth Ann sat because an aftershock of trembles kept her from standing.

"What did you give Iris?" Christian asked curiously as he pulled up a chair and straddled it, putting a bowl of water on the table. He experimentally touched the corner of her eye with the wet cloth.

Beth Ann flinched.

"I won't hurt you," he said quietly.

"I know," Beth Ann replied. She did know. "It stings."

"I'll be careful," he promised and tried again.

This time she could barely feel the brush of the cloth, but when she looked down she could see her blood stain the water as he rinsed out the cloth.

They sat that way for a long time, Christian tending her wound, Beth Ann savoring his attention.

"A sedative," she said suddenly.

"What?"

"A sedative. I gave Iris a sedative. I bet she's asleep now."

"Does this happen a lot?"

Beth Ann shook her head. "You've been here for a while now. How often have you seen this?"

"Since the fried egg episode this is the first."

"They used to be further apart. Months. I'd actually forget. Sometimes they'll happen in a bunch. Other times they're isolated incidents. The sedatives seem to work pretty well."

"What happens if she gets worse?"

It seemed like an innocent enough question, but Beth Ann felt her throat tighten. She didn't want to think about Iris getting worse. She couldn't think about this. She stood up abruptly and took the washcloth away from him.

"Thanks so much for helping out," she said hurriedly. "You should really soak that shirt."

"Beth Ann," Christian asked insistently, his voice all business. "That wasn't a polite, disinterested question. What happens if your grandmother gets worse? What if you're alone?''

Beth Ann didn't want to think about being alone, about how much easier life had been the past month, about the fact she had painted more since Christian had come to stay than she had in the past year. She wanted to continue to paint, to let Bernie enjoy the first everyday father she had ever known. Most of all, she wanted him.

"I don't know!" She wrung her hands and fell silent. She finally ventured a glance his way and saw that his gaze hadn't wavered.

"Do you want me to get you some permanent help?" he asked.

She bit her lip. She didn't want permanent help. She shook her head.

"You need someone," he persisted. "To help. So you don't have to deal with Iris alone."

"I don't need *someone*. I need you."

Christian's heart jumped at her words, spoken so softly that he had to lean toward her to hear them.

She didn't look at him but spoke rapidly, "I reacted badly to your, er, gifts." She waved in the direction of the stove. "I don't want you to leave because of that." Her words came out in a rush, "and I want you to know that if you'd like to stay longer then I would more than appreciate it. I can't pay—"

Christian cut her off. "It's not about pay."

Beth Ann nodded. "I know. But I'd like some way to pay you back for all that you've done for us these past few weeks. I don't know many people who would have taken on the responsibilities you have and not gone stark raving mad. The television was a stroke of genius...." Her voice drifted off.

Well, it wasn't a declaration of undying love, but Christian was willing to take what he could get.

"You can do something to pay me back," Christian said, adopting a deal-making voice. He put an arm on her shoulder and had her sit down again so he could apply a Band-Aid.

Beth Ann looked at him warily. Christian gently taped up the broadest part of the cut with a bright bandage. Her eye was already turning a dark shade of purple. "You're going to have one hell of a shiner there," he remarked.

"So how can we pay you back?" Beth Ann asked.

"Not we, you."

Beth Ann suddenly looked very vulnerable and Christian resisted the temptation to kiss her. Instead, with his hand tangled in her hair, he gently placed his mouth over her swelling eye. But when she turned to him, her mouth parted, he couldn't resist and settled his mouth on hers, his hand tightening on the nape of her neck. She tasted like toothpaste and smelled like paint. Her sigh caused his insides to tighten, his heart to pound in his ears. Reluctantly he pulled away.

"Was that how I can pay you back?" she asked, her head tilted provocatively. Even with a black eye, she was sexy. Beth Ann put her small hand over his. It was rough, stained with color. He picked it up and examined it. This hand had probably never seen a professional manicure in its entire life.

"No," he answered slowly as he turned her hand over and kissed her palm.

Her good eye widened.

Christian chuckled. "No. Not that. Though the thought has kept me awake many a night."

"Then what?"

"I want to see your studio."

She pulled her hand away. "My studio?" Her voice squeaked.

He nodded.

"When?"

"Whenever you're ready."

"Why?"

"Because I want to share that part of you as well."

"If I show you my studio, then you'll stay?"

Christian gave a single nod. "Yes. If you show me your studio, then I'll stay."

CHAPTER ELEVEN

BETH ANN STARED at him for a long time, trying to ignore the throb in her eye, trying even more to ignore the tingle in the palm of her hand where he had kissed her. He was staying. She felt like shouting with joy from the top of the house. She got up and pushed open the swinging door to the living room.

"Grans is out like a light," she whispered, excitement welling through her. She quietly walked down the hall and gestured for Christian to follow her.

"Where are we going?" he asked.

She stopped. "My studio."

"I didn't mean—"

"What?" Disappointment flooded through her. Perhaps she had been wrong about why he wanted to stay. "You don't want to see what I've been working on?"

"No, it's not that." He stopped halfway down the hall.

"What then?"

"I didn't mean you had to show me now. I know it's very personal. You can show me when you're ready."

Beth Ann thought about what he was saying and then shrugged. "I'm ready now." She held out her hand to him and pleasure wafted through her when he took it.

Christian entered the attic cautiously. It had the smell of a studio. He saw paper and paint. Three easels. And color. Lots and lots of color. Beth Ann didn't use the subtle pastels he often associated with the medium. Instead she favored dramatic, tropical colors. Vivid blues and greens. Fuchsias, teals. He was immediately captivated by what he saw. He walked around the edge of the studio, his hand behind his back as he studied what she had done over the past month, feeling very much as if he were in a gallery. He was awed by her talent, the world she saw. How lovely it was. Optimistic, cheerful.

"These are great," he said quietly.

She looked pleased. "Well, it's coming. Slowly, but surely. The time you've given me has helped a lot."

"No, I'm serious. These are wonderful." He smiled as he saw one of Bernie trying to catch a purple fluorescent beetle the size of her hand. Beth Ann had captured the fearlessness of the little girl's reach. He walked toward another set and then flushed with self-consciousness, as he stared at a series of pencil sketches.

"These are of me." A shiver passed through him. They were pages of eyes—his eyes. Wary eyes, pain-filled eyes, then laughing eyes, teasing eyes, intense eyes. The last few made him bite his lip. Beth Ann had caught his eyes when he looked at her, when he'd thought she wasn't watching him. She had captured the eyes of a man clearly in love.

He turned to Beth Ann who was blushing up to the very roots of her hair. "I'm flattered," he said with a quick smile, and tried to calm his rapidly beating heart.

"You're a good model," she said roughly and fiddled with an envelope.

"Are those the slides of the ones that you're going to submit?" Changing the topic was good. For her and for him. He had signed for the envelope when it was delivered earlier in the week.

She nodded.

"They're due soon, right?"

"Next Tuesday."

Christian looked at her in surprise. "Tuesday? Don't you think they should be in the mail? Saturday's just a few days away."

"They're only going up the road. If I mail them on Saturday, they'll get there by the deadline."

"Isn't that cutting it a little close?"

Beth Ann took a deep breath, then exhaled and said quickly, "I'm having second thoughts. This is a new style for me and I don't—"

"Send them," Christian said.

"But—"

"Don't nothing beat a miss but a try."

"What?"

"Don't nothing beat a miss but a try. It means you've got nothing to lose. Trying is what it's all about. And you might be pleasantly surprised." He moved away from the pencil sketches and continued to walk around the perimeter of the attic, pausing at another full watercolor.

"I didn't know you saw this," Christian said.

Beth Ann put her hands behind her back, completely silent, letting him study the painting before him. *Naptime,* she'd labeled it. It was a precious piece of Bernie and him napping under the large oak. The painting was so well rendered Christian swore he could actually see a wayward butterfly weaving its awkward pattern across the two of them. And the slight rise and fall of their chests. She had caught Bernie's small mouth in a round yawn, her head propped on his shoulder, her own shoulders tucked protectively under his arm as he wedged her next to his chest.

Christian was overwhelmed and stiffened his spine, trying to dampen the emotion that threatened the back of his throat. Beth Ann had painted him as an ordinary subject. He could be any man. Any man. More significantly, she had made him a father.

Beth Ann motioned to the round window. "You'd be surprised at what I manage to see."

"Glenn was right." Christian sat on a stool and wondered how she kept all this color locked in the attic. Her work needed to be out in public, enjoyed, bought, hung in places of honor.

"What?" she asked.

"You have tremendous talent."

She smiled. "Lots of people have tremendous talent. It's all about those who are dedicated enough to work at it."

"You don't look as if you're afraid of hard work."

Beth Ann shook her head. "I'm not. I just haven't felt like painting for a while."

"I don't think anyone can blame you. After all, you became a mom." He cleared his throat. "You took on Bernie when Caroline wouldn't."

"Of course, I did," Beth Ann said simply. "Who couldn't care for such an itty-bitty thing? Though—"

she paused ''—I never expected Carrie to leave. After about a week, I thought she was adjusting. She even spent time with Bernie, changing her, feeding her. Carrie loved sleep and that was what I think bothered her most. That and being confined. And having nowhere to spend money. And being fat.'' Beth Ann laughed as the list grew longer.

Christian found himself laughing, too, and felt a little bad. Everything Beth Ann said was absolutely true. Caroline hated all of those things.

''I guess she did show some early signs of stress,'' Beth Ann conceded.

He didn't want to talk about Caroline anymore. He just wanted to be with Beth Ann. He had missed their talks and since the television had arrived, this was the first time they'd had to recover their old camaraderie. ''Your work is wonderful,'' he said sincerely.

Beth Ann felt a rush of pleasure at his words. ''Well, you're responsible for them.''

Christian shook his head. ''No, I'm not. The work is all yours.''

Beth Ann smiled. ''Yes, you are.''

''All I did—''

''All you did was give me time. Peace and security knowing my two favorite people were being taken care of by someone who truly cares about them. I think that's what's made me able to paint.''

''It wasn't anything,'' Christian mumbled.

''It was everything.''

They fell silent.

''Beth Ann?'' His voice was oddly strained. He got up and crossed the room toward her.

"Yes?" she whispered.

She knew it was coming, she could feel it coming, but when it happened, the softness of his lips startled her. This kiss was a gentle, intimate caress. And she didn't back away. She couldn't have backed away to save her life. Instead, she pressed herself against him as her mouth opened to his subtle pressure.

Her breathing became shallow. He groaned and deepened the kiss as he pulled her close. She could feel his control and strength, and the solidness of his body made her dizzy. She moaned and he moved away suddenly.

"Is it your eye?" he asked.

Her eye? She had forgotten about her eye.

"No," Beth Ann said with a small smile. "You're a pretty good kisser."

Christian stared at Beth Ann, her good eye glowing with an emotion that filled him with warmth. He gave her a hug.

"So I showed you my studio," she said as she touched his face. "Now, you need to stick to your side of the bargain."

Christian couldn't speak. He just held Beth Ann tightly in his arms. "I thought you'd never ask."

CHRISTIAN SAT on the antique cherry bed and called Max the next morning, the memory of Beth Ann's kiss still imprinted on his lips. He'd slept more soundly than he could ever recall, not even disturbed by the physical ache caused by an intense wanting. He could be patient. If her kiss was any indication, her lovemaking would be as earthy and wonderful as she was. He'd fallen asleep half-speculating whether she would recycle condoms and woke with a deep sense of peace. He was in love, a love that burst with joy and renewal, with all the vivid hues of Beth Ann's watercolors.

"My friend!" Max exclaimed. "Are you enjoying the wine and women of the beautiful Napa Valley?"

"Not yet," Christian said and then continued. "I've decided to stay for a while."

"Where?"

"Mercy Springs."

"You're still there? It's been what two, three weeks?"

A month. "About that," Christian said.

"So what's up?"

"I just wanted to let you know where I'll be."

"You're kidding." Max didn't bother to hide his disbelief. "I can't imagine what's keeping you there. Have you been scouting new investment opportunities?"

With Max, it was always about money.

"No," Christian replied. "I'm just enjoying the scenery. I like spending time with Caroline's family."

"What are they like?" Max asked curiously.

"Normal people."

"Normal how?"

"Just normal, normal." Christian didn't feel like explaining. "I'm going to call Mrs. Murphy next. I just wanted to give you an alternative number in case of emergencies."

"No emergencies, remember. Doctor's orders," Max said, then he added more seriously, "Are you okay? You're not being held hostage or anything? I don't have to collect a ransom, do I?"

Max's mind worked in strange ways.

Christian laughed. "No, Max. I'm not being held hostage."

"Did they tell you to say that?"

"No, Max."

There was silence on the other end. Christian felt his friend thinking. They had known each other for far too long.

"Just to be sure, maybe I'll fly up this weekend," Max said.

"No need for all that." Christian tried to make his voice casual.

"I've been meaning to take the Cessna out anyway. This town got an airfield?"

Christian should have said no, but admitted, "Yes."

"Fine. Expect me about noon on Saturday."

"Max. I don't need you to check up on me. This really isn't necessary."

"Consider it a favor. It's not a bad idea for me to be out of town this weekend."

"It's hot here."

"Then it'll be that much more interesting to see what's keeping you there."

Christian disconnected his cell phone with a feeling of dread. It wasn't that he didn't want Max to come, but it was. He hit the redial button.

"Yes?" Max asked in a clipped tone.

"It's me."

"What'd you forget?"

"Don't come."

"Don't come?" Max laughed. "Now, I really want to come. I'll be there by noon so don't leave me hanging. I bet I won't be able to get a taxi to save my life.''

Max hung up. Christian shook his head. Max was like a small terrier that never let go if something was interesting, even if it was better for everyone if he would. Come to think of it, whenever he and Caroline had got in a disagreement when Max was around, Max had seemed to egg it on, siding with whoever was about to capitulate.

Christian shook himself. But that was just Max.

''Christian?'' Beth Ann poked her head in to the bedroom.

''Yes?'' He glanced up surprised at how familiar she looked to him. She didn't have Caroline's stunning beauty, but she was very pretty in her own right, even with a swollen eye. He smiled.

''I'm going to paint and Bernie's ready to hit the garden trail.''

''Iris?''

''Grans is watching television. I think she'll be okay. I'll listen for her while you're outside.''

''Maybe she'll want to come.''

''Maybe,'' Beth Ann sounded hesitant.

''Anything wrong?''

Beth Ann leaned against the door frame. ''I don't know. But since her last bout, she hasn't had a lot of energy.''

''I imagine it takes a lot of energy to panic the way she did.''

Beth Ann nodded. ''I know, but usually the next day she's back to normal. She's still very tired.''

Christian didn't know what to tell her. ''You could have her checked out.''

Beth Ann nodded. "Maybe I'll try to make an appointment for Monday."

"Beth Ann?" Iris called.

"I'm here, Grans," Beth Ann said over her shoulder. "I'm just talking to Christian."

"Unckiss!" Bernie, accompanied by Fluff, wriggled between Beth Ann's legs and ran to him. "Garden?" She batted her long lashes at him.

"Yes, garden."

Bernie twirled with excitement and Fluff flew out of her hand.

"You'd think she didn't spend every morning there." Beth Ann looked at her daughter fondly and then looked up at him.

Beth Ann felt a tingle shimmy down her spine as she met his light eyes. He was staring at her, a half smile on his handsome lips, looking so perfectly at ease. Beth Ann swallowed hard, his kiss still vivid in her mind. Bernie went to pick up Fluff and chattered to him about dirt and bugs. Beth Ann bit her lip when she saw Christian place a large hand on Bernie's head to calm her down slightly. She went to Beth Ann's open closet and carefully laid Fluff on the floor.

"Fuff seeping! Garden!"

"Well," Christian said seriously. "If Fluff is sleeping then you should put him in a real bed."

"Bed?" Bernie asked, her forehead puckered.

Christian nodded. "Yes. A bed."

Beth Ann backed out of the doorway unfamiliar with the raw desire that began to flood through her body as she listened to their conversation. She had been withered and dry for so long and after one or two, okay, three kisses, she felt as if she was sixteen.

Christian stood up, lifted Bernie easily and tucked her under his arm like a football. Bernie screamed with laughter.

"Let's go to the garden while Mommy paints."

"Garden!"

"You've got Iris?" Christian asked, with a raised eyebrow.

"I've got Grans." Beth Ann nodded as she pulled the baby monitor out of her back pocket.

"Let me see first if she wants to go to the garden. Beep, beep!" He crowded his way past Beth Ann, using Bernie as the lead. Bernie chortled. "Iris. Do you want to go to the garden with us? Bernie says please."

"Peas!" Bernie echoed.

Beth Ann felt sad when Iris just shook her head with a frail smile and weak wave of her hand. "No. I know I should, but I'm just so tired this morning. Maybe later. Be sure to pick the zucchinis and trim back the tomatoes. They're growing so big."

"Will do."

"And can you be sure to give a deep water to the fruit trees? They're looking a little parched."

"Yes, ma'am. Anything else?" Christian looked at Beth Ann.

Beth Ann shook her head and then her heart lurched when Christian held Bernie down to kiss her great-grandmother. "Tell Nana, hope you feel better."

"Feo bedder," Bernie said and then ordered, "Garden!"

After the two had charged out of the house, Beth Ann sat next to Iris on the couch, putting her arm around her. "How are you doing, Grans?"

"Just tired."

"Do you want to go to bed?"

Iris shook her head. "No. Though if you got me a pillow and a blanket, I might not object to laying down on the couch, if you could find me a movie rather than these long commercials."

"Infomercials."

"They're awfully long whatever they are. I never knew anything to work nearly as well in real life as it does on television."

Beth Ann laughed and went to get Iris a pillow and a light blanket. It was already eighty degrees, but Iris was chilled. Beth Ann hid her frown.

"Thank you, Beth Ann."

Beth Ann watched her grandmother lean back, her heart tearing as Iris sighed with relief. Apparently just sitting took too much out of her. "Are you sure that you'll have enough energy for Bernie's party Saturday?"

"Bernie's having a party?"

"Yes. It's her birthday. Fred and Glenn are coming out for the day."

"Then I have to make her a cake," Iris said.

Beth Ann looked at her doubtfully. "We'll see how you feel then."

"By Saturday, I'll feel fine," Iris said positively, her eyes already closing.

"How do you know that?" Beth Ann asked with a smile as she tucked the end of the light blanket under Iris's hand.

"Henry told me." Iris yawned and then drifted off to sleep.

Henry? Beth Ann hadn't heard that name forever. She smiled and kissed Iris on the forehead. If Bernie could carry on extensive conversations with Fluff, then Iris should be able to talk to the long-deceased Henry.

Beth Ann turned on the monitor and balanced it on the end table, taking the other monitor with her as she went to the attic. It was a great feeling to be back painting. Christian's appreciation of her work made her efforts that much more rewarding. Beth Ann smiled and picked up her detail brush. She unpeeled the plastic wrap from her palette and tested the paints. A little stiff. She swirled water in one well and tried it on the strip of paper that hung next to her easel. The first stroke of the day was always the hardest.

"LUNCH!" came out of the baby monitor.

Beth Ann jumped and her hand slipped across the paper, extending the branch of the old oak another three representational feet. Damn. She stretched and her stomach rumbled. She glanced at the clock, still surprised that it was working. She'd been compelled to replace the batteries now that she spent so much time here. Already twelve-thirty and she was sweltering. She covered her palette with a fresh length of plastic wrap and ran a generous amount of water through her brushes, popping them into an old tomato juice can filled with fresh water to let them soak through lunch. Too often, she had failed to rinse out her brushes completely only to find one color contaminated with another. It occasionally led to a happy accident, but that was very rare.

As she entered the kitchen, she smiled at Bernie, already strapped into her high chair.

"Cheese!" she said pointing wildly at Christian.

"I see," Beth Ann said as she gave Bernie a noisy kiss on her cheek. She smelled freshly scrubbed. "Uncle Christian is making grilled cheese sandwiches." Beth Ann greeted an alert and refreshed Iris by dropping a kiss on her silver hair, and then, fought the urge to wrap her arms around Christian's waist and give him a kiss, too. "Want some water, Grans?" she said hastily, as Christian slid her a look that seemed to tell her he knew everything she was thinking. Her cheeks flushed and she told herself it was from working in the hot attic.

Iris nodded.

"Shoot!" Christian said, glancing at the table from the stove. "I meant to have that done."

"No need. I can do it. How many ice cubes?"

"One," Iris said.

"Two," Christian said over his shoulder.

"And two for me, too." Beth Ann plopped the cubes into the glasses.

"Ice coob!" Bernie called.

Beth Ann looked at her daughter in surprise. "You want some water? In a glass with an ice cube?"

Bernie shook her head. "Ice coob."

"Plain?"

Christian grinned sheepishly at her. "Sorry. I gave her some yesterday. I figured it was fluid."

Beth Ann laughed. "It is fluid. One ice cube for Bernie, too." She slipped one onto Bernie's tray. Bernie laughed as she chased it around, finally caught it with two hands and then brought it up to her mouth.

"Cooolddd," she said with a shiver.

"Yes," Beth Ann agreed. "It's cold."

"Cheese," Bernie said as Christian put two triangles of grilled cheese in front of her. "Ott."

"I don't know if it's too hot, Berns," Christian said. "Try it."

Bernie poked at it. "Ott."

"Okay, if it's too hot then eat your apple now," Beth Ann suggested.

"No." Bernie looked at Beth Ann defiantly.

"No?" Beth Ann was so surprised by Bernie's mutiny she almost laughed.

"No."

"Okay. Then wait for your sandwich."

"No."

"So everything's no today?" Beth Ann touched Bernie's grilled cheese. "It's not hot anymore."

"No."

Christian grinned as he slipped a sandwich on Iris's plate and then Beth Ann's. "She's in a lovely mood today, isn't she?"

"You've dealt with this?"

"All morning." He rolled his eyes. "She didn't want to pick peas, she wanted to pick tomatoes. Then she didn't want to go in. Didn't want to get her face and hands washed. Didn't want grilled cheese."

"She seems to like it well enough now," Iris commented with a twinkle in her eye as Bernie took a small bite out of the corner.

"Not ott."

"Cucumber and tomato salad?" Christian offered.

"I'd like a little," Iris nodded.

Beth Ann watched Christian dole out a small spoonful.

"Is that enough?"

"This is Henry's favorite salad," Iris murmured.

"Does he want some, too?" Christian asked jokingly.

Iris smiled. "Oh, no. He had a large breakfast."

Beth Ann felt a surge of love swirl around the kitchen. Halfway through her sandwich she said, "It's Bernie's birthday Saturday."

"I'm going to make the cake," Iris reminded her.

"I'm counting on that," Beth Ann said.

"Oh, and Max is coming, if it's not too inconvenient," Christian added.

Beth Ann cocked her head at him. "Really?"

Christian said quickly, "He decided to fly up for the weekend."

"Do you have to pick him up at the airport?"

Christian nodded and went back for an extra portion of cucumbers and tomatoes. "Did you taste the mint? I decided to try it."

"Is that what it is?" Iris asked. "I thought I tasted something other than basil."

"Which one?" Beth Ann asked curiously. "If it's San Jose maybe Fred and Glenn can pick him up on their way here."

Christian looked a little uncomfortable.

"What?"

"He's flying into the local airport."

"How can he do that?" Beth Ann looked puzzled.

"He has a plane."

As if she were hit by a blast of cold water, Beth Ann suddenly realized, again, that the man sitting across from her was not ordinary. Even though she drew him as an ordinary man, he wasn't. His friends had private planes. No matter how ordinary he looked, no matter how simply he had learned to live, he was Christian Elliott, heir and CEO of a billion-dollar multinational corporation. "Oh." She looked down battling her feelings of doubt, then forced a smile. "He's more than welcome."

THAT EVENING long after Bernie and Iris were asleep, Beth Ann sat in the attic and stared at the slides she would be sending to the hotel jury. Under the glow of several lamps, Beth Ann squinted at them and tried to see the paintings as Christian saw them. She just saw risk and lots of bright colors. She put the slides away and moved restlessly around the attic. No matter what she felt for Christian, no matter how long he extended his stay, she couldn't ignore the fact that they were from different worlds. Eventually, he would leave her, leave Bernie and return to a life that promised all the glitter and trappings that had pulled Carrie away. She swallowed hard. Loving him was a risk.

A soft knock made her look up.

"Come in," she called. "Can't sleep, Grans?"

"It's me."

"Christian!" She looked around and then rose hesitantly to open the door. He stood hovering in the doorway.

"Is it okay if I come in?" He looked perfectly prepared to leave if she said so.

She nodded. "Sure. Come in."

They stood apart from each other.

"How's the eye?"

"Blurry."

"Beth Ann?"

"Yes?"

"Do we need to talk? If you don't want Max to come, I'll just tell him not to come." Christian moved close to her, his hand resting gently on her elbow. "If you feel uncomfortable."

Beth Ann shook her head. "It's not that. He's more than welcome."

"Then what is it?"

Beth Ann took a deep breath and said, "I just couldn't stand it if you left us." She pressed her lips together to keep back the tears.

"Why would I leave?"

"Because you live in a different world." She turned and tried to walk away, but Christian held on to her, reeling her into his embrace.

"I know that it might be hard for you to believe, but I've never been happier. I will do anything in my power to protect you and Bernie," he whispered fiercely. "If I have to give up my name and my money, I will. I would never willingly leave Bernie. Or you."

Though she wanted to, Beth Ann couldn't believe him, but she took comfort in his tight embrace anyway.

CHAPTER TWELVE

THE DAY OF Bernie's birthday dawned bright. Beth Ann woke with a mixed sense of dread and anticipation. Christian was staying, but his friend, Max, would be coming. What if Max made Christian change his mind? Made him realize what he was missing? Beth Ann gingerly tested her eye. It was less sore. She took a deep breath remembering the tender kiss Christian had placed on it. *I will do anything in my power to protect you and Bernie.* She believed him. She loved him.

Beth Ann heard a little voice. "Mommy?"

"Bernie?" she asked in the same voice.

"Mommy!"

"Bernie!"

"Mommy." Bernie held her arms out to Beth Ann.

Beth Ann yawned and pulled herself out of the daybed and then hoisted Bernie over the side of her crib. Then she went back to bed, pulling Bernie close and giving another loud yawn. "Are you still sleepy, Bernie? Mommy is."

Bernie yawned, too, and snuggled her head into Beth Ann's underarm, her small body wriggling, her heels poking into Beth Ann's stomach. Beth Ann fended off the small feet and Bernie giggled.

"So guess what?" Beth Ann asked, before throwing off the covers suddenly and making Bernie laugh.

"Guess whose birthday it is today?"

Bernie just kept trying to get under the covers.

"It's Bern-Bern-Bern's. It's your birthday. And you're *two* today."

"Two!" Bernie shouted and started jumping on the bed.

"Yes. You're two. And Pop-pop and Fedman are coming. And a friend of Uncle Christian's."

Beth Ann squelched the uncertainty that welled up inside her again. Carrie would have died of embarrassment if any of her friends had come to the house. Would Christian be embarrassed when his friend arrived and saw the old bungalow? Would they embarrass him?

"Mommy?" Bernie patted her face, her little fingers touching Beth Ann's eyes and mouth. Beth Ann winced when Bernie poked her black eye.

"Bernie."

"Birf-day?"

Beth Ann got up and pulled Bernie with her. She put her on the changing table.

"Yes, sweetie. It's your birthday. How old are you today?"

Bernie looked at her blankly and then looked as if she was thinking hard. Then she shook her head.

"You're two." Beth Ann took her hand and formed it into the peace sign. "You're two. So when people ask, you hold up two fingers and say you're two."

"Two." Bernie nodded and stared at her fingers.

"Just like we've been practicing." Beth Ann

kissed her on the forehead, and pretended to eat her neck.

Bernie giggled and held up her fist, her fingers pointing in three different directions. *"Two!"*

Beth Ann helped her put her fingers in the correct position again. "Two."

"So how old are you?"

Bernie said loudly, *"Two!"*

"Who's two?" Christian poked his head in the door, fully dressed, his hair damp from his shower, his hands behind his back.

Lord, he was beautiful. Beth Ann's heart flipped over. She bit her lip and turned away, attacked by a fit of shyness. With a deep breath, suddenly conscious that she was hardly dressed, she casually looked up and was surprised by the intensity that burned in his gray eyes.

"I two!" Bernie held up all five fingers.

Beth Ann put her hand back into the two position.

"I two!" Bernie repeated and held up two fingers.

"Really?" Christian feigned surprise. "If you're two that must mean it's your birthday!"

"Birf-day," Bernie echoed. "Garden?"

Beth Ann and Christian laughed at the same time, and then Christian cleared his throat. "How about a present first?"

"You didn't—"

"I wanted to," Christian said quickly and produced a medium-size box from behind his back.

Beth Ann ducked her head, and finished changing Bernie's diaper. Then she smiled and said, "Thank you. What did you get her?"

"Why doesn't she open it and see?"

Beth Ann put Bernie back onto the bed and Christian put the box in front of her.

"Open it," she instructed Bernie.

Bernie pulled off the metallic pink bow.

"Good. Now tear the paper." Beth Ann slowly started to rip the pretty paper and Bernie squealed, pulling off the paper in little chunks.

Christian gazed at Beth Ann and Bernie, tenderness swelling inside his chest. This was what family was about. He studied Beth Ann's rumpled hair. Even though her nightgown wasn't the see-through one, he could almost physically feel the soft curve of her breasts. His hands itched to hold them, feel their weight. Bernie laughed as she threw the bright wrapping paper, covering herself and Beth Ann with self-made confetti.

"Let me open the box," Beth Ann told Bernie, who seemed more intrigued by the pretty pieces of wrapping than the present itself.

"Don't be mad," Christian warned Beth Ann.

She looked up at him with her dark eyes crinkling in the corners. She tilted her head. "Why in the world would I be mad?"

She opened the box and gasped. She stared at the contents for a long time.

Christian shifted his weight, even though he knew it made him look defensive.

"I told you to not be mad."

Slowly Beth Ann shook her head. She licked her lips and shook her head again. "I'm not mad. It's beautiful. I'm afraid to touch it."

"It's just a dress. For her birthday."

Just a dress. Beth Ann slowly picked up the small hand-smocked garment. It was pristinely, terrifyingly white, with delicate pink and yellow embroidery.

"Pitty," Bernie said, her hand grabbing the corner of the dress.

"Be gentle," Beth Ann replied, undoing Bernie's grip. "Soft." She used Bernie's hand to stroke the beautiful fabric. "Soft."

"Toft."

"This is for your birthday."

"Birf-day!" Bernie struggled to get down off the daybed. "Garden?"

"A one-track mind," Beth Ann said, then addressed Bernie who tottered on her descent to the floor but didn't fall. "Let's have breakfast first, sweetie."

"Beckfast," Bernie echoed as she searched around the room for her bear. But there was no Fluff. "Fuff?" Bernie called, expecting him to answer.

Both Christian and Beth Ann turned their heads looking for the bear.

"Where's Fluff?" Beth Ann asked. She looked behind the crib, while Christian looked under it and the bed.

"Don't see him."

"Fuff?" Bernie's voice was full of sorrow, her lips trembled and her eyes filled with tears.

"Don't worry, sweetie. Fluff couldn't have gone far," Beth Ann said reassuringly. "Why don't you go look in the kitchen? Maybe you left him there."

Christian looked at Beth Ann puzzled. "He was gone last night."

Beth Ann shook her head. "I know, but..."

"Where could he be?"

Beth Ann laughed. "Well, you never know. This place is like the Bermuda Triangle." She paused, finding herself very near him. She could smell his aftershave. She could hear the thumping of his heart. Or was it hers? She looked up, feeling his hand in her hair.

"Wrapping paper," he said, his voice uneven, his eyes uncertain.

It took nothing for her to step into his embrace. His arms immediately wrapped around her, his hug deep and reassuring.

"Thank you," Beth Ann said softly. "The dress is beautiful."

"You're beautiful."

And Beth Ann believed him, as much as she believed in the gentleness of the kiss he gave her.

PEOPLE WERE scheduled to arrive around noon. It was going to be a small party, but Christian felt the air of anticipation. It was as if the old bungalow knew that company was coming. In the kitchen, he helped Iris pull a beautiful applesauce cake from the oven.

"Thank you so much," Iris said.

"Don't mention it," Christian said, glad the real Iris was back this morning.

"Henry thanks you also."

"Henry?"

"Yes, Henry. Don't you see him?" Iris looked at Christian inquisitively. "He's standing right next to you."

Christian nodded in the direction of Henry and then glanced at his watch. Iris was starting to make icing, while she waited for the cake to cool, so he wandered into the living room where Beth Ann was blowing up balloons. Bernie was having the time of her life, chasing the bright objects, punching them into the air. As their numbers grew, Bernie became more excited as she struggled to pick up them all at the same time. She looked darned cute in the dress, though he now wondered whether white had been such a good idea. He frowned when he saw her old blue sneakers.

"Sorry," Beth Ann said between breaths.

"For what?"

"I don't have shoes to go with the dress. Accessories, you know."

Christian didn't know, but he made a mental note to remember accessories in the future. Maybe socks with the little frilly stuff around the ankle, too.

"Watch this, Berns," Christian said as he took a balloon and rubbed it across her head a few times and then stuck it to the wall.

Bernie squealed and hit it off the wall, then tried to stick it up again.

"You have to rub it on your head," Christian said and then impulsively ran the balloon over Beth Ann's hair midblow, her face turning progressively redder. The friction of the balloon made her carefully tamed curls go awry. She just gave him an exasperated look and gave one final blow. He stuck the balloon on the wall and a laughing Bernie hit it down. Then, Bernie made an attempt at rubbing the balloon on her head, but only ended up smashing her face against the latex.

"Don't you have something else to do?" Beth Ann asked, looking meaningfully at the clock.

Christian glanced at his watch. "Yep. I guess I should go get Max."

"What time is he landing?"

"Twelve-thirty."

"So you better go."

"It's only twelve-ten. How long does it take to get there?"

"Ten minutes," Beth Ann admitted. "But you don't want him waiting around."

"Why not?" Christian asked, but went in the bedroom to grab his keys.

He came back and paused, his eyes following Bernie, still absorbed in the balloons. He almost wished he had been more assertive with Max. This was a special day, and he didn't want Max to spoil it. Max had a tendency to be cutting to those he perceived as the less fortunate. It had never bothered Christian before. But now— With a rattle of the keys, he shoved his wallet into his back pocket.

He went up to Beth Ann. "Before I go, I wanted to ask—who's Henry?"

Beth Ann looked at him blankly and started another balloon. When it didn't inflate, she pulled on it, stretching it out several times. "Henry?"

"Iris mentioned him."

Beth Ann nodded with a smile. "He was a very close friend of the family."

"Was?"

"He died, oh, I don't know, probably ten years ago."

"Oh," Christian nodded. Bernie had Fluff. Iris had Henry. He had Beth Ann. It all worked out perfectly. "This shouldn't take too long. I'll take him to the hotel and then we'll be back."

"Take your time," Beth Ann said between breaths. A red balloon was getting bigger. "Fred and Glenn should be here pretty soon."

He paused again, then leaned over and gave her a quick kiss on the cheek, sorry the chaste gesture didn't convey what he really wanted to do, how he really felt, but with Bernie in the room, it would have to do. He laughed when her balloon deflated, but his smile faded after the mock annoyance in her dark eyes turned to an emotion not chaste at all.

Christian muttered goodbye, as an unsettling sensation—a cross between soul satisfying calm and tense physical frustration—emanated through every blood vessel, every vein, every artery, until he shoved his hand in the pocket of his jeans to hide the physical evidence of his own unchaste thoughts.

EVEN THOUGH Christian was early, Max was waiting for him, a brown leather garment bag slung over his shoulder. He looked just the way he always had at school, smooth and cool, despite the ninety-five degree weather.

"Hey, buddy, long time no see," Max said as he lay his bag down flat in the trunk of the Jaguar.

Christian waited until Max got in.

"Air-conditioning!" Max looked at him with a shake of his head. "I can't believe it's this hot and it's only noon. What's it going to be like by five?"

"Hotter," Christian said briefly.

"Ha, ha." Max grimaced. "So, how're you doing?"

"What are you doing here?" Christian asked, getting straight to the point. He knew Max well enough to be sure he had an ulterior motive.

"Aren't you glad to see me? I'm hurt." Max feigned a pained look.

"Always."

"Man, I had to come." Max stared out into the scenery, at the fast-food restaurants, the open fields and propane store. "This place sure ain't San Diego, is it?"

"No. But it grows on you."

"Obviously."

Christian felt Max's amber eyes on him. He turned and looked at his old friend. "What does obviously mean?"

"When Christian Elliott calls to tell me he's extended his stay from a morning to a month, I say, humor the man, he's had a hard time of it. When he calls again at the end of that month and says he's staying for two more, I say, get in the plane and find out what's keeping him here." Max shook his head. "I don't know. I thought you might be a prisoner or something. I had to check it out myself."

Christian held both hands up before placing them back on the steering wheel. "You can see I'm free. How long are you planning on staying?"

"A couple of days."

"Need to check in to a hotel?" Christian was already turning into the parking lot of the motor inn he'd stayed at when he'd first arrived.

Max made a face when he saw the establishment. "Please, you can do better than this, can't you?"

Christian just got out of the car.

"Okay, so you can't."

Christian was already in the trunk and handed Max his garment bag. "We have a couple of things to talk about."

"Yeah?" Max's eyes lit up.

"No. It's not what you think."

"So is Caroline's sister as hot as she was?"

Christian pressed his lips together. This was exactly why he didn't want Max here.

"Okay, okay," Max backed down. "So she's a dog."

"Don't say that about Beth Ann."

"Don't say that about Beth Ann," Max mimicked him, his gaze missing nothing.

Christian had never felt so scrutinized.

"So it's Beth Ann, is it?" Max continued. "I was wondering when you'd get back into the fray. I guess it beats the manual alternative."

Christian let Max's words pass. He'd been like that their entire friendship. And Christian admitted he'd once been a willing participant in such conversations. Now, it just seemed crude and he wondered about the cutting edge of Max's tone.

"We miss you at headquarters," Max said, as he handed over his credit card to the desk clerk. From the flicker in his eyes, Christian knew he was lying. Christian wasn't completely out of the loop. When he had talked to Mrs. Murphy to tell her about his change of plans, she had filled him in on things. Max, apparently, was very much enjoying being the man in charge. But he had done no harm, so Christian said nothing.

"I'm not supposed to be back until the end of September. Joe and Pete are supposed to be helping you take care of things. Are they?"

Max spoke noncommittally, "Sure they are. So, what is it you wanted to tell me?"

"I want you to be nice."

"Nice?" Max looked innocent. "I'm always nice. I'm a charmer."

"This is Carrie's—"

"Carrie?" Max raised an eyebrow.

"Caroline," Christian corrected himself. "This is Caroline's family. I want you to be on your very best behavior."

"If you tell me what that is, I'll be sure to do it."

"Beth Ann's daughter is turning two."

"The D-Tech heiress?"

Christian nodded. "But don't say anything about that, I haven't fully negotiated the transaction yet."

Max shot him a surprised look. "What's there to transact? It's hers or it isn't."

"Beth Ann doesn't really want it."

"That's what we want, right? Just get it back from her. Easy. You can send her a small stipend every year and promise to put the kid through college."

Christian shook his head. Max's logic scraped against his nerves. Would Beth Ann like him? "Just be nice. They're not like the people we know."

BETH ANN surveyed the dozens of balloons scattered across the floor, completely satisfied with the way the living room looked. It was definitely worth nearly hyperventilating. Bernie was in color heaven. Beth Ann left her and went into the kitchen to carefully cut the cake in half horizontally. Then with her hand trembling, Iris started the arduous task of frosting her great-granddaughter's birthday cake. Glenn, who had studied calligraphy, volunteered to do the lettering on it. But they weren't here yet.

A sharp rap on the screen door had Bernie yelling.

"Pop-pop! Fedman! Mommy, mommy, mommy! Pop-pop! Fedman!" Bernie ran around in circles until she fell over, her world whirling around her, the balloons fluttering away as Glenn swung her up and gave her a big kiss.

"The birthday girl!"

"I *two!*" Bernie told him proudly and held up four fingers.

"Yes, you are two," Glenn said agreeably. "And don't you look nice! I don't think I've seen you in a dress before."

"Pitty." Bernie plucked at the smocking on her bodice.

"Hey, Bethy." Glenn leaned over and stopped. "Whoa! Who gave you that shiner?"

Beth Ann grimaced. "Iris. Long story."

Glenn inspected it. "It's a few days old, but you'll be wearing it for a while still."

"Thank you so much."

He gave Beth Ann a less hearty kiss, his eyes on Bernie's new attire. "I can't believe you shelled out the money for a dress."

Beth Ann made a face. "I didn't. He did. Can you believe white? For Bernie?"

"Give old Mr. Fedman a kiss," Fred said, taking Bernie from Glenn, who left with bounding steps to go back out to the car. Bernie wrapped her arms around Fred's neck and gave him a big kiss, wrinkling her nose at his beard. Fred looked like a big bear, with his furry brown beard and mustache. He was a few inches shorter than Glenn, but his hazel eyes were kind and friendly.

"Tikko." Bernie giggled.

"The beard tickles?" Fred said and rubbed his

beard on her cheek. She shrieked and wriggled to get down, soon intent on chasing a balloon, until she bounced up against the sofa and lay on her back for a rest. Glenn came back with a large box topped with presents. Bernie ran toward the pretty packaging and Glenn lifted her on his shoulders before heading outside for the rest of their things.

"Don't get her dress dirty," Beth Ann called. She shook her head at all the packages. "These are too much. Fred, you guys shouldn't have."

Fred ignored her comments and leaned over to give Beth Ann a kiss on the cheek. "Time flies, doesn't it? What happened to your eye?"

"Iris," she said briefly. "I'll tell you all about it later. I can't believe Bern's two. Just a little while ago, she wasn't even crawling. Now look at her. She's going to go to school!"

Fred patted her hand sympathetically. "Not yet, Mommy. Let's not have her grow up too fast." Fred looked around the house curiously. "Where's Christian? I'm dying to meet him."

Beth Ann flushed. "He went to get his friend at the airport."

"Which airport?"

"The one in town. His friend has a private plane."

"I guess he would now, wouldn't he?" He gazed frankly at her. "Are you okay?"

Beth Ann nodded as she looked out the window, almost expecting to see the silver Jag. She then glanced up at Fred and said quietly, "I never expected to like him so much."

"Carrie had good taste?"

"Excellent taste. I know why she liked him—he's

very good-looking, very rich, very charming, polished." Beth Ann shook her head. "He's someone I'd avoid with a ten-foot pole. But I like him for different reasons."

"Which are?"

"He's kind and he's just so good with Bernie and Iris. He treats them like they're people and even though he's got all the money in the world, he does the best job cleaning toilets I've ever seen. And he's lonely."

Fred gave her a big hug. "And you're lonely, too."

"Is that a reason to fall in love with someone?"

"Well, it's not a reason, but when you meet someone that makes you feel less lonely, then it's worth it to fall in love." Fred stared at her consideringly. "It is love between you, isn't it?"

Love? Beth Ann felt her face flush at the thought of Christian's increasingly intimate kisses. She took a deep breath. Yes. It wasn't just like love, it *was* love.

With his arm draped casually around her shoulder, Fred walked her through the swinging door into the kitchen and stopped dead. "Oh, my goodness. What happened in here?"

Iris flashed him a pleased smile. Her cake was half-frosted and looked very good.

"A small gift," Beth Ann said wryly, seeing her shiny appliances from Fred's eyes. A shout and squeal in the living room told her Glenn and Bernie had returned.

Fred whistled as he turned around a full three hundred sixty degrees. "I'll say. Several small gifts. I can't believe this. Look at this equipment. Do you have any idea what kind of stuff you have?'' He regarded it with an appraising eye and whistled again. ''This must have set him back a bit. He must have custom-ordered it.''

''Custom-ordered?'' Beth Ann hadn't even let herself dwell on that aspect, though she had suspected as much.

''Sure. How else would they have fit so perfectly into your already existing spaces? Believe me these models are usually built for much bigger kitchens.''

Beth Ann rolled her eyes. Of course, Christian would never say anything about custom-ordering. She said conversationally, ''You know I've been cooking with Iris's stove my whole life. This one came with an owner's manual an inch thick.''

''Has Glenn seen all this?''

Beth Ann shook her head. ''I don't think so. I'm still getting used to them.'' She pointed to the stove. ''It's smart.''

''Smart?''

''It won't run without an access code. It was Christian's idea.'' Beth Ann's eyes motioned in the direction of her grandmother.

Fred nodded with a quick glance at Iris. ''He's a good man. Let me say hello to this lovely young lady.'' Fred crossed the kitchen to where Iris was still frosting the cake and put his hands around her eyes. ''Guess who?'' he asked, even though Iris had greeted him already. It was a game the two of them had played for years. Beth Ann smiled, feeling a little teary.

''Prince Charles?'' Iris guessed and then giggled.

''Almost, but not quite.''

''Prince Fred?''

"Close enough." He gave her a big hug and then kissed her cheek. Warmth passed through Beth Ann and she actually wiped her eyes. With Fred and Glenn behind her, as they always were, Beth Ann knew she could do anything. Even raise her sister's child. Or be in love with her sister's husband.

Bernie squealed. "Unckiss! Unckiss!"

Beth Ann looked at Fred. "Christian is back." And the two of them went out to greet him.

"Christian, I'd like you to meet one of my best friends, Fred," Beth Ann said lightly, as she and Fred walked into the living room.

Christian shook hands with him and Beth Ann was struck again by his charm as he said, "I'm glad to finally meet you. I've heard a lot about you."

Fred nodded. "You, too."

Christian turned to his friend, who surveyed the disarray in the small living space. "Beth Ann, this is one of *my* best friends—"

"And Caroline's," Max put in, shooting a meaningful glance at Beth Ann.

Hiding the shudder that ran down her spine, she smiled the perkiest smile she could and shook his hand, which was cool and a little soft. "Glad you could make it for Bernie's birthday." She released his hand quickly.

"Wouldn't miss it for the world," Max said, his voice too silky, too smooth. He stared down at Bernie who looked up for the briefest of moments before dismissing him.

Bernie turned to Christian and asked with the sweetest little-girl voice, "Fuff?"

Christian bent down to pick her up, and Bernie gave him a big hug and snuggled into his shoulder.

Beth Ann's heart grew warm again. It was hard to imagine the two of them hadn't always been doing that, rather than for just the past month.

"Fluff is still missing?" Christian asked, his tone telling her how concerned he was about the fate of the bear.

Bernie nodded seriously.

"Where could he have gone?"

"Don't know!" Bernie gave an adorable shrug of her shoulders.

All the adults laughed except for Max, who continued to assess Bernie with his sharp eyes.

Beth Ann looked at Max, then back at Bernie, her stomach tightening as her eyes took in what he was seeing. She stepped back and shook her head. Surely not. She shot a quick glance at Glenn, to see if he saw it, too. But he wasn't looking at Max. Her gaze returned to Christian's friend. She hadn't spent the past few weeks drawing faces without memorizing every curve, every feature of Bernie's face.

Beth Ann felt her throat close and she shut her eyes tight, trying to fend off the implications of what she saw. She gave a quick prayer. *Carrie, please say you didn't. Please say you at least had the dignity to sleep with a complete stranger, not your husband's best friend.* Beth Ann opened her eyes again to see Max grinning at her.

Laughing, Christian put Bernie down. She tore through the living room looking for Fluff, calling his name. His grin faded when Beth Ann wouldn't look at him, her posture suddenly tense. Fred and Glenn continued to play with Bernie and she shrieked, becoming even more hyper with all the attention, as they took their antics into the kitchen.

Christian was concerned. Beth Ann was staring at Max, her face pale and withdrawn. Max, his hands shoved in his pockets, studied the photos on the shelves. Christian crossed the room to her.

"Are you okay?" he whispered.

The pain in her eyes stabbed at his own heart.

"What's wrong?" he asked, steering her away from Max.

She just looked up at him helplessly. "I'm so sorry. I'm so sorry, Christian."

He had no idea what she was talking about. None.

"Beth Ann, you're not making sense. What are you sorry about?"

"He's her father." Her voice was barely audible.

His heart flip-flopped, but his brain refused to process what she was saying.

"Who is whose father?"

"Max. Look at him," she whispered. "I swear. Carrie never told me."

Christian glanced toward Max and then dismissed her observation. "No, you've got to be mistaken."

She shook her head. "No. I've been drawing Bernie's face all month."

"Max has one of those faces that's very common," he rationalized.

Beth Ann was silent.

Christian looked at Max. There wasn't a resemblance at all. Bernie looked much more like Caroline. Hell, she could look like him.

He glanced at Beth Ann and saw that her good eye was welling up.

He swallowed hard. No. It couldn't be. Caroline wouldn't—Max?

"Glenn, don't eat all the icing!" Iris's voice came

from the kitchen followed by a burst of laughter, as
Glenn shot out the swinging door with the bowl of
left-over frosting. Bernie ran behind him, demanding
that he share his booty.

Christian felt his stomach wrench. There was no
denying it. Bernie, who followed Glenn through the
living room, down the hall, and back into the
kitchen, looked exactly like Max.

The appearance and disappearance of her daughter pushed Beth Ann into action.

She stepped toward Max with a friendly smile.
"Make yourself at home. Would you like something
to drink?"

"Hot around this area, isn't it?" Max said conversationally. "I'd love something to drink, thank
you."

"There's not much planned for today except lots
of food and drink. Feel free to watch television. We
get a bunch of channels."

"No thanks." Max looked around. "Your place
is, er, nice."

Christian could have kissed Beth Ann as she
smiled with her general disregard to her poverty and
said, "We like to think of it as homey. I'm sure it's
not what you're used to."

Max had the grace to let that pass.

Another burst of laughter came from the kitchen.

Beth Ann headed in that direction flashing Christian a reassuring smile. His own returning smile was
stiff enough to break off.

"I better go see what all the fun is about," Beth
Ann said.

Then Christian and Max were alone.

"You son of a bitch," Christian said quietly.

"What?" Max gave him a speculative look, his eyes almost yellow. He had adopted a bland, innocent expression.

"You know what. Now I know why you were so eager to come."

"I have no idea what you're talking about." Max shook his head. He got up and looked out the living-room window with a whistle. "She probably doesn't have to buy any food at all. Does she slaughter her own chickens and pigs as well?"

Christian found Max's humor offensive.

"You should relax more," Max said, his voice tinged with condescension.

"You couldn't leave her alone."

"Leave who alone? I just got here." Max finally looked at him and Christian saw a coldness in his best friend's eyes. He had seen it many times before but never directed at himself.

Max continued, "Not that I really know what you're talking about, but let's just say you're talking about Caroline. You're a fine one to talk about leaving her alone. You did it all the time."

"I had to work. She liked the cruises."

Max gave him a mocking smile. "Yeah, right. Mr. Elliott of the Elliott family empire. You are such a liar. You could not work forever and your great-grandchildren would have enough money to live whatever kind of life-style they wanted. You didn't have to work. You *chose* to work. You chose work over everything else, your wife and your family."

"I didn't see you complaining."

Max shook his head. "Me complain? Never. You're my ticket. Caroline was delicious. You have excellent taste in women." Max wrinkled his nose.

"Though I'm not quite sure what the attraction to the sister is."

"You did sleep with Caroline." Christian could barely think straight he was so angry. His stomach soured at the thought of Caroline and Max together. All of Max's smiles and gestures of friendships—

"I wasn't the only one," Max said, seeming to take delight in Christian's shock. "Do you actually think she was celibate on all those cruises? You took the vow of chastity, not your wife. You should have seen her, been with her."

"So it was my fault?"

Max nodded pleasantly, his eyes sparking with malice. "Yes. I think it was."

"Well, you can start looking for a new job." Christian said in a low undertone.

"I don't think I need to."

"What do you mean by that?"

"D-Tech, my man."

"What about it?"

"I think the company will be enough to keep me satisfied. I won't ever have to work for you again. Ever. I won't have to be your right-hand man. I won't have to bow to your kingship. I kind of fancy the idea of being CEO of my own software company."

"DirectTech is Bernie's."

"And if I prove paternity, I think I would have a good case for making it mine." Max gave him a nice grin. "You know. I think I'm going to enjoy this birthday party."

"I won't let you have it," Christian said through gritted teeth. "Caroline wanted Bernie to have it."

"What's Bernie's is mine, apparently."

It took every bit of control that Christian had not to slam his balled fist into Max's leering face. The muscles in his shoulder twitched as he fought the reflex that coursed through his body.

"You want to hit me so badly, don't you?" Max said mockingly. "But Christian Elliott is always in control. He can never show emotion. He can never be happy or sad. Besides, we're in his girlfriend's house and he's too polite."

"You can't have DirectTech."

Max nodded and gave him an audacious wink. "I think I can."

"So how about lunch?" Beth Ann called as she walked into the room, her voice cheerful. "Glenn's almost done with the cake. It only took four people to make a cake that Bern's not even going to remember."

Max laughed and uttered to Christian under his breath. "Saved by the bell." And then with his voice projected said, "I'd love some lunch, Beth Ann."

"This isn't over," Christian murmured, his jaw hurting because he was clenching it so tightly.

Max said under the smile, "You're right, my friend. I think it's just beginning."

CHAPTER THIRTEEN

BETH ANN CHOSE to ignore the tension that bristled in the living room. She put out all the food on the kitchen table, broke out the paper plates and bade everyone to eat. Fred and Glenn did their best to make light conversation, and the mystery of the vanished Fluff remained a topic of much speculation. As Bernie ate her lunch, Christian reverted back to the man he'd been when he'd first arrived, reserved and distanced from whatever was going on. His handsome face smiled, while his eyes were shuttered closed. It broke her heart, because he couldn't even look at Bernie, not even when she tugged on his shirt to be lifted on to his lap.

After lunch, Beth Ann found him in the garden, his hands shoved into his pockets.

"I think we have some unfinished business," she said, not shrinking from the chill in his eyes.

"Yes?" His voice was urbane.

"Yes," she said forcing her voice to be cheerful. "You said you were going to stay."

He nodded.

"Are you still up for it?" She moved as close to him as she could without touching him. "I'd love the extra time to paint."

He was quiet for a long time. "I don't know anymore."

Beth Ann didn't know what that meant, but dread settled in the middle of her chest. Now wasn't the time to be coy, so she asked bluntly, "What don't you know anymore?"

"I don't know if I can stay on. There might be things I need to take care of."

"Something you didn't have to take care of last week?"

He shook his head. "Max changed my mind."

Beth Ann nodded, although she had no idea what he was talking about. Christian turned away from her and studied the tomatoes.

"I was thinking you should probably trim those back," Christian said. "I was reading you could get another crop of fruit in late summer if you do." He was definitely changing the subject.

"Sure, okay. I'll trim the tomatoes back," Beth Ann said agreeably. "Do you want to tell me what it is that you need to take care of now that you didn't have to take care of yesterday?"

Christian rocked back on his heels and turned his attention to the beans.

"Don't talk to me about the beans." Beth Ann shook his arm. "Talk to me."

"I can't."

"You can't or you won't."

"Can't, won't. It doesn't make a difference." He looked back at the house. "It's not too hot. I think Bernie will really like it out here. She missed her morning trip to the garden."

"Christian."

"What?" His voice was hoarse and Beth Ann could tell how hard he was fighting to keep control.

Beth Ann sighed. During his time with them he'd

been open, honest and straightforward, but now he'd reverted to someone who could barely communicate. Is this what had frustrated Carrie? Beth Ann suddenly felt a rush of sympathy for her sister. It was hard to take when Christian turned into a statue every time he was given a difficult emotional task. But the difference between Carrie and herself was that Beth Ann always stuck around to finish the battle. She wasn't a runner. Carrie had been and from the looks of it so was Christian. No wonder they'd never spent any time with each other.

"I'm not going anywhere, Christian," Beth Ann said quietly, fighting her own urge to cry. She could feel him slipping through her hands, slipping away from her and from Bernie. And she felt as helpless to keep him with her as she did keeping Iris in the present.

"What?" He looked at her sharply.

"I'm good old dependable Beth Ann. I don't have Carrie's beauty or glamour, but I don't have her flight shoes either. I'm not going anywhere and this home isn't going anywhere. So you can go take care of what it is you have to take care of and when you're done, we'll be here."

Christian fought the lump in his throat. "You make it sound so easy."

"It is easy," she replied simply, breathing deeply, hoping that he could feel what she was saying. "It's just knowing what's real and what's not. This garden is real. Bernie is real. I'm real. This is all real. Max isn't real. Money isn't even all that real. Your not being able to look at that little girl, even though she wanted your attention—" she shook her head as tears spilled over ''—that's made up. You made that up all by yourself.''

Her words made the lump grow larger. She couldn't understand. She didn't understand.

''I'm going to get Bernie,'' he said with a forced smile and walked away from her.

''Christian?''

He paused, a pulse pounding so hard in his temple that he couldn't see straight. ''Yes?''

Beth Ann looked as if she was going to say something more but then she shook her head again, as she dabbed her index finger around her black eye, wiping away her tears. ''Nothing. I think I'll go and invite the Marquezes to share some birthday cake.'' She started walking briskly toward the dairy.

Christian didn't know what to think. All he knew was there was no way Max was going to get his hands on DirectTech. It wasn't his and it didn't belong to him. It was Bernie's.

''Max, let's take Bernie to the garden,'' Christian said, his voice clipped as he strode into the living room. Fred and Iris were talking quietly and Glenn was playing with Bernie.

''*Garden!*'' Bernie squealed and started to run around.

''Why don't you change her first?'' Glenn suggested.

''*No!* Pitty!'' Bernie pulled at her dress.

''It's hot out there,'' Max said warily. He was well into his third beer and watching golf on television.

''You can stand under a tree. It's not so bad.''

''I think I'll pass.'' Max waved the beer bottle in the air with a nod.

"No, I don't think you will."

"Garden!" Bernie said imperiously and tugged at Christian's pant leg.

"Max. Please join us." Christian didn't care that Fred and Glenn exchanged a glance.

Christian walked out, holding open the screen door for Bernie as she took the steps. Bernie pulled her arm from Christian's protective grip. *"I* do stairs."

"Okay," Christian said, keeping a watchful eye on her. "But be careful." He tucked a light finger into her collar just in case she slipped, but Bernie did just fine. As he looked over his shoulder, he was grimly pleased to see Max slowly following.

"Cute little beggar, isn't it?" Max said as he took a deep swig of beer. He watched Bernie start to collect a pile of dirt clods.

"She. Bernie is a she. She's not an it," Christian corrected him, the inflection of his voice belying his calm.

"What kind of name is Bernie?" Max asked rhetorically. "It sounds like the name of a deli manager." Max belched and then turned his tawny eyes on Christian. Insolence emanated from him. "What is it you wanted to talk to me about?"

"DirectTech."

"Oh," Max nodded, finished the beer and just tossed the bottle aside.

Christian bristled. "This is not a country club with people who'll pick up your trash."

"Pick it up yourself."

Christian had to choose his battles and fighting over a strewn beer bottle wasn't the one he wanted to engage in.

"About DirectTech?" Max asked. "I didn't think there was any discussion needed. You give me D-Tech, I resign and we're happy."

"Why in the world would I give you Direct-Tech?" Christian asked, his voice deceptively even. He was seething inside. Apparently, he hadn't calmed down as much as he'd thought. He could feel his pulse in his temple, his adrenaline high.

"Because Caroline wanted me to have it," Max said simply.

"That's impossible."

Max shook his head. "I don't think so. I think eventually she knew I would see, er, Bernie and I would know."

Christian shook his head. "That's not true. Caroline left before Bernie looked like anybody. And," he added, "if she really wanted you to have DirectTech, she would have told you about the child."

"What if I say she did?" Max's eyes were red.

"Then I'd say you're lying."

"She did. The night she died."

"You were with her."

Max looked away, for the first time he appeared angry. "I begged her to get a divorce from you. She wouldn't. She was with me, but she loved your money. She had *my* child, yet she wanted to be with you—even though you never loved her."

"What do you mean I never loved her?"

Max shook his head, his face tight as he spoke bitterly. "You never loved her. You never saw what she needed. You never cared."

"And you're saying you did?"

"I did from the first time I saw her." Max's eyes

glittered. "If you remember, I introduced you to her. Not to have her dump me for you, but to show you the one woman I would have settled down for."

"I didn't take her from you."

Max laughed and rolled his eyes. "You never do, do you? They just like you because you're rich. That's all it is. That's all it was with Caroline. I know that because she told me."

Christian could barely take it all in. "How long?"

"How long were you married?"

Christian longed to wipe the smirk off Max's face, but simply asked, "The night she died?"

"I gave her an ultimatum. Divorce you or I would tell you about our affair."

Christian stared at him in disbelief. "You'd lose either way."

"I *loved* her," Max snarled. "You have no idea what it's like to love someone so fully that your soul is ripped out when you discover she loves someone's money more than she loves you. You have no idea, because you've got the money."

"You'll never see a penny of DirectTech money," Christian said flatly.

"Yes, I will." His voice was confident.

"What makes you think so?"

"Because if I don't, I'll take your precious Beth Ann to court for custody of Bernie. I have no idea if she's formally adopted the kid but even if she has, these things are overturned all the time. I think I can tie her up in a nice, nasty custody battle."

"A snowball in hell has a better chance of winning such a suit than you do."

Max's amber eyes gleamed. "Ah. Who said anything about winning? I'll just take her to court, have the authorities put young Bernie in foster care while my paternity is established. Then maybe I'll have a few people dig into Beth Ann's past. Anyone with eyes can see Bernie's become attached to two gay men. Hardly an appropriate environment for such a small thing to be raised in. Also the grandmother looks a little on the fragile side. Could Beth Ann be overworked? Actually—'' Max gave him a steely smile ''—come to think of it, I could probably give that snowball a run for its money. I could win and I could make Miss Beth Ann pretty miserable while I'm at it.'' He added as an afterthought, ''And you, too.''

''And why would you want to do that?'' The thought of Beth Ann's world being invaded by such ugliness sent a chill into his soul. Everything she held dear would be ruined by the intrusion Max threatened. No matter what Beth Ann thought, Max *was* real.

''Call it payback.''

''Payback? For what?'' Christian was surprised.

''*Bug!*'' Bernie interrupted them, holding up a fat snail between two fingers.

''Yes.'' Christian had to concentrate to change his voice for the toddler. ''That's a snail.''

''Nail?''

''Snail.'' Christian squatted down next to Bernie and turned the snail over so she could see the muscled foot.

She wrinkled her nose. ''Ewww.''

''Yes, that's what I say. Ewww.''

''Nail.''

''Snail.''

Satisfied, Bernie headed toward the grapevines by the shed.

"Bernie, play over by the beans where I can see you better," Christian instructed. She changed directions midstride and Christian watched her find her way to the beans. He turned his attention to Max, only slightly satisfied to find that Max had actually picked up the beer bottle and balanced it on a short fence post.

"So tell me what you're paying me back for, my friend?" Christian asked, his voice silky.

"Your friend?" Max laughed with disbelief. "You have no friends. You have people who are convenient to you. You married Caroline because she was beautiful and looked good on your arm and could play your wife perfectly. You had good old Max on the side to give the illusion that you could maintain a friendship. I don't think you even know what friendship is."

Christian was silent. He could feel a vein throb in his temple.

Max shook his head. "See? Even when I insult you, you just take it. It's like you're a robot. That's what Caroline said about you. Said you were a robot in bed. You didn't have the slightest idea how to please a woman because you never let yourself become close to anyone in your entire life."

Christian fought the urge to walk away.

"You want me to tell you something? It was easy to sleep with your wife. All I had to do was pay attention to her. To comment on how nice she looked or say her hair had changed or that she looked healthy. That's how easy it was to sleep with your wife." His face was flushed.

"So this is payback." Christian could barely talk.

"Yep. For all those years I've had to play second to your first. Even in school, girls liked me because I was your friend. Business associates took me seriously because I was your VP. For once, I'd like to be the president. I'm not greedy, D-Tech will do just fine. Give me the company and I'll leave this little bubble intact." Max gestured to the bungalow and the garden.

"And what guarantees you won't try for custody anyway?" He hated it but he had to ask the question.

"I'm sure our attorneys could draw up a suitable agreement."

"You know, I don't deal with blackmailers."

"Then you'll have to find a way to explain that to Beth Ann, because I can make it last forever." He shrugged, then said candidly, "What's the big deal anyway? You said she didn't want Direct-Tech."

Christian shook his head, forcing his voice to be calm, undisturbed. "No deal, Max."

"Then you should have a talk with your lawyer and prepare for—"

Everything happened so quickly. One moment, Christian was damned near ready to deck Max and then, out of the corner of his eye, he saw Bernie disappear into the grapevines, as she climbed up a set of crates he had stacked.

"*No!*" he yelled. "Bernie!"

Startled, she looked at him, guilt passing across her plump cheeks. Then she lost her balance, her arms flying in different directions. Christian rushed toward her but not quickly enough to catch her before she hit the ground, forehead first. She lay still and Christian felt his throat close in terror. *Not Bernie. Dear God, not Bernie.* As if God answered his prayers, Bernie lifted her little head and got up on all fours, screeching in pain, blood from the split in her forehead streaming down her face and splattering onto the white dress. She couldn't see and she clawed at the wound. Christian grabbed her and held her close, his hand pressed tightly against her forehead as he ran into the house.

He burst into the kitchen and Glenn was the first to rise.

"What happened?"

"She fell."

"Let's see." Fred came close and Christian gently lifted his hand off Bernie's forehead. She screamed and writhed in pain.

"I think it's pretty bad."

"I'll drive you to the hospital," Glenn said. "Let's go."

"Hold on, Bernie-Bern-Bern. Pop-pop and I are going to take you to the hospital."

"Mooooommmy! Moooommmy!" Bernie sobbed.

"Where *is* Beth Ann?" Fred asked.

"She went to the Marquezes to invite them for cake."

"The Marquez's phone number is on the wall," Iris said, her voice clear. "You and Glenn get going. We'll call Beth Ann."

On the way to the hospital, Christian cursed himself. It was his fault Bernie was hurt. If he hadn't been wrapped up in talking to Max, he would have followed her, kept her safe.

At the hospital, they were seen immediately and

once the gash was cleaned and exposed, both men saw that it would take several stitches to mend it.

"It's the middle of her forehead," Christian said. "Is it going to scar?"

The doctor held a needle. "I'll do the best I can."

"Is there a plastic surgeon here?"

"Not that we can get to immediately."

"Where can we get a plastic surgeon?"

"Stanford," the doctor joked. "Don't worry. The scar will fade in time."

"But it's her *face*." Christian was appalled. It was bad enough he had allowed her to fall, for her to be permanently scarred was worse. "Can you do something temporary?"

"We can but I don't think it's a good idea to—"

"I saw a helicopter."

"We need that for emergencies."

"This is an emergency. Please," Christian asked. "How long would it take?"

"About thirty minutes."

"I'll pay for everything and when this is over, I'll donate another helicopter to the hospital." He looked at Glenn. "What do you think?"

Glenn shrugged with a smile. "It's your money."

"We do have two helicopters..." The doctor was bending.

"Please. You can call this number and they will wire your hospital any amount this afternoon."

The doctor looked at him doubtfully. "You'll have to talk with billing."

"I'll talk with billing."

BETH ANN ran up the back porch frantic to see Glenn's car gone. Had she missed them? There was no one in the kitchen, and the balloons were still, as if a party had never existed. Max lay snoozing on the couch and the television blathered on about golf.

"Christian! Glenn! Grans?" she called.

"It's me." Fred poked his head out of Iris's room.

"Where is everybody?"

"On their way to Stanford Children's Hospital. Glenn just called."

"Stanford?" Beth Ann shook her head. "You said she only had a small cut."

"Christian and Bernie are in a helicopter."

Beth Ann thought she was going to pass out. "What do you mean? Oh, God. Is she dead?"

Fred shook his head. "Beth Ann take a deep breath. She's okay. Just a bump on the head."

"A concussion?"

Fred conceded. "Maybe."

"Then why is she being flown to Stanford?"

"To see a plastic surgeon."

"*A plastic surgeon?* I can't believe this. What happened?"

"They were out in the garden and she fell and split her forehead. There was blood everywhere. I've never seen anyone act so quickly. Christian stopped the bleeding, but it was a pretty bad gash. Christian didn't want her to be sewed up by a hack so he had her mediported. Glenn's meeting them at the hospital to drive them back. They took your car seat. I think Bernie's going to be pretty knocked out."

Beth Ann sat down, her mind whirling, guilt and terror stabbing at her heart. She'd been selfishly stewing in her own problems when—"I should have been here."

"Why?" Fred asked sensibly. "There were five adults on the premises."

"How's Iris?"

Fred made her sit down at the kitchen table. "Iris is fine. She's just tired from all the excitement, so she decided to lie down for a nap."

Beth Ann exhaled sharply. "He did it again."

"Did what?"

"Whose idea was it to fly her to Stanford?"

"Christian's."

"I'm never going to be able to pay those bills. Can you imagine what that must cost?"

Fred looked at her, concern clouding his eyes. "I don't think he's going to ask you to pay for it."

"I can't let him pay for it. I wish he wouldn't make these decisions without me."

"We didn't have time. She had to be sewn up, so she might as well be sewn up by the best in the business."

"Did he ever consider Fresno's children's hospital?"

"I don't think he was shopping for the best hospital at the time. He thought Stanford and off he went."

"Can they get a plastic surgeon on a Saturday?" Beth Ann fretted. "I'm sure they didn't have an appointment. And I'm sure the hospital is going to be p.o.ed that it's not an emergency."

"Well, there was an awful lot of blood. It looked like an emergency."

"And what about him?" Beth Ann lowered her voice as she looked at Max.

"I think he's waiting for a ride back to his hotel," Fred whispered back. "Christian told me under no circumstance to leave Iris alone. Max tried to find Christian's keys, but then figured he must have taken them with him. Basically, he was stuck until you got back.''

Beth Ann didn't care that Max was stuck. She stared morosely at Bernie's cake. ''I don't suppose Bern'll be in any mood to open presents when she gets back. Oh, Christian...''

She couldn't believe it. Once again, he'd done the most wonderful thing that cost the earth. The fact that he'd go through all that to ensure Bernie wouldn't have a scar, but couldn't see what he had before him...

Beth Ann glanced at the living room where Max still lay prone. He had shown no affection toward Bernie at all. Beth Ann walked noisily around the living room, pacing. She desperately wanted to drive to Stanford and see what was happening, but Glenn called often to update them. Yes, Bernie was all right. They were waiting for the doctor to come. Now, the doctor wanted to talk with her, and Glenn put the doctor on the phone. Then Bernie was squalling to high heaven in the background so Glenn put Bernie on. Bernie was having none of it. Finally, the doctor gave Bernie a little anesthetic where he was going to stitch. Bernie didn't like that much either.

All the time, Beth Ann most wanted to talk with Christian. She could just hear his low tones talking to Bernie.

''Sucker?'' she heard Bernie say between sobs.

''Things are going to be fine,'' Glenn assured her in his last phone call. ''We're on the way home.''

Beth Ann hung up the phone with relief. ''She's

going to be fine. They'll be home in about two hours," she reported to Fred, who had fixed himself another plate of food. "How can you eat?"

Fred grinned. "Crises make me hungry."

"Thank God!" a cool voice said from the couch. "Now, someone can drive me to my hotel. All that fuss for a cut."

Beth Ann looked at Max, who stared back at her with the funny amber eyes that gave her the willies. Bless Fred, he immediately got up and wrapped up his full plate and said, "Where're your keys Beth Ann? I'll drive him back. You stay here in case Glenn calls again. Iris is sleeping."

Beth Ann thanked Fred with her eyes while he gave her a grin that disappeared into his neatly trimmed beard.

IT WAS DARK when the trio arrived home, Bernie, looking like a wounded war veteran complete with bandage on her head, was out like a light. Her beautiful smocked dress was ruined.

"She slept most of the way home," Christian whispered, refusing to relinquish his hold on Bernie. "I'm going to put her to bed."

Beth Ann nodded and gave Glenn a hug. "Thank you so much."

Glenn hugged her back, his strong arms reassuring. "She's going to be fine. I think she had a lot of fun, actually. She kept making chopper sounds before she fell asleep. The doctor said she'll be cranky for a couple of days, and that sleeping was normal but you should check on her during the night and try to wake her."

Beth Ann nodded. "I've got to go see her. Get something to eat. You must be starved."

"We stopped for something on the way home."

Beth Ann shook her head. "But we've got tons of food."

"We'll be here tomorrow to eat it."

"You're staying?" Beth Ann felt better just knowing that.

"I decided we should get a room for the night and then come back tomorrow. Bernie didn't even get to blow out her candles or open her presents."

Beth Ann gave him another big hug. "You guys are priceless."

BETH ANN WALKED quietly down the hall to Bernie's room where she found Christian carefully diapering the toddler, the stained dress in a small heap on the floor. Bernie was fast, fast asleep. As he put her in her little pajamas, her head lolled like a rag doll. When he placed her in the crib, Beth Ann went up beside him and studied her daughter. Except for the bandage, she looked none worse for the wear. She touched a smooth cheek.

"Thank you," Beth Ann said softly, placing a hand on his arm.

She was surprised when he took both her hands and held them tightly between his. They stood that way for a long time watching Bernie, her mouth open, breathing evenly.

Eventually Christian looked at her, and Beth Ann gasped. His smoky gray eyes were red with unshed tears. "You shouldn't be thanking me," he said roughly.

"Why not?" Beth Ann asked puzzled. "You

went far beyond the call of duty. At least I'm not in a huff anymore, about you commissioning the Air Force to take her to the doctor.''

"It was my fault."

"Your fault." Beth Ann looked at him in disbelief. "I find that hard to believe."

"I should have been watching her more carefully. One moment she was by the beans, the next she was climbing near the shed. It happened so fast."

"As it always does. She's going to be okay, right?"

"Yes, but she'll have one heck of a headache."

"So I'm not sure how this is your fault."

"I was responsible. I should have been *paying attention.*" Those last words wrenched from him.

"Children get hurt. That's their job. I stopped painting when she was in the hospital for five days. The longest days of my life. Almost made me start smoking. Kids get hurt and we watch. And no matter how much we want to protect them from everything, we can't. Actually, it's amazing how many things we can't protect them from."

"She's really his, isn't she?"

Beth Ann could barely hear his voice. "I'd bet my life on it."

"You know, I was okay with the fact that Caroline wasn't faithful. But to know that she wasn't faithful with my best friend—"

"No wonder she kept the baby a secret."

"It's worse than that."

Beth Ann waited for him to continue.

"Max wanted her to get a divorce and she wouldn't."

Beth Ann swallowed. "Because she loved you."

"Because she loved my money. It was never me." Christian's voice was hard.

"That's not your fault."

Christian finally said, "Yes, it was. I think I always knew that. We hadn't been intimate in months. She stayed married to me because she needed my money to travel. If she had shown up pregnant, I would have known immediately Bernie wasn't mine."

Beth Ann waited a moment and then ventured. "But she is yours. Just like I was Grans, even though I wasn't."

"No, she's not," Christian muttered. "She's anything but mine. Caroline, my wife, was her mother and Max, my best friend, is her father. And every time I look at her, that's what I see."

Beth Ann couldn't believe what she was hearing. After all the time he'd spent with her, he couldn't possibly reject Bernie. Not Christian. She tried again, "But Bern's yours in every other way. Carrie spent ten days with her and then decided she didn't want her. Max looked like he could barely tolerate her. You know Bernie like no other person knows her. You've seen her moods, rocked her to sleep, watched her tantrums, been persuaded to give her another fig bar even though you know you shouldn't. All these things, these experiences, these acts, make her yours. You're her father in every way that counts."

"It's not that easy, Beth Ann." His voice was very final.

Beth Ann looked at him, her heart breaking, feeling the same way she had when Iris and her stepfather had argued the night before he left. "I know it's not that easy. It wasn't easy for me when I was suddenly a mother. And it wasn't easy for me to think about the time when I would eventually have to give Bernie back because Carrie suddenly was ready to play mommy.''

She looked at him and confessed, telling him something she had never revealed to anyone. ''You know, there were times that I wished, no prayed, Carrie would never come back.'' Her eyes filled with tears. ''And then when I found out she died—Well, it's almost as if I wished it upon her. What more permanent way to guarantee that Bernie would never know her real mother?'' She swallowed. ''But what makes me angriest is that some day Bernie will know that her mother chose money over her. Ten software companies can't make up for that. But you can.''

Christian didn't speak.

Beth Ann bit her lip, the events of the past few days washing over her, leaving her drained and beaten. She exhaled as the silence lengthened. He was going to run away.

''So when are you leaving?'' She could barely get the words out.

CHAPTER FOURTEEN

CHRISTIAN WAS OVERWHELMED by her simple question. He didn't know what to do. The little girl he had come to care for as his own, wasn't, couldn't be his. She belonged to Caroline and Max. He couldn't help seeing Max every time he looked at Bernie, especially while she slept.

The longer he stayed with Beth Ann's hodge-podge family in their rickety bungalow with only a swamp cooler and a big oak tree to fend off the heat, the more entrenched he would become, the more he could delude himself that there was actually a place for him here. But this could never be home as much as he loved it, as much as he loved the occupants. Bernie's acute resemblance to Max made that painfully clear. He shut his eyes tightly. His place was as head of a multinational corporation, rattling around in a mansion thirty times larger than Beth Ann's house.

Give me the company and I'll leave this little bubble intact. Christian clenched his fists. He would not let Max destroy Beth Ann. He'd promised her that he would do anything to protect her and Bernie and he would, even if that meant he had to walk away from them, from the best sleep he had ever known, to fend off Max's threats.

He couldn't put Beth Ann in such a vulnerable

position. She had no idea how nasty Max could become if provoked. Even if Bernie's adoption was final, Max would find a way to contest its legality and her small paradise would be ripped to shreds—because of him. He needed to take care of this in his own way. If he was successful, she would be happy, content, never knowing how close she had come to losing it all. He would find some way to buy Max off and keep DirectTech for Bernie and Beth Ann. Even if Beth Ann didn't want the company, he would keep it for Bernie until she turned twenty-one.

Beth Ann tugged at his arm. "You don't have to go."

Christian couldn't look at her face, her tears. "I do have to go."

Beth Ann shook her head. "We want you here. You're the missing piece to our family."

Those were the words Christian didn't want to hear. "Don't say that," he said, his voice harsh.

"Why not?" Beth Ann asked.

"If I were paying more attention—" He couldn't finish his sentence.

Attention. All that Caroline had wanted from him was attention. If he had been paying attention, rather than fighting with Max, then Bernie would have never been by the shed.

"Neither of us can watch Bernie all the time. We're human. We do the best we can."

The best we can. Could he really say he did the best he could? Had he with Caroline? Could he have taken more time off? Or just taken more time? Would it have mattered?

"You don't need to run from this. Just stay here."

"There are things you don't know."

"Like what?"

"Like—" He started to tell her everything and then stopped, his mind contracting and expanding with his thoughts. Finally he simply turned and started to walk out. But she caught his arm with both hands and pulled him back.

"Don't you do that, Christian Elliott."

"What?"

"Walk away from me. Tell me what's wrong. There's nothing the two of us can't figure out together."

"No. I promised I'd protect you."

"From what? Does it have anything to do with Bernie? And Max?"

Christian closed his eyes and gently loosened Beth Ann's grip on his arm. "No," he answered quietly. "I need to protect you from *me*."

Beth Ann cleared her throat and immediately put some physical distance between them. Somehow, standing three feet away helped her from feeling dread at the thought of him actually leaving. Christian had become a part of her and she felt his hurt all the way down her throat, the pain awakening the young girl who had never really healed from her stepfather's desertion.

"Please, don't go," she said quietly. This time, she could ask. Maybe if she had asked her stepfather he would have stayed. The tears were back, along with the sick feeling of helplessness.

"Beth Ann." Christian's voice came out ragged. "Don't ask that of me."

"You said you weren't going to leave. That you'd never leave Bernie." She couldn't keep her voice from sounding accusing. She added quietly, "You said you'd never leave me."

"I'm sorry, Beth Ann," was all he could say before he turned and walked out of the room.

BEFORE BETH ANN went to sleep, she checked on Iris, who stirred awake as Beth Ann straightened the light coverlet.

"Do you want the fan on, sweetie?" Beth Ann asked.

Iris shook her head and then smiled. "Henry says hello."

Beth Ann smiled. "Tell Henry hello back."

"He says your paintings are going to be the best in the show."

"And how does Henry know that?" Beth Ann inquired, plumping up Iris's pillow. The slides were probably already in the mailroom of the hotel.

"He saw them." Iris settled back into the pillow, her eyes alert. "What's wrong, Beth Ann?"

Beth Ann shook her head. "Nothing's wrong. Why would you ask that? It's been a busy day."

"Is Bernie okay?"

"Bernie is fine."

"Did she really take a helicopter ride?" Iris looked like she wasn't sleepy at all.

Beth Ann nodded. "He did it again."

"He's a good man. Carrie was lucky."

"I don't think Carrie appreciated what she had." Beth Ann swallowed so she wouldn't cry again.

Iris nodded. "I don't think she ever stopped long enough to appreciate anything."

"He's leaving, Grans," Beth Ann said finally, pulling up a chair to sit next to her. She leaned against the bed, her forearms bearing most of her weight. She couldn't believe how much it hurt to say that.

"Not for long."

"I don't know for how long."

"Not for long," Iris repeated. She pulled one of Beth Ann's curls and watched it spring back. "He loves you and Bernie."

"If he loved us, he wouldn't leave."

"He has to. Be patient, Beth Ann. Be patient and he'll eventually catch up to you. He will—Henry says so."

Beth Ann laughed and gave Iris a kiss on the cheek. "Thank Henry for me and you have a good night's sleep. I'll see you in the morning."

CHRISTIAN TOOK the coward's way out. He blindly threw his few things into his bag and set the leather duffel in the hallway, before creeping down the hall for one last peek at Bernie. Moving as quietly as he could, he pushed open the door to her room, letting his eyes adjust to the dark. Bernie lay sleeping, the white bandage glowing, her mouth open as she breathed. He tread softly to the crib and couldn't resist touching her rounded cheek one last time. Remorse choked him.

As he turned to leave, he saw Beth Ann lying on the daybed, wide awake, staring at him, studying his clothes.

"Drive carefully," she whispered before she turned over and faced the wall.

Christian felt terrible, her words piercing him, but he couldn't say anything, and he needed to leave before he crawled into that daybed with her and stayed forever.

He paused at the front door, staring out into the warm night.

"You don't have to leave."

He whirled and saw Iris sitting on the couch, dressed in her nightgown.

"Yes, I do."

Iris smiled. "But you can always come back."

"I don't think it's possible to go back," he said shortly. He didn't want to talk to her. He wanted to leave and just drive.

"It's not possible to go back, but sometimes *coming* back means going forward." She rose unsteadily and walked over to him resting her hand on his arm. "Just remember that you should always go in the direction of love. And know that you will never be loved more than Beth Ann and Bernie love you now."

Unable to speak, Christian grabbed his bag and left.

BERNIE'S CRY awoke Beth Ann from a restless, dreamless night.

"Oh, sweetie. You had a bad accident yesterday," Beth Ann crooned as she lifted her out of the crib. She pulled Bernie close and lay back on the daybed, her head still groggy.

"Mommy!" Bernie clung to her.

"I know, you hurt your head. On your birthday even."

"Birfday!"

Bernie touched her head and started to cry again.

"I know, Bernie-Bern-Bern. You've got the biggest hangover ever. See that's what happens when you indulge in too much of that birthday punch. Mommy's got some medicine for you.''

Bernie whimpered and let Beth Ann carry her to the kitchen. Intending to give the toddler baby aspirin, she found a prescription on the kitchen counter. She tried not to be surprised by the note, written in Christian's scrawl, underneath the medication.

Beth Ann,
   Forgot to give this to you.

Christian

Then like an afterthought, he'd put a phone number at the bottom of the note. Not an invitation to call him. Nothing. Just the phone number. Beth Ann swallowed hard and supposed he thought he was doing what was best. No tearful goodbyes, no closure, not for her, not for him. At least she had new appliances. She measured out a portion of the medicine and tasted it. It was pretty awful.

Bernie looked at it suspiciously.

''Punch,'' Beth Ann said.

''Punch?''

''Drink it just like punch.''

Bernie twisted her head away and then bumped her forehead on Beth Ann's shoulder and started to cry again. Beth Ann tucked her close and rocked her. ''I know. Bernie doesn't feel too good this morning.''

''Appo juice,'' Bernie finally said.

''I can get you apple juice. The brown one?''

Beth Ann put the medicine down and opened the refrigerator. Bernie pointed to the grape juice.

"That's grape juice."

"Gape juice."

"Okay, sweetie." Beth Ann nodded. At least the grape juice would mask the taste of the medication. One-handed, she opened the dishwasher and found Christian had run it before he left. She got a clean sipper cup, put in the grape juice and poured in the medicine.

"Here you go." She handed Bernie the cup. After a moment she asked, "Can Mommy put you down?" She tried to put Bernie down, but Bernie protested.

"You're so heavy, Bernie. Mommy's got to sit down." Beth Ann sat at the table and studied Christian's note. At least he'd left a phone number, something Carrie didn't do.

"UNCKISS?" Bernie asked as she searched the house. "Fuff?"

"I'm sorry, sweetie," Beth Ann said as she loaded the washer with Christian's linen. Bernie's temperament had changed miraculously as the painkiller set in. She still looked battle scarred, but Beth Ann had decided to leave the bandages on for at least the rest of the morning. She didn't want to disturb any newly formed scabs. "Uncle Christian had to go to work."

"Werk?"

"Yes, work. And I have no idea where Fluff is." Beth Ann wrinkled her forehead. "Usually he's not gone for such a long time. He'll be back." She didn't know if she was talking about Fluff or Christian.

When she had ventured in the room he'd slept in for the past month she expected there to be some sign of him, a sock, something. But there wasn't. It looked like her room, untouched, everything in neat order. He hadn't left anything. Nothing to indicate that he had occupied the room at all. Be patient, Beth Ann. *Be patient and he'll eventually catch up to you.* Beth Ann pressed her lips tightly together, refusing to cry again. She doubted Iris's words.

"Deggs," Bernie informed her.

"Eggs? You want eggs for breakfast?" Beth Ann asked. She looked at the clock. "I guess it is breakfast time. Let's go see how Nana is this morning. We all had a very exciting day yesterday."

Bernie ignored her and kicked a few balloons not yet deflated.

Beth Ann knocked quietly on Iris's door.

"Grans? I'm fixing eggs for breakfast. Do you want some?"

Beth Ann heard no stirring. It was good that Iris was getting some extra sleep. She was probably exhausted. She knocked again lightly, then pushed open the door a crack. Iris was still fast asleep.

Beth Ann walked over and placed a light kiss on her forehead and then stepped back in disbelief. She picked up Iris's frail wrist and felt for a pulse, the stiffness in Iris's limbs telling Beth Ann what she didn't want to know.

"Oh, Grans. You, too?" Beth Ann whispered and pushed back Iris's hair. "Why are you all leaving me?"

"Mommy?" Bernie hovered near the door.

"Hey, sweetie."

"Deggs," Bernie reminded her in an imperious tone.

"I know, honey. I'm going to fix your eggs. Come say goodbye to Nana."

"Nana, bye-bye?" Bernie walked closer to investigate. She looked up at Beth Ann puzzled, then shook her head. "No bye-bye."

Beth Ann pulled Bernie up onto her lap so she could see Iris. "Yes, Nana went bye-bye. She's gone to heaven."

"Broke?"

Beth Ann nodded, then said, "Well, not exactly broke. I'd say worn out."

"Wore out." Bernie patted Beth Ann's leg. She smiled and then said, "Deggs!"

"I guess so," Beth Ann smiled, blinking back tears.

While Bernie ate her eggs, Beth Ann called Fred and Glenn, who advised her to call 9-1-1. Thank goodness, her old friends knew what to do because she certainly didn't. Surely, she should have been more prepared for this. It had been bound to happen. Iris was nearly ninety. But somehow, when the days are the same and the body chugs along, it's difficult to think of the end.

She fingered the message with Christian's phone number wondering if she should call him as well. He'd be in Napa by now. She desperately wanted to talk to him, cry on his shoulder. Christian was someone who really knew how special Iris was to her, to Bernie. But she didn't want to hear his polite words. She just wanted him to come home. She put the number aside.

Fred and Glenn arrived at the same time the coroner did.

"What time do you think?" Fred asked him.

"By the amount of rigor mortis, I'd say early this morning. Would you like a few minutes with her before we take her?" the coroner asked gently.

Beth Ann nodded and walked into the bedroom, remembering this bedroom, oh so many years ago. She was lucky to have had Grans for as long as she had. Not everyone lived to be nearly ninety. And she was lucky Grans had had a very good life until near the very end. No homes, no lasting, painful infirmities.

Iris looked very peaceful.

Beth Ann pulled up a chair. "Well, Grans, I guess this is it." She couldn't resist smoothing back Iris's hair, tucking it behind her ear. "I just wanted to thank you for taking me in all those years ago. And I wanted to thank you for teaching me to draw and to plant gardens and cook. I—I hope you and Henry are having a t-terri-fic time—" Beth Ann broke off and gave her a quick kiss. "Goodbye, Grans."

She left the room and went straight into Glenn's arms. His eyes were rimmed in red and he hugged her tightly. "I'm so sorry, Bethy."

"She was almost ninety," Beth Ann hiccuped. "It had to happen sometime."

"But we never think of sometime as right now."

"I'm going to miss her," Beth Ann sobbed. "Even though she was a lot of work, I'm really going to miss her."

TIME PASSED in a blur for Beth Ann. Glenn stayed on while Fred went back to San Jose, planning to be back for the small service they would have at the end of the week after Iris was cremated.

"When is Christian coming back?" Glenn asked bluntly. Bernie was safely installed in front of the television, happily reciting an alphabet song.

"He's not."

"I can't believe he'd miss Iris's service," Glenn said, his voice reproving.

"I haven't told him," Beth Ann said simply. She was wiping down the chrome on the new refrigerator. Although most of Iris's peers had already passed on, there would be a few guests coming to the house after the service and Beth Ann wanted the house to look nice.

"Why not?"

"I didn't want to bother him." She couldn't get rid of the lump in her throat.

"I don't think telling him Iris has died is bothering him."

Beth Ann felt her eyes well with tears. She stubbornly shook her head. "He left because he said he needed time. I thought about it and then figured—"

"Call him now."

"What do you mean?" Beth Ann looked up.

"It's not that hard. Just call him and tell him there's a service for Iris at the end of the week. He should know."

Beth Ann bit her lip. "This is too complicated."

"No, it's not. This isn't about your love life, Bethy. This is allowing someone to pay his respects to a loved one who's moved on. You owe him that. After what he did for you, you owe him."

"I know." Beth Ann felt like she was going to choke, just so she wouldn't cry again. She'd been crying nonstop for two days. Her sinuses hurt. "But—"

"There's are no buts," Glenn said. "Can you imagine how terrible he'll feel, if he knows you didn't want to call him?"

"He *left* us."

"And he can come back. Isn't that the point? That we can leave but then we can come back? Even Carrie knew that. In her time of need. Where did she come? Home. You've got to give Christian a chance to come home."

"It's only going to hurt when he leaves again," Beth Ann whispered.

Glenn got up and took the washcloth from her. "But that's a risk you'll have to take. If you don't risk, you can't change, you can't allow yourself new experiences." He paused significantly, then said, "Look at your paintings."

"My paintings?" Beth Ann shook her head. "I haven't even thought about those."

"I looked at your stuff for nearly an hour. Both Fred and I did. We love what you've done. Look how much your art has changed, evolved because you've changed." His praise was genuine and Beth Ann felt a glow of pride inside her fog of sadness.

"Grans taught me."

"She did?"

Beth Ann nodded. "She said I needed movement." She sighed greatly. "Okay, so I need to call him."

Glenn gave her a big smacking kiss on the cheek. "I'll go learn my alphabet with the Bernster. Give you some privacy."

"Thanks." She caught his arm before he was able to leave the kitchen.

"Glenn, thank you."

Glenn's smile never wavered. "You're welcome."

CHRISTIAN SAT in the middle of the expansive living room in the beautiful chalet in the Napa Valley and stared at a small brown bear that had been packed way at the bottom of his leather duffel bag. He suspected that Bernie had found the perfect bed for her beloved friend and then promptly forgot about him. What he didn't expect was the pain he'd felt when he'd found him late Sunday. He'd spent most of Monday wondering what to do with him. Couriering Fluff seemed to be the most practical solution, but somehow inhumane.

He examined Fluff thoroughly and found nothing spectacular about the stuffed animal. Fluff stared back at him, not giving Christian the answer he was looking for. He was just a brown bear, worn thin on one ear where Bernie always carried him. Despite Fluff's physical imperfections, there was no denying that he was Bernie's best friend. She sat with him on Mrs. Potty, read him books, told him to go to sleep. She scolded him, laughed with him, and discarded him, only to hunt for him later, hugging him with abandon and relief when they were finally reunited. He was nothing but Fluff, not even real, but her love for him was more real than most—

It's just knowing what's real and what's not. This garden is real. Bernie is real. I'm real. This is all real. Max isn't real. Money isn't even all that real. He heard Beth Ann's voice, soothing him. He heard

Bernie's laughter and Iris's gentle conversations. His hands automatically squeezed Fluff. *Sometimes coming back means going forward.*

The phone rang.

"Hello?" he answered, his voice clipped.

He suspected it to be Max, asking for an update on DirectTech. Christian had briefly talked to him, letting him know he was working on the details of the transfer, when in actuality, he was stalling for time, using his enormous legal base to try to find a way out of this mess. Even though his attorneys had found ways to divert Max, there was no denying that if Max ever decided to pursue paternity of Bernie, there was no way for Beth Ann to be spared a lengthy and painful court battle.

"Christian?" The voice over the phone sounded very uncertain.

"Beth Ann!" Christian was surprised, his heart beating rapidly. His hold on Fluff tightened. "What can I do to help you?"

He hated how formal his voice sounded. It was his work voice, austere and distant. He'd spent years cultivating that voice. Now, he used it so she would never know how much he wanted to come back and finish the summer with her, sleep in her bed and listen to the cows moan in the distance. How much he missed Iris and how much it was killing him to know he had Fluff when Bernie had a headache.

"If this is a bad time, I can call back la—" she started and he could hear her drift away.

"No, no! This is fine," he said hastily, the work voice disappearing. He winced at his eagerness. So much for staying away. "How are you?" He tried for friendly, but sounded a little desperate to his own ears.

"Not so good," she said.

Did her voice waver?

"Not so good? Bernie? Is she okay?" His heart started to pound, unspecific guilt beginning to pulsate.

"No, no," Beth Ann assured him. "Bernie's fine."

"Is Fluff still missing?" He tried to joke and stared at the bear.

"Yes. We've torn the house apart looking for him."

"He'll show up," Christian said slowly and nodded to himself, the solution suddenly very clear. Yes. Fluff would show up, even if that meant he would take him back himself.

Beth Ann was silent.

"What is it, Beth Ann?" He felt a terrible sense of foreboding.

"I don't want you to think I'm calling to persuade you to come back. Glenn just thought you'd like to know what happened."

Did her voice waver again?

"What happened? Of course, I want to know." He made his voice as gentle as he could.

"It's Grans." Now he could tell she *was* crying.

"Tell me, Beth Ann," Christian said gently. "What happened to Iris?"

"She died early Sunday morning. I found her."

"She died? Early Sunday morning?" A shiver passed through him. Was their conversation the last Iris had had?

"Y-yes." Beth Ann sniffed. Then her voice came

over the connection stronger as she spoke rapidly. "I just wanted to let you know the service for her is at the end of the week. But I'm not telling you this to make you feel obligated to come home. I just thought you needed to know."

Christian was silent for a long moment, just because he didn't know how to say what it was that he was trying to say.

"I just wanted to let you know," she repeated.

"I'll be there in four hours."

"The service isn't until the end of the week."

"I'll find a hotel."

"You don't need to do that, if you don't mind—"

"I don't mind."

"Okay, then." She sounded relieved.

"Is someone with you?"

"Bernie and Glenn."

"Good. I'll be there this afternoon."

"Thank you, Christian."

He felt a warm feeling spread through him. "No, Beth Ann. Thank you." Suddenly, as if the weight of the world was lifted off his shoulders, he knew the answer. There was nothing he could do about Max, there was nothing he could do to prevent him from filing for custody, but there was something he could do for Beth Ann. He could be there. He could be there and pay attention to her. The realization was liberating.

When he arrived in Mercy Springs, the bungalow was still, although the television was on low. He plucked Fluff from the passenger seat before walking up to the door, not knowing whether to knock or just enter. He did both. He knocked and entered at the same time, poking his head through the screen.

"Unckiss! *Fuff!*" Bernie screamed from the floor, jumping up. "No werk?"

"Work?" Christian looked at Beth Ann who looked gorgeous in her shorts and baggy T-shirt, her eyes puffy from a week of crying, her skin pale and drawn, her black eye fading slightly. She looked at the stuffed animal in surprise.

"I told her you were at work," Beth Ann said, then added, "I had to say something. She asked."

Bernie ran to him and threw her arms around his leg. He lifted her carefully and she pulled Fluff against her. "How's the old noggin?" he asked her, though he looked at Beth Ann inquiringly.

"She's fine, like it never happened. Sunday was the roughest day."

He nodded. "In more ways than one. How are you?"

She smiled, but it didn't reach her eyes. "I'm okay. I miss her. It sure is quiet around here."

"Pop-pop sleeping," Bernie said in an exaggerated whisper.

"Glenn's here?"

Beth Ann rose and stretched. "He's staying in my room until the service. They didn't think I should be alone with Bernie so fussy and all."

Christian felt a sharp pang. No, she shouldn't have been alone when she discovered her grandmother had died. He should have been here. But he wasn't. He'd left her and he didn't know if he could ever forgive himself for that.

"It's kind of macabre, but you're welcome to sleep in Gran's room," Beth Ann offered.

"The couch is fine."

Beth Ann nodded and then grinned. "I don't blame you." She shuddered. "I wouldn't want to either. Sooner or later, I'll need to clear it out, but it just seems way too soon."

Christian exhaled in relief that Beth Ann wasn't going to banish him to a hotel. His place was in her house, even if it was on the couch. She had asked him to come home. He kissed Bernie on the cheek and set her down.

"So sometime, when all this has settled down, we need to talk."

Beth Ann looked at him. "About?"

"About Max and Caroline, me and you and Bernie."

Beth Ann felt her pulse quicken. "Now?"

Christian shook his head. "Not now."

"Before you go," Beth Ann ventured.

Christian nodded. "Okay. Let's say before I go."

"And when are you planning on leaving? After the service?" She knew her voice sounded whiny, needy. But she wanted to prepare herself, for when she and Bernie were alone. Although she missed Iris terribly, she would now be able to get adequate day care for Bernie and she would be able to go back to painting. Christian had reignited that spark in her.

Christian cleared his throat and walked in the direction of the kitchen.

"I was thinking," he said as he left the room, "about the end of the summer."

Beth Ann didn't think she heard him right but refused to follow him. She sat down on the couch and waited. A few minutes later Christian came back with a glass of iced tea and sat on the couch. Bernie immediately crawled into his lap, dragging the bear with her.

"So what do you say?" he asked.

He waited for Beth Ann's response. She was very quiet.

When she finally spoke, her voice was barely audible. "I know you feel sorry for us because of Grans, but there's really no need—"

"It's not about need. It's what I want to do." Christian took a deep breath. "I should have been here. You shouldn't have had to find Iris by yourself. I should have been with you."

"I wasn't alone. I had Bernie."

"At the very least, I should have stayed for a few days more just so you wouldn't have to deal with Bernie, too. She must have been cranky."

"Well, I gave her a lot of that medicine," she smiled shyly. "It worked wonders."

"I shouldn't have walked away," Christian said. "But I'd like to come back. Just like we agreed. I'll stay until the end of summer and then—"

"Then?" She looked at him strangely.

"And then, we'll take it from there."

Beth Ann wrung her hands.

"What's wrong?"

"I'm not sure I can take you leaving at the end of summer."

Christian's heart quickened at her soft confession.

"And?"

"And if you don't want to stay for good, I'd rather that you leave sooner instead of later."

"For good?" Christian's heart pounded.

Beth Ann nodded. "For good."

After a minute, he started to smile and said teasingly, "Are you asking me to marry you?"

Beth Ann looked away, her face as red as the tomatoes in her garden. "Well…"

"I accept."

She stared at him for the longest time. "For good?"

"Forever."

"I don't want to move."

"You won't have to. I'll move here."

"What about your work?"

"Max reminded me that I don't have to work. Besides there's plenty of work to be done here."

A glimmer of a smile hovered on Beth Ann's lips. "We have guests coming at the end of the week and I think the toilet needs a scrub."

"I'm on it tonight," Christian promised. "Is this for real? Am I staying?"

Beth Ann swallowed hard. Was it for real? Did she want him to stay forever? Then, she nodded. "Yes, I want you to stay but—"

"But what?"

She couldn't think when Christian looked at her so intimately.

"But you have to be able to be Bernie's father." She looked at Bernie who had settled into Christian's lap, her mouth yawning open. Her eyelids drooped and she clutched Fluff.

"I am Bernie's father."

"What?"

"I was Bernie's father in the hospital. That was the only way they would grant her treatment. Glenn said so."

Beth Ann laughed softly. "What's Bernie's name?"

"Bernadette Bellamy Elliott." Christian grinned and then sobered. "I was very stupid when I thought I couldn't love her. She's yours and mine in every way. You taught me that. And Iris beat it into me."

"Grans?"

Christian nodded, his voice gruff. "Iris told me that sometimes coming back means going forward."

"When did she tell you that?"

"The night she died."

Beth Ann felt Iris's presence in the room.

He looked at her pensively. "But you know who really taught me about love?"

Beth Ann had no idea.

"Fluff." Christian smiled. "Fluff is nothing but polyester and cotton and stuffing and he means more to Bernie than the world. Bernie is a giving, loving individual. How can I not love her? You were right. She's mine and she'll always be mine."

"And what about Max and Caroline?" Beth Ann watched his face grow grim.

"I didn't want to talk about this now," Christian said his voice very low so as not to wake Bernie who had drifted off into a sound sleep. "It still makes me very angry."

"What?"

"Max threatened to sue for custody of Bernie."

Beth Ann felt a shiver go down her neck. "He can't have her."

"Well, according to my team of lawyers, if he turns out to be the father, he has every legal right."

"What does he want? He can't want Bernie."

Beth Ann shook her head. "I saw them together. He didn't even look at her the whole time he was here."

Christian sighed heavily. "He doesn't want Bernie."

"What does he want?" Beth Ann's heart was pounding hard.

"DirectTech." Christian pronounced it like it was the end of the world.

Beth Ann blinked and asked again, "What?"

"Max wants DirectTech," Christian said heavily.

"Is that all?" Beth Ann asked, relief flooding through her.

"What do you mean, is that all?" Christian looked annoyed.

"Give it to him," Beth Ann said simply.

"What?"

"Give it to him. We don't need it. I never wanted it anyway."

"It's not your company to give away. It's not my company to give away. It's Bernie's."

"Find a way. DirectTech did everything it was supposed to do," Beth Ann said seriously.

Christian looked warily at the woman who had just agreed to become his wife. "What?"

"It brought you to us." She smoothed back her daughter's hair. Bernie snuggled deeper into his arms. "Give Max DirectTech with our blessing and get him to sign lots of documents saying he'll never, ever think of trying to get custody of Bernie."

"It really means nothing to you," Christian asked. He brushed his finger over her cheek.

Beth Ann shook her head, clicking her tongue impatiently. "You are the densest man, I've ever met. DirectTech, your money, your privilege aren't real.

This—'' she gestured around her ''—is real. You are real. I'm real. Our love is real. If DirectTech is eating you alive, then I want you to give it up, let it go, because we have far more than any software company can offer. You promised me.''

''I promised you.''

Beth Ann nodded, her eyes serious. ''You told me you would do anything in your power to protect us, even if that meant giving up your name or your money. Did you mean that?''

Christian felt love move through his body. ''Yes, I meant that.''

''Then walk away from the software company. Don't walk away from us.''

''Never,'' Christian whispered as he pulled her close, shifting Bernie's weight so he could kiss Beth Ann. How had he ever thought he could walk away? He had finally found himself a family. Forever.

EPILOGUE

Two years later.

RAAAH! Raaah, raaah! *Raaaahhh!*

Beth Ann groaned and woke to the wail.

"Mommy, mommy, mommy! Iris is crying!" Bernie informed her, her button nose right up against Beth Ann's.

Beth Ann squinted at a blurry child and croaked, "I hear her. Thank you, Bernie. You can go back to sleep."

"No, I can't," Bernie said logically. "Iris is crying too loud."

"I'll get her," Christian whispered from the other side of the bed. Beth Ann felt the bed creak as he got out. "Go back to sleep, Bernie," he instructed the four-year-old.

"I will if you carry me!" Bernie wheedled.

Christian lifted Bernie up and carried her to her room, talking soothingly as they went down the hall.

He put Bernie back into the daybed and kissed her on her forehead, a hairline scar barely visible. He searched around and found Fluff jammed between the iron bars and the wall. He reached down and pulled him free.

"I told you she was crying just like you asked,

Daddy,'' Bernie said proudly as she accepted the bear from him.

Christian kissed her again, tucking them both in. ''Thank you for being such a good big sister.''

BETH ANN heard Christian and Bernie talk and smiled sleepily. She was exhausted. She now had more sympathy for Carrie, understanding why she'd been so crabby while she was pregnant. At least, Beth Ann had had Christian participating in every stage of the pregnancy. Beth Ann felt truly blessed. Although he had resigned as the CEO of the company, he still kept his hand in most of the business through the extensive telecommunication system he'd set up. The bungalow wasn't quite the same bungalow.

To accommodate his electronic needs, they'd added on another room, made the kitchen bigger and even though Beth Ann initially had protested replacing the old swamp cooler with central air-conditioning, it was something she, grudgingly, appreciated in her last weeks of pregnancy, during the uncharacteristically hot May they'd just experienced.

With the recent slump in computer stocks, rumor had it that Maximilian Riley was working harder than he ever had before just to keep DirectTech afloat. And Bernie remained no wiser that she was almost the heiress to the floundering company.

Christian gently lay little Iris next to Beth Ann.

''Hey, there, sweetie,'' Beth Ann greeted the infant.

Little Iris stared up at her, her mouth puckering

when she was presented a breast. She latched on and suckled quietly.

"I'll take her back when you're done," Christian said as he crawled back into bed.

"She can just sleep here," Beth Ann said, shifting closer to him, using his broad chest to support her back. He wrapped his arm around her waist to pull her against him, then gently caressed the nearly bald top of Iris's head. Iris continued to suckle greedily, her eyes closed.

"You've got a long day ahead of you." Christian squinted at the clock. "You should get as much sleep as you can."

Beth Ann nodded in agreement, but said, "I don't think I can sleep anymore."

"You're excited."

She smiled. "Yes."

"You should be. You've earned this. What time did Fred and Glenn say they were coming?"

"About noon."

"Good. You guys go ahead and make sure everything is perfect. I'll bring the girls about five. We'll go to dinner before your show opens."

Beth Ann smiled and put her hand on her husband's face. Her very own show in a real gallery. Her husband. Her girls. She snuggled Iris closer to her. There was no place like home.

HARLEQUIN®
SUPERROMANCE®

You are now entering

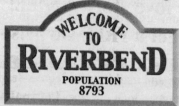

WELCOME TO
RIVERBEND
POPULATION
8793

Riverbend…the kind of place where everyone knows your name—and your business. Riverbend…home of the River Rats—a group of small-town sons and daughters who've been friends since high school.

The Rats are all grown up now. Living their lives and learning that some days are good and some days aren't—and that you can get through anything as long as you have your friends.

Starting in July 2000, Harlequin Superromance brings you Riverbend—six books about the River Rats and the Midwest town they live in.

BIRTHRIGHT by **Judith Arnold** (July 2000)
THAT SUMMER THING by **Pamela Bauer** (August 2000)
HOMECOMING by **Laura Abbot** (September 2000)
LAST-MINUTE MARRIAGE by **Marisa Carroll** (October 2000)
A CHRISTMAS LEGACY by **Kathryn Shay** (November 2000)

Available wherever Harlequin books are sold.

HARLEQUIN®
Makes any time special ™

Visit us at www.eHarlequin.com

HSRIVER

If you enjoyed what you just read,
then we've got an offer you can't resist!

Take 2 bestselling love stories FREE!

Plus get a FREE surprise gift!

Back by popular demand are

DEBBIE MACOMBER's
MIDNIGHT SONS

Hard Luck, Alaska, is a town that needs women!
And the O'Halloran brothers are just
the fellows to fly them in.

Starting in March 2000 this beloved series returns
in special 2-in-1 collector's editions:

MAIL-ORDER MARRIAGES, featuring
Brides for Brothers and *The Marriage Risk*
On sale March 2000

FAMILY MEN, featuring
Daddy's Little Helper and *Because of the Baby*
On sale May 2000

THE LAST TWO BACHELORS, featuring
Falling for Him and *Ending in Marriage*
On sale July 2000

Collect and enjoy each MIDNIGHT SONS story!

Available at your favorite retail outlet.

HARLEQUIN®
Makes any time special™

Romance is just one click away!

love scopes

➤ Find out all about your guy in the Men of the Zodiac area.

➤ Get your daily horoscope.

➤ Take a look at our Passionscopes, Lovescopes, Birthday Scopes and more!

join Heart-to-Heart,
our interactive community

➤ Talk with Harlequin authors!

➤ Meet other readers and chat with other members.

➤ Join the discussion forums and post messages on our message boards.

romantic ideas

➤ Get scrumptious meal ideas in the Romantic Recipes area!

➤ Check out the Daily Love Dose to get romantic ideas and suggestions.

Visit us online at

www.eHarlequin.com
on Women.com Networks

HARLEQUIN® SUPERROMANCE

COMING NEXT MONTH

#924 BIRTHRIGHT • Judith Arnold
Riverbend

Aaron Mazerik is back. He isn't the town's bad boy anymore, but some people still don't think he's good enough—especially not for Riverbend's golden girl, Lily Holden. Which is fine with Aaron, since he's convinced there's even *more* reason he and Lily shouldn't be together.

Riverbend, Indiana: Home of the River Rats—small-town sons and daughters who've been friends since high school. These are their stories.

#925 FULL RECOVERY • Bobby Hutchinson
Emergency!

Spence Mathews, former RCMP officer and now handling security at St. Joe's Hospital, helps Dr. Joanne Duncan deliver a baby in the E.R. After the infant mysteriously disappears a few hours later, Spence and Joanne work closely together to solve the abduction and in the process recover the baby girl—and much more!

#926 MOM'S THE WORD • Roz Denny Fox
9 Months Later

Hayley Ryan is pregnant and alone. Her no-good ex—the baby's father—abandoned her for another woman; her beloved grandfather is dead, leaving her nothing but a mining claim in southern Arizona. Hayley is cast upon her own resources, trying to work the claim, worrying about herself and her baby.... And then rancher Zack Cooper shows up.

#927 THE REAL FATHER • Kathleen O'Brien
Twins

Ten years ago, Molly Lorring left Demery, South Carolina, with a secret. She was pregnant with Beau Forrest's baby, but Beau died in a car crash before he could marry her. For all that time, Beau's identical twin, Jackson, has carried his own secret. Beau *isn't* the father of Molly's baby....

#928 CONSEQUENCES • Margot Dalton
Crystal Creek

Principal Lucia Osborne knows the consequences of hiring cowboy Jim Whitely to teach the difficult seventh graders. Especially when Jim deliberately flouts the rules in order to help the kids. Certain members of the board may vote to fire Lucia and close the school. But Lucia has even graver consequences to worry about. She's falling in love with Jim...and she's expecting another man's child.

#929 THE BABY BARGAIN • Peggy Nicholson
Marriage of Inconvenience

Rafe Montana's sixteen-year-old daughter, Zoe, and Dana Kershaw's teenage son, Sean, have made a baby. *Now what?* Rafe's solution—or rather, proposal—has Zoe ecstatic, but it leaves Dana aghast and Sean confused. Even Rafe wonders whether he's out of his mind.

CNM0600